INTO THE FIRE

INTO THE FIRE

THE CAITLIN CHRONICLES BOOK TWO

DANIEL WILLCOCKS

MICHAEL ANDERLE

DISRUPTIVE IMAGINATION

THE INTO THE FIRE TEAM

Thanks to the JIT Readers

Kim Boyer
Mary Morris
Micky Cocker

If we've missed anyone, please let us know!

Editor
Lynne Stiegler

For the Willcocks five.
—Dan

To Family, Friends and
Those Who Love
To Read.
May We All Enjoy Grace
To Live The Life We Are
Called.

—Michael

CHAPTER ONE

Silver Creek, Old Ontario

Caitlin woke to something she never thought she'd ever say.

"*Hoooly* fuck. That is one comfy-ass bed."

She sat up, delighting in the soft linens stroking her body, and for the first time ever, agreed with the bastard of an ex-governor on something. Living in luxury was goddamn nice compared to the conditions she'd lived in her whole life—and that was something she could now share with the rest of the town.

After taking down Trisk, the first thing Caitlin had done was open his quarters up to Silver Creek's poor and homeless. The luxurious rooms decorated in golds and finery now hosted souls who were infinitely happier out of the cold and inside the warmth.

Caitlin had wanted to head back to her own, simple home with Dylan. But the townspeople were having none of it.

"Don't be silly," Mother Wendy said as Caitlin argued

the point. "If you want to be treated like a leader, people need to see you as the leader. Go. Take it. You've earned it."

And who was Caitlin to argue?

Not that she intended to enjoy the luxury forever, mind. She still had a job to do, and she still had a governor to track down. Plus, if everything went according to plan, the entire world would someday live like this. Not merely one man selfishly hoarding all the goods.

It had been several days since Caitlin had led her Revolutionaries—a group of folks she had liberated from a small hamlet under the governor's rule, which also included a friggin' vampire and a werewolf—to Silver Creek to topple the governor's regime of bullying and oppression. That was something she had never truly set out to do when she became one of the first female rangers to join a night-time mission into the Mad-infested wilds.

Though she had been chased by what everyone was calling zombies—Mad-infected humans with glowing red eyes and a taste for human flesh—and had lost her friend in the process, she had found a calling in her life which she never knew existed.

Caitlin took to the role of leader as easily as the Mad took to chasing anything with blood pulsing around its body.

Caitlin stretched, rose reluctantly from the bed, and the covers slipped off her like water. She walked over to the window where a thick curtain was drawn, its corners moth-eaten and faded. They made a stark contrast to the rest of the governor's finery. She pulled them open and looked out over the town—*her* town.

Silver Creek was a wooden fortress of sorts. It provided

a safe haven for those who lived inside its walls, wishing for protection against the Mad who roamed the pines and foliage beyond. Though dusk was falling and the last rays of the sun stroked the canopy of trees, along the tops of the parapets, she spied the silhouettes of guards, armed with bows and arrows, ready to take down any Mad who might decide to take a chance and charge the walls.

On the ground level, she could see the market square. Folks wandered to and fro, haggling and bargaining, all with smiles on their faces. Caitlin felt her own smile grow. Barely weeks before, she had been down there amongst them, never quite feeling at peace. Never quite feeling at home. Now that the governor had fled and his number one henchman had been killed—*his own fault, really, for trying to turn me into a lamb kebab*—there was an air of calm around the town. It was nice. It almost made Caitlin feel like she could stay there forever.

Almost.

Except she still had a job to do.

Even though peace had been restored to the town and the guard force now accepted both men and women under the careful watch of the new captain of the guard—her brother, Dylan—Caitlin felt a distinct restlessness.

The governor was a madman. A disgusting, obese, jellied excuse for a human. She still remembered how she felt when she had punched him, and he had tossed her back. His foul stench as he leered at Caitlin and told her she was dispensable still lingered unpleasantly in her memory. She had simply been another tool for him to play his power games with. For Trisk, her life had no meaning whatsoever.

And he was still out there, somewhere out in the wilds, oppressing, hurting, and manipulating.

That was something that Caitlin couldn't allow.

If only she had a map which detailed the extent of his reign of terror. She needed something which showed the direction of the other small towns and villages within the governor's rule. The reality was that there were places Caitlin had never imagined existed outside Silver Creek's borders. She was told that the world had died and her town was practically the last one standing.

Perhaps even a map which identified places where possible Weres and vamps—though they were few and far between these days—potentially still existed in the vicinity. Only a couple of weeks ago, Caitlin had thought them to be fairytales until she met one of each.

Oh, wait!

Kain *had* found a map nestled clumsily on the top of a dresser unit in Trisk's living room.

Shit-eating idiot.

Armed with that knowledge and having had a taste of the world beyond Silver Creek's borders, Caitlin wanted to see more of it. To feel the freedom of travel and see new things. Her heart thumped with excitement.

It was almost dark. Almost time to wake the vamp and the Were and get to work. But first, there was someone else she needed to see.

Caitlin got herself dressed, placed her silver-tipped sword at her side, and headed into the town.

"Dylan, wake up," Caitlin said, shoving her brother playfully but so hard that he had to grab onto the sides of his bed to keep from falling off. "It's morning."

Her walk across town had left her in a good mood. It was nice to see so many people smiling as she made her way to her old home in the suburbs, which Dylan refused to leave. She had given him the option of sleeping in comfort in one of the governor's other rooms or staying in their old quarters and, true to his nature, he had chosen home.

Dylan rubbed his eyes and looked out his bedroom window to the bruised colors of the sky. The moon already peeked wanly over the treetops, pale and watery against the muted shades of nightfall.

"In a manner of speaking, I suppose it is morning."

Dylan was nocturnal, still on "ranger time." As the former captain of the rangers, it had been his job to traverse the forests at night with his crew and eliminate any hordes of Mad which may have stumbled through the forest to make their way to Silver Creek. They hadn't seen any bandits in the forest in years, but the rangers also kept an eye open for them or other dangerous creatures which posed a threat.

Since he had taken over as captain of the guard, Dylan had tried to adjust to now working to daylight hours, but clearly, he still struggled with the change.

It didn't help, Caitlin realized, that she and their wolf friend, Kain, maintained the night time schedule for the sake of the vampire she had rescued. Mary-Anne had quickly become one of her most trusted friends, but it did mean a reversed routine if they were to spend time together.

Caitlin hit Dylan with a pillow, then ran from the room. With a chuckle, he gave chase.

She couldn't remember the last time they'd played with such carefree abandon. Before Ma and Da passed, perhaps? As they laughed and chased each other around their poor excuse for a house, a small part of Caitlin begged for her not to leave. To stay and keep watch over the town.

It could be like this. Fun and simple and easy. What are you leaving for?

But she knew that could never happen. Not now. Not really.

"Do you really have to go, sis? You've proven your point to the town. You can handle yourself against the Mad. Stay here with me, let's lead together. Me and you, bringing happiness and peace to Silver Creek."

"N'aww, ickle Dylan is going to miss his wittle sister too much?" Caitlin teased, looking down her nose at her brother.

Dylan raised an eyebrow and waited.

She sighed and put the pillow down. Jaxon, their black-eyed German Shepherd, entered the room, looked up at Caitlin, barked, and sprinted over. She bent down and stroked his back. Her affection for the pooch had grown stronger after seeing Jaxon's loyalty over the last few weeks. She would never forget how he had chased her halfway through the woods and saved her from several attacks.

"You know I have to go, Dill. It's not a case of proving myself. It never has been," she said. It was strange to feel like they'd swapped roles. Not too long ago, she had been concerned for her brother's welfare when he had been unlawfully imprisoned by the governor. "There are people out there under Trisk's thumb who may be in worse situations than we were. That map showed other towns, other villages, and other lives. Who knows what kind of squalor they're living in? There'll be no happiness and no peace until the wider world is fixed and free."

Dylan raised an eyebrow. "And it's got nothing to do with the fact you have unfinished business with the man?"

Caitlin feigned a thoughtful face. "Erm...well...maybe a little. But mostly the freedom thing." She smiled, then hopped over to the door. "C'mon, the whole town will be waiting for us."

Dylan disappeared into his room and emerged a few moments later in his traveling cloak. He did his best to hide the armor of the guards he wore beneath it. As captain, it was now his duty to wear the same uniformed protection as the rest of his crew. Caitlin could just make out the embossed markings across the front of his chest—a large, wide leaf with a waterfall pouring down its middle and off the tip.

The emblem of Silver Creek.

"Looking sharp there, Hank," Caitlin said, poking her tongue out. Hank Newman had been the former captain, a terrible man whom Caitlin had been forced to kill when he had attacked her directly after she had offered him life.

Dylan stuck his middle finger up in response.

"Hey, that's no way to treat a lady," a voice called from the corner of the room where a large casket now lay open. Mary-Anne sat upright, looking at them both.

"A lady? Have you *met* Cat?"

"She may be rougher than a straw jumper, but she's still a lady," Mary-Anne said. "So if you don't put that finger down, I'm going to bite off the tip and use it as a straw."

Caitlin laughed, knowing that Mary-Anne's humor had a tendency to make people feel uncomfortable, but she didn't often mean it. Dylan, meanwhile, went pale. His laugh sounded hollow.

He hadn't quite gotten used to the vampire yet, though he tried to pretend otherwise.

They made their way across Silver Creek, Jaxon trotting excitedly at their heels. It was a clear night, which worked perfectly for Monica Chapman's plan to host a farewell meal on behalf of the entire town.

Monica had really come out of her shell since the liberation of Silver Creek. Seen by many before as nothing more than a deranged lunatic who had lost her husband when Hank shot him with one of what they believed to be the only working guns left in existence, she had taken to a hermit's lifestyle. What no one knew, however, was that she'd worked in secret on the spares and parts of guns and weapons of the old world that her husband had salvaged during his lifetime.

Caitlin and Kain couldn't believe the number of weapons she had hidden in the basement beneath her house. Whether they all worked or not was a different matter, but the Colt Python she had given Caitlin to aid her in her quest to topple Trisk's regime had worked a treat.

Granted, she had only used one bullet, and that had been shot into the sky rather than at Hank's face. She preferred to play pokey-pokey with her sword rather than bang-bang-gunpowder with explosives.

But now, as they heard voices and rounded the corner, they could see the old woman bustling up and down the lengths of the long benches with a large pot in one hand and a ladle in the other. Her hair, which had previously been a mass of gray frizz, was now tied back in a ponytail, and though her smile was nearly toothless, she grinned more broadly than any other time Caitlin had ever seen her.

The benches were packed. There was a smaller table at the head of them all where Alice, Ash, Kain, and Sullivan already sat. Ash and Alice were deep in conversation, their heads a hair's breadth away from each other as they went all gooey and romantic on each other. A match made in heaven, really, but it still made Caitlin feel queasy.

It was Kain who first saw them approach. He stood up, looking like a changed man in his fresh clothes with his hair combed and washed. Though his face was still a mass of scars, from afar, he almost looked like a normal human being and not a scraggly, skinny wolf-man ripped from the wilds.

He bashed his hands on the table hard several times to grab everyone's attention.

"Hey, fuckwads!" he boomed. Caitlin rolled her eyes and laughed. Kain always did have a way with words. "Your guest of honor has arrived."

"Hear, hear!" came the shouts and claps of the townspeople. Several stood and raised their cups, sloshing dark liquid everywhere.

Caitlin felt herself blushing. Everyone joined in:

rangers, former guards, current guards, carpenters, traders, blacksmiths, and friends and neighbors she had known for years. Though she had never chosen her path for glory, she had to admit, it was nice to feel appreciated for her work and to know that she had done something good for the betterment of her hometown.

This was what it was all for. This was how life should be. Not only for her but for everyone both inside *and* outside of the walls.

The food was as great as it could ever have been. Though provisions were still scarce, the townspeople, led by Monica, really went all out in putting together the best meals they possibly could. Caitlin felt slightly guilty eating, knowing that the town would have to spend several weeks on tighter rations to manage this feast, but it was all worth it to see people's happiness. There were even plenty of scraps which Caitlin fed to Jaxon who had taken residence under the table.

"Hey, stop wasting food on the dog," Kain said, ripping a chicken leg to shreds with his teeth.

"Why? *You're* eating it, aren't you, Pooch?" Caitlin retorted.

Mary-Anne scoffed, almost choking on her drink.

As the night rolled on and the moon rose high, Caitlin turned to her two closest but unlikely friends. Everyone was involved in their own conversations now, and it had been their plan all along to sneak out when the festivity was at its highest. Though Caitlin could not have been more thankful for the help of her Revolutionaries, they belonged there, ready to help protect and guard Silver Creek on her behalf.

And keep those guards who previously served under Hank in line. Those were the ones she *still* didn't trust.

"You guys ready?" she asked quietly.

Mary-Anne nodded, then looked at Kain and sighed. As he raised another cup full of mead to his lips, she pushed his arm back down. His head followed the cup like a child chasing a spoon until he could no longer reach it.

"*Hey,*" he whined, hurt in his eyes. He hiccupped and swayed as he sat.

"I think that's enough for now, don't you?" Mary-Anne scolded.

"That's not your decision to make, is it? You're not my *Ma.*" He paused, thought about his words, then chuckled. "Ha ha, 'Ma.' M.A. Mary-Anne. You are, aren't you? You're my *Maaa.*" He wrapped an arm around her shoulder and was met with a look of mild contempt. "You're old enough to be my Ma, aren't you sweet-fangs? How old are you... *Ooh—*"

He stopped talking and did his best to keep from shouting as Mary-Anne took one of his fingers and bent it back until there was an audible snap. Jaxon let out an empathetic yip from under the table.

Ash and Alice both leaned forward and gasped at the awkward angle Kain's finger was bent in.

"What are you doing?" Ash whispered, glancing at the other tables to check no one was listening.

"It's rude to ask a woman her age," Mary-Anne replied, looking as if butter wouldn't melt on her tongue. "Besides, he's a Were. He'll heal soon enough."

Kain whimpered as they slipped out and headed for the gates. The night air was cool, and they could hear the festivities from halfway across town now. The sky above glittered with a million bright white stars.

"You be careful out there, Kitty Cat," Alice said, smiling affectionately and coming in for the hug. They wrapped each other tightly in a hug. Alice placed a small kiss on Caitlin's cheek. "We need you back in one piece."

Ash was next, his hug warm and supportive. "The world isn't ready for you, Caitlin," he said, reaching into his pocket and pulling out a small leather belt with four throwing knives attached—a small gift inherited from Mary-Anne's treasure trove of weapons. "Take these and watch yourself. You'll do great things, I just know it."

Caitlin could feel tears rising but did her best to pull them back. How could she have found such wonderful people out there in the place where the governor had told them only Mad existed?

"You two take care of each other, okay?" Caitlin said, pointing one of her new knives between the two. "If I come back and you're, like, dead or something, there'll be hell to pay. I need you guys to be my eyes and ears. No getting beaten up and making yourselves vulnerable. I mean it. Top form."

Alice and Ash grinned. He wrapped his arm over Alice's shoulder. "Sure thing."

Sullivan and Dylan looked at each other. Dylan nudged Sullivan ahead, clearly uncertain of what to say to Caitlin. In all honesty, he hardly knew her.

"Erm…you…" He took a deep breath. "You do you."

Caitlin laughed and pulled Sullivan in for a hug. Her hands barely met around his huge frame, and she had to stand on her tiptoes to whisper, "Without you, I know my brother would be dead." She kissed his cheek, and he blushed.

When Sullivan stepped away, Dylan approached.

"Oh, enough of the goodbyes. Can we get going already?" Kain complained between hiccups.

They all snorted, a mixture of mockery and amusement. Dylan bent down and patted Jaxon's head. The dog snuggled into his palms, whined, then licked his face. "I wish you didn't have to take this one with you, too," he said.

Caitlin smiled. "He's the best Mad detector around."

Dylan reached forward and pulled Caitlin in for her final hug. They held each other for some time before he let go. "My little sister, out to tackle the world."

"You know it."

Dylan held her shoulders. "There was never a part of me that doubted you belonged at the front of it all."

Caitlin looked confused. "What do you mean?"

"Who do you think it was who convinced the governor to make Hank allow women on the ranger patrol?" His smile stretched ear-to-ear.

Caitlin's eyes lit up. "You?" She thought for a moment. "Not that he needed much convincing in the end, though."

Dylan nodded. "Still, Ma and Da always said it. Great things will come from you. Great things already have. I have no doubt that everything you touch will turn to gold, and before long, this town will be flooded with people saved, trading routes will open, and a whole world will fall at your feet."

Caitlin blushed.

Dylan smiled. "Now, head on out there and bring some color to this miserable gray-scale fuckery of a world."

Caitlin stared at her brother, overwhelmed with emotion. She felt she could stand there forever, savor the feeling, and be with them all for eternity.

That was until there was a sound of chains and scraping metal from the large wooden gates behind.

"Er...guys?" Kain said, a note of definite alarm infusing his voice.

They all turned to see the gates now wide open and Kain on the floor next to the heavy chains which operated the mechanisms. He scrambled backward as a handful of Mad looked at them as if in surprise, then began to run.

"That's what we get for inviting the gate guards to dinner," Caitlin said, reaching for her sword.

Dylan stayed her hand with his own. "We got this, sis," he said with a cocky grin on his face. "Sully, go right. Matt, you take left."

"It's *Ash*, dufus!" Ash said with a laugh as he ran at a woman whose body had half rotted away from the Madness. A moment later, his sword had sliced across her hip, causing her to buckle and fall sideways.

"Great. Alice, take front and center with me. We'll grab the big boy."

"Oh, *her* name you get right," Ash said, spinning in a half circle and stabbing his sword through the Mad's back.

Sullivan used the flat side of his sword and batted his target back. The man was huge, with strength that even he was unaware of. He swatted the Mad like a bear might swat a fly.

Caitlin gritted her teeth, tried again to draw her sword, and felt resistance where there should have been none.

She looked down and saw Mary-Anne's hand on hers.

"What are you doing?"

"They've got this, Kitty-Cat," Mary-Anne said softly.

But Caitlin found it hard to stand by and watch. Even after Ash floored his Mad and stabbed her in the chest, forcing the red eyes to extinguish. Even after Sully clobbered his enemy with a rock and watched until he stopped twitching. Even after Dylan and Alice paired up and took down a Mad who looked like he'd eaten quite enough out there in the forest. Fresher than the others, his stomach was the size of a beach ball, and when he was felled, Caitlin swore she felt the ground shake.

"See," Dylan said, a little breathless as he wiped his sword and sheathed it once more. "Piece of cake."

Caitlin looked from her brother to the forest outside.

"We got this, Cat," Dylan smiled.

Then, feeling more confident than ever that her brother had things handled, she gave Dylan a final hug and whispered, "I know you do." With new resolution, she kissed him on the cheek and headed off into the forest with Mary-Anne and Kain.

CHAPTER TWO

Silver Creek Forest, Old Ontario

Caitlin took the lead, slightly ahead of her friends, with Jaxon sniffing the ground by her side. They all wore dark green cloaks—gifts from her brother from his old duties—which helped them blend in with the surrounding forest. The trees were thick, though as they walked along, they often passed signs which showed them that the world hadn't always been as confused and overgrown as it now was.

At one point, they passed what looked to be the remnants of an old tarmac road on their left, its surface thick and black with faded white lines painted along its center. Trees had taken root and eaten into it, leaving crumbling chunks as a brittle reminder of the past. Caitlin tried to remember what she knew of the old world, way before the Mad or the fall had happened and thought back to a book which told of the days when people had supposedly ridden in metal vessels with wheels at unimaginable speeds.

She could hardly believe it now. That this might once have all been roads choked with traffic.

A short while later, a large metal pylon loomed over the trees. Years ago, it might have spiked all the way into the clouds, towering higher than any tree she'd ever seen. But now, the thing was rusted and folded over. A giant metal flower, devoid of water and sunlight.

They stopped for a short while in its shadows, Kain using the pylon's thick metal beams as a lean-to. Jaxon used it as a peeing post.

"What was it for?" Caitlin asked Mary-Anne. Though she was sure that Kain was much older than he looked, she was more confident that Mary-Anne was the eldest of the three and would therefore be the most knowledgeable.

"What makes you think I know a damned thing?" Mary-Anne's false protest preceded a hand placed dramatically across her chest. "How dare you suggest that I'm old enough to know the ways of the old world?"

"Because she's smart," Kain scoffed. "Know anyone else with an entire stockroom of weapons from over two centuries ago? Those swords in your attic. What are they? Relics you've found?"

Mary-Anne shrugged coyly.

"I didn't think so," Kain said and bent down to pick a particularly long piece of grass and place it between his teeth. "You watch her, Cat. She's your encyclopedia from the old days, I guarantee." He grinned at Mary-Anne. "C'mon, sugar. How old are you, really? Two-hundred-and-fifty? Two-seven-five?"

Whatever Caitlin thought, it certainly wasn't anywhere near those numbers. No matter what breed of creature you were, how the hell could anyone live for that long without turning to dust or drying up?

Mary-Anne waved a hand and said, "Oh, you're too kind. To think of me as such a young lady."

Caitlin's mouth fell open. "You're older than *that*?"

"How old are *you*, Kitty Cat?"

"Nearing thirty summers."

"Aww, cute." Mary-Anne turned and looked up at the pylon. "Let's just say I'm old enough to remember a world when these stood fully erect."

Kain obviously couldn't help himself as he tried to capture his laughter but failed. "I bet you do."

Mary-Anne whispered to Caitlin, "Poor choice of words, I know. Still, he's a kid, really. You've got to do what you can to keep them engaged."

When Kain eventually finished laughing, they continued through the forest. Mary-Anne explained that once, the country had been dotted with tens of thousands of those metal structures for the people to communicate with each other. Miles upon miles of wire once connected the world, creating communication channels in nearly every single home across the world.

The thought of it blew Caitlin's mind.

"You're telling me that you could dial a combination of numbers and speak to your friend halfway across the world in a matter of seconds?" Caitlin demanded as they climbed over a small pile of vehicles that lay like abandoned corpses in the thick undergrowth of the forest. Though they made a quick examination, there was no way in hell any were remotely able to work anymore.

"Yeppers. As easy as that. Though that wasn't even the

most impressive part of it all. Towards the end, in the final years before everything fell apart and a century or so before the Madness came, humans figured out how to do everything wirelessly." Mary-Anne emphasized that last bit and waited for a reaction from Caitlin.

Caitlin's mind worked double, trying to process it all. In a time long past, if she wanted to stop in the middle of the forest and communicate with Dylan, all she had to do was press some buttons and wait?

What kind of futuristic society existed back then?

Could something like that ever exist again?

"Okay, that all sounds fantastic," Kain said, also seeming to try to wrap his head around it all. "But if the world was that freakin' great, why the hell did everything implode? We all know the world blew itself up. But why? I mean, look at that."

Kain pointed through the trees. For the first time, they all noticed that they could see much further ahead. The trees had begun to thin, and in the spaces between trunks were whole bundles of what appeared to be junk.

Metal piled on metal. Rubber tires and tin cans. It looked like some kind of garbage disposal service had unloaded its contents all around the forest. Caitlin walked forward and accidentally kicked a can. It clanged around so loudly that they suddenly became aware of how much noise their discussions were already making.

"What is this place?" Caitlin said. She did her best to evade the trash on the floor, but as they moved further into the thick of it, avoidance became more and more difficult. Huge, precarious piles of varying colors of junk and garbage sprawled around them. Some looked like they had been deliberately shaped into huts and cabins, while others seemed to have simply been piled and left.

Mary-Anne sniffed the air, and her fangs came out. "I don't know, but something smells funny to me."

As if in agreement, Jaxon began to growl.

"Might be you," Kain said, pulling out his two short swords from their sheaths—gifts from Mary-Anne's stocks. He danced them around in figures of eight and kept his body low and his knees bent.

Caitlin looked around, unable to see any imminent danger. As they passed a cabin made from garbage, she poked her head inside. The place was small, only big enough for the small stack of rotten leaves in the corner which might once have been a bed.

"Not exactly the comfiest place in the world," Kain grumbled. He took a big sniff and recoiled at the stink of old urine which even Cat's limited human sense of smell could identify.

"Who the hell would sleep here?" she asked, reaching down to pick up a can with a faded and half torn label. It showed a grayed picture of ripe red tomatoes on the side, but inside was nothing more than a thick cluster of mold.

"I don't know," Mary-Anne replied, her eyes alert and glowing.

Jaxon suddenly let out an explosive bark. The sound of a shotgun being cocked came from behind them.

"I'lls tell yas where yas are," the man said, whistling through the gaps in his teeth as he spoke. "Ya's trespassing on my God dang propertys, and it woulds do ya well ta keeps that dog under control, steps away, and leaves."

. . .

Silver Creek, Silver Creek Forest, Old Ontario

Dylan and Sullivan watched the new recruits with great fascination as they drilled.

The training facility was little more than a small fenced-off area of Silver Creek. It was the place where all the town's guards would come to practice their swordsmanship as well as their hand-to-hand combat. There were dummies set up around the area, made up of thick wood, to take the sword blows and seating areas for rest when required.

Not that these guys seemed to want a rest at all. If anything, they seemed pissed off, and Dylan couldn't quite work out why.

The closest to Dylan—a young woman with a fierce attitude, whom Dylan had come to know as Belle—toyed with a dagger in one hand and a sword in the other. She grunted, stabbed the dagger into the dummy's neck, then played a deadly combination with her blade, twisting around in a full circle before the sword lodged in the dummy's hip.

Where the hell had she learned that combination?

He actually knew where, though he didn't understand it. His sister had always been a fast learner, but to see and watch what some of these guys could do made his head spin. They outshone the guards that Hank had trained and, even more surprising, their camaraderie seemed unshakeable. Since the liberation, he had hardly seen Caitlin's Revolutionaries separated for longer than a few hours.

But there was one vital mistake the girl had just made.

"You know, you should never turn your back on your enemy," Dylan said, leaning against the fence. Belle turned, as did a guy to her right, Vex. "The last thing you ever want to do is leave a big meaty marker open while you're dancing around with your sword."

"Ooh, saucy," Vex said. "What are you doing watching my mighty meat?"

Belle took a moment to reply, perhaps evaluating Dylan's words. "They're mighty big words from a guy who found himself captured and taken into the governor's prison for weeks." Belle caught Vex's gaze, and they both grinned.

"Watch your tone around the captain—" Sullivan began.

Dylan hushed him with a hand. He knew Belle's words didn't mean any harm. "Still, they're the words of a guy who has spent his nights out in the wild with the Madness. I've probably taken down more of those sons-of-bitches than you've seen days, and the last thing I'll *ever* do is turn my back on one of them." Dylan moved closer. "All it takes is one bite. One scratch. One tiny droplet of their blood to enter your system, and its bye-bye humanity, hello Madness."

"That's not all it takes," Vex said.

Dylan turned, looking Vex up and down. "Excuse me?" He wasn't sure he liked the tone that Vex used. Though they had all fought together, Dylan had to play this carefully. It was his job to watch the town in Caitlin's absence, and he wanted to make sure that people respected him and knew their place.

Dylan squared up to Vex.

Vex began to square up, too. He glanced over Dylan's shoulder at Belle who must have shaken her head because he slowly relaxed.

"Not that you're wrong," Vex said, stumbling a little over his words now. "It's just that we've seen stuff out there, y'know? Me, Belle, and the others who lived out in the shitty wilds with nothing more than a length of barbed wire fence the governor had given us as 'protection.' We didn't have your walls or guards. We had to survive out there, and we've seen stuff." Vex walked around Dylan and stood next to Belle, playing with the sword in his hand. "It's not always blood and biting. Sometimes it just…happens, y'know?"

Dylan pondered this for a moment, trying to gauge if Vex was playing him for a fool. When he saw that there was a genuine honesty on his face, he relaxed a little.

"What do you mean, it just happens?"

"I mean exactly that. I can't explain it. Sometimes people just…turn."

Vex moved back to his training, then, patting Belle on the shoulder as he went. A shadow crossed her face, and she nodded at Dylan before returning to her own.

Dylan stayed a while longer with Sullivan at his side, discussing what exactly Vex had meant. In all their experience, they had only known the Madness to affect people who had come into direct contact with a Mad-infected person. Spread was caused by direct contact and an exchange of fluids.

But there had to be more to it than that, surely? It didn't explain the rise of the Madness, and how so many of the population died out so quickly. Could the Madness simply affect people? Could it merely be a switch that went off in people's heads and turned them into feral creatures?

Dylan watched Vex and Belle a little longer before heading off around town to continue his rounds.

Psycho Joe's Garbage Lot, Silver Creek Forest, Old Ontario

"I ain'ts goin' t'ask again," the man said, raising the shotgun to shoulder level.

He was a strange guy to look at. A dark-colored ten-gallon hat, riddled with holes and grime, perched on his head. He wore a tank top that drowned his form, exposing skinny arms that seemed too long for his body. His shorts left little to the imagination, and his beard grew in patches.

Caitlin struggled to determine the guy's age. Judging by his size, he could've been in his twenties. But in his filthy state, he looked to be sixty.

"Gets the fuck off ma land, 'fore I lets old gunnie 'ere do the talkin'."

Kain raised his hands in the air almost instantly. Mary-Anne growled, and Caitlin took a deep breath and stepped towards the guy.

"We didn't mean to trespass, friend," she began, giving him her warmest smile. "We're merely wanderers through this land, trying to find our way to the nearest town. Could you maybe help us with some directions, and we'll be on our way?"

The man eyed Caitlin suspiciously. "Wand'rers, you say? Ain't hads wand'rers round 'ere in s'long as I can 'member. Only folks round 'ere who wander are those goshvermant lunas. All hours of ta day. It's a full-time jobs ta keep ol' Violet safe 'n sound."

Kain lowered his hands and shrugged. Caitlin studied the man, noting that the shotgun in his hands was shaking.

"How about you tell us your name, and a little about these…'lunas'…and maybe we can help you?"

"Yeah, help the madman with the gun. That's smart," Mary-Anne said, her eyes burning red now.

The man saw Mary-Anne's eyes and a look of terror fell across his face. He struggled with the gun, tried to cock it back—obviously forgetting he had already done so a moment before—then aimed it her way and fired.

The blast exploded through the trees, the bullets finding their mark in a tree trunk directly behind where Mary-Anne had stood moments before. Jaxon burst into a fit of barks, his hackles raised and teeth bared.

"Luna! Luna!" the man cried, cocking the gun back again, his hands fumbling and most likely sweating given his lack of control of the weapon.

Caitlin took her chance and darted forward. Jaxon ran beside her, leaping into the air and catching the barrel of the gun in his teeth. As the weight of his body came down, the gun came with him, and Caitlin seized the moment to place her sword against the man's neck. From up close, she could see the tendons stretched across his throat and could smell the staleness of his breath. He looked up at her, his eyes pooling with tears.

Jaxon shook the shotgun like a stick, yanked it from the now limp hands, and cast it aside. He turned instantly and growled again at the strange man.

"Good work, Jax," Kain said, appearing at Caitlin's side with his swords at the ready. "Who in their right mind would give a psycho a shotgun?"

Caitlin pressed the blade against the man's skin. "Okay, here's the situation now. Tell us who you are. Tell us what the fuck 'lunas' are. And if you try to shoot any of us again, we'll aim the barrel at your own dick and force you to pull the trigger."

The man nodded his understanding. "I sorry, I sorry, I sure am. It's justs, it's been so long since Joe's seens folks who ain't turned, y'knows? The gov'nor trusted Joe, he sure did, and alls I gots to do is keep the lunas away, that's right, so it is."

Kain rolled his eyes and smacked the man in the face.

"Kain!" Caitlin scolded.

"We need answers, right? What the *fuck* are lunas?"

Joe looked at them both as if *they* were the crazy ones. He brought a hand to his nose to dab at the tiny beads of blood that began to trickle. "Y'all tellin' me y'alls ain't never seens the crazies with bright eyes and blood on their teeths? Goshvermant lunatics everywhere."

"Oh…" Kain said as realization dawned on their faces. "You mean the Mad?"

"Ev'ry which ways I look it's madness, for sure." Joe seemed to remember something then, his eyes growing wide again. "Your friend, I hates to tell you, she's turning, for sure she is. I seen them looks before on those folks, and that's how its starts. Red eyes, red teeth, black hearts. Now, where'd she go?"

He tried to whip around again, but Caitlin held his arm firmly.

Mary-Anne appeared behind Joe, her eyes blazing red now. She leaned forward and whispered into his ear. "I'm not a lunatic, Joe. But if you try to blow my body to smithereens again, I will be your worst fucking nightmare."

Joe swallowed and nodded.

Caitlin watched the man with pity. Maybe he had been a regular nobody at some point in the past. Maybe he had been this way since he was born. Either way, it was hard to tell. All she knew now was he was a guy protecting his property and scared shitless of the Mad. Understandably, he was ready to pump his gun and blow anything that came close to causing him and his 'Violet' harm apart.

"Come now, Joe. We've been on our feet all day. Would you mind showing us a place to shelter and rest up? If Kain, here, doesn't rest up, he'll look worse than he would if you'd shot his face off." Caitlin yawned a little too theatrically, but Joe didn't seem to notice. "You've got to have a place around here somewhere, right?"

She waited for Joe to answer, but instead, her attention was drawn to Jaxon's growls. A couple of barks were followed by a few more growls as Jaxon faced into the trees ahead. In Caitlin's moment of distraction, Joe twisted away and grabbed his gun from the floor. They all turned towards where Jaxon stared, seeing then that several pairs of red eyes now hung suspended in the darkness.

Joe cocked the gun, a hideous grin on his face. Kain smacked it out of his hand.

"What are you thinking, fuckwad?" Kain hissed through his teeth. "Your last shot is probably the reason they're coming this way. Mad are attracted by sound. How do you not know that?"

They were still some distance away, but the sky was beginning to lighten. The four Mad wandered clumsily through the brush, making no effort to hide their noise. One of them stumbled and caught their foot on something on the ground. Another bumped into a tree, spun a one-eighty, then began walking away from its companions.

The entire time, their eyes didn't blink. Those red dots seemed to scan for them like lasers, all their instincts apparently telling them to chase after the thing that made the big boom in the forest.

What kind of backward-ass logic is that?

Caitlin leaned close to Joe. "Hey, Joe. About that shelter?"

Joe nodded, turned, and with surprising speed, began running into the thick of the garbage piles.

Jaxon streamed off after him immediately.

Mary-Anne and Kain followed while Caitlin hung around for a second longer. The Mad kept a steady pace, seemingly unable to see her from where they were. She noted that one had a missing arm, while the other seemed to have lost half of its face at some point along its journey.

For a half-second, Caitlin found herself back at the Carter Manor, staring down the wide steps as the Mad entered Mary-Anne's house. Only then, Caitlin had been unaware of her own abilities, her heart thumping as she struggled to take down the Mad. She'd nearly been bitten from behind until a vampire had saved her.

Now, with a sword at her side and confidence she could only have dreamed of, she strode towards them. A silent assassin in a whispering wood.

She'd return to Mary-Anne, Kain, Jaxon, and Joe in a moment. Just as soon as she'd taken out the trash.

CHAPTER THREE

Psycho Joe's Garbage Lot, Silver Creek Forest, Old Ontario

Caitlin caught up with them several minutes later, slightly out of breath and with a thin veil of sweat on her head.

"Subtle," Mary-Anne side-mouthed.

"What?"

Mary-Anne tapped her ears. "Super vampire hearing, remember?" She looked around conspiratorially. "They didn't touch you?"

"Didn't even get close." Caitlin winked.

Kain walked ahead of them both, keeping his eyes locked on Joe as he twisted and turned through the labyrinth of his own creation. The strange man's internal compass was nothing short of impressive.

They passed toppling piles of scrap and what looked like deep holes which had been filled to the brim with junk. The closer to the center of it all they got, the more the trash turned into structures that looked akin to walls, doors, and bridges. They marveled at it all as they jogged and kept pace. How had one man managed such construction? It was beyond reason.

Joe slowed as he removed his hat and passed through a doorway which the rest of them had to squeeze to get through. Flanking the sides of the entrance were semi-decomposed bodies, corpses, and bones—presumably from the Mad Joe had defended himself against over the years. At least, they hoped that was what they were. From the outside, the whole thing looked like a large igloo, and when they entered, they found the image apt.

They were inside what appeared to be a house. Several doors led off to different rooms, but the outer shell was made of compressed metal, alloys, and various other compound materials mashed and merged together with craftsmanship that left them in awe.

Joe waited for them, his expression stern, a finger over his lip. "Y'alls best be nice and quiets, yes? No wakin's Violet, no way, no how, or Joe 'ere is goin' get mighty pissed."

"Sorry, Joe, but who is Violet?" Caitlin asked.

Joe pottered around as if he hadn't heard her.

He showed them to a room off to the right. The doorway was tiny, but the space inside was impressive. Though Joe watched Mary-Anne suspiciously as she went ahead, he played nice and left them to it. Maybe he wanted to ask about her red eyes, but maybe he didn't want to know the answer. Whatever it was, Kain and Caitlin certainly weren't ready to tell him that she was actually a vampire and the glowing pupils were kind of *their* thing first.

It was so unbecoming for zombies to steal vampires' style.

They took it in turns to sleep while one person stayed on watch. Even though Joe had opened his home to them, they would be stupid to trust a stranger.

Caitlin took the first watch, sitting by the door with Jaxon's head resting on her lap and listening to Joe pottering around and mumbling to himself on the other side of the wall. A couple of times, she heard him call out to Violet but heard no response.

Caitlin let her mind wander over who the hell this Violet might be. Perhaps she'd be introduced when they all woke as the sun set. They didn't plan on staying long, but she had to admit that they were lucky enough to find shelter before the sun came up and roasted Mary-Anne to cinders.

They had discussed it at length before they had set off from Silver Creek. The logistics of traveling with a nocturnal companion were part of the reason that Caitlin was determined to keep the company's number small—that and the fact that she had already saved the twenty or so Revolutionaries from New Leaf, so she was hardly ready to put them at risk again.

One suggestion had been to take the casket they had forged out of the components of the abandoned airship. They had used this to transport Mary-Anne from the ship to Silver Creek before the liberation. Even with Kain's strength, though, it didn't make sense for them to carry a coffin around during the day when they could just as easily walk together at night.

At some point in the early afternoon, Kain awoke and

switched places with Caitlin. They heard Joe head out through the front tunnel, still mumbling, then all went silent.

"Strange kind of bloke, that Psycho Joe, don't you think?" Kain said, taking a seat with his back to the wall while Caitlin lay down in his place still warm from his body heat. Jaxon trailed behind Caitlin and settled down beside her, his ears down, and eyes shut the moment he rested his head. "Madder than a box full of zombies in a nuthouse."

"I'd watch what you call him while he's around." Caitlin sighed. "Might not take that much to set him off, and as strange as he is, he's given us his hospitality. I doubt many people around here'd do that for a stranger these days."

"Yeah, well. He's not around, so I can call him whatever I want," Kain said and stuck out his tongue. "You should hear what I call you when you ain't around." He paused and chuckled. "'Lunas.' Can you believe it? We've not even made it to the next town yet, and we've already crossed the language barrier."

But Kain's words fell on deaf ears. Within minutes, Caitlin slid into sleep, tension easing from her body with each breath.

In her dreams, she found herself playing among the trash, hunting for relics from the past that she could give to Monica—pieces of guns and old parts for machines she could never comprehend. Occasionally, she'd find another weapon, a sword, an ax, or a crossbow, but even in her dreams, she chose her own sword every time. Nothing else compared—at least, not to her.

She found herself wondering what the purpose of the

scrapyard was, and what kind of man guarded a rubbish pile for years on end. What was it the governor had offered in return for Joe's service? Money? Love? Power? What promise could make a man so fiercely loyal for years on end, even when there was no sign of hope that the promise would ever come to fruition?

As Caitlin snored gently, Kain laid his head back and yawned.

He closed his own eyes, still tired from their trek.

He needed to rest them for a little bit.

Just a little bit.

Silver Creek, Silver Creek Forest, Old Ontario

"You know, I don't think this will ever get old," Alice said, rolling over in bed so the thin cloth outlined her womanly curves. The sunlight filtering through the windows reflected off her body, making her look like a canvas painting.

Ash lay on his back, his bare chest exposed to the world as Alice cuddled him. "You know, I think you're right," he said and kissed her forehead and held her close.

She looked up at him, her eyes twinkling.

It was almost impossible to think that a short while ago, she had woken up at the crack of dawn to see her 'man' off to work. She'd made breakfast, cleaned the house, and lived in fear of the guy many called 'Big Bill' who would rather clobber her with a slap of the hand than kiss her cheek.

Back then, she could never have dreamed that one day, she'd wake in the arms of a fella she actually liked, let alone a man who had proven himself worthy enough in combat of the honor of his new position as the new second in command at Silver Creek. Ash was now the new deputy captain of the guards, and Alice knew he deserved it.

Oh, and not to mention her discovery of how badass she was with twin daggers, though that seemed to come second now to how good she seemed to be in the sack.

It's always better with somebody you like.

Alice stood and let her bare body absorb the late-morning air. She strode to the window, deliberately swaying her hips, and pulled the curtain wide. A man outside with a large ginger beard looked up, caught sight of her, and flushed bright red. She waved, and he lowered his eyes to the ground, running off down the street and almost bumping into several people as he went.

"I hope you're not giving away all the good stuff," Ash said as his arms appeared behind her and wrapped around her stomach. "You know you're mine, and mine only, right?"

He kissed her neck, and she melted.

"I belong to no man. Not anymore," she replied with little conviction, turning around to plant a deep kiss on his lips and push him back onto the bed. She straddled his lap.

"You know I can't go for round two," Ash said as she began to gyrate on top of him.

"Two? I thought we were on four? Or was it five?"

Alice loved to watch him squirm. There was something

powerful in being able to manipulate a man with nothing more than touch.

Even if Ash was a darn sight stronger than she was.

He grabbed her hips, lifted her up, and placed her back on the bed, sealing the movement with a kiss.

"Look, why don't you accompany me on my rounds? I'll show you the town, and you can meet the folks of Silver Creek. It'll be good to get some fresh air."

Alice sighed, smiled, then stood up. "Fine. But when we get back, we can make the air stinky again, okay?"

Ash's nose wrinkled. "Bad choice of words."

"You know what I meant." She grinned.

They both dressed and headed outside.

The sunlight was bright. It was certainly a beautiful day, especially with the view that greeted them as they headed along the parapets. Back in New Leaf, the most Alice ever got to see was trees, trees, and...

Oh, wait.

Guess what?

More trees.

But here, as she looked down at the patchwork of streets to her left and the canopy of forest over the walls to her right, she felt like a queen of the world.

"They're really out there somewhere?" Alice asked, shading her eyes and doing her best to see the furthest reaches of the forest. She thought of Caitlin, Mary-Anne, and Kain and wondered where they were right now. Somewhere out there kicking ass and taking names. She had been a little vexed to discover they had gone without her, but after Dylan had spoken to her and the other Revolutionaries, she kind of understood why.

"Yup, though I hope they've found somewhere to hide from the sun, for Ma's sake," Ash said, squinting and shading his own eyes.

A flock of crows exploded from somewhere in the nearby trees. Dotted across the sky, they flew in a large circle before heading over the town and off in the opposite direction. Somewhere in the distance, he thought he could see the faint trails of smoke.

"What was that?" Alice asked, stepping closer to the edge of the wall to look below. Two guards on either side did the same, nocking an arrow into their bows as they took aim. One of them glanced sideways at Ash—a gaunt man with greasy hair—an expression of contempt on his face.

"Probably nothing," Ash said, conscious that he was on precious time and wanted to get moving around the town. It was important to keep his face fresh and in people's minds, Dylan had told him. After all the changes in leadership, if the chiefs of the town didn't show their faces enough, chances were that somewhere down the line, there would be a mutiny.

And that would not end well—for them.

They needed strong leaders, ready to keep the peace. No more governors hiding inside their quarters. It was all about building trust now.

"It's probably just a deer or a fox."

But Alice wasn't convinced. She waited, staring down below.

"Come on."

"There." Alice pointed.

They heard frantic footsteps before a man appeared

from the shadows of the trees. His hair was dark with patchy bald spots all over. His breath came in loud gasps. He paused as he neared the walls, surprise written on his face as though he had no idea that he would find a town through the trees.

"Who goes there?" one of the guards shouted.

He looked up at them with a mixture of fear and elation written all over his face. Alice saw that his clothes were scratched—badly. Blood ran down his left arm, and even from up high, they could see the telltale red sores popping up across his skin.

Alice had seen those sores before, and that frenzied look. They were symptoms of a man who had limited time before the Madness took him.

"Please!" the man shouted, clutching his hands together as if in prayer. "My name is Toby Dobell. I'm lost, hungry, and in desperate need of aid. My wife and the others, they're not far behind, but I needed to run ahead to find... something, to find *you*...and warn you."

The guards tensed their bows.

"Warn us of what?" Ash called down.

Toby looked at Ash. "First, please promise that you'll be kind to them. They're all good people, I swear. I must ask that you promise to take care of them in your town in my absence. We escaped from the Madness. Well...*they* did. I saved them from a group of five using just my bare hands. But I fear my time is limited." He fell to his knees. "Please, can you promise me this?"

"And how do we know that they're not also infected?" Alice asked. "How can we guarantee the safety of our people with only your word?"

Toby stood with great effort and spread his arms. "Because I'm asking you to shoot me. Promise me my family will be cared for, and I offer you my life in return."

The guards looked at each other, perplexed.

"And your warning?" Ash asked. "It doesn't do well to hold back secrets when we could end your misery with a simple loose of the bow."

Ash nodded to the guard on his right. The guard pulled his bow taut and closed one eye as he took aim. Alice could hear the bow creaking.

"What are you doing?" Alice asked, suddenly afraid for Toby.

"He is infected. He'll die either way," Ash replied, not taking his eyes off the man. "At least this way, we can stop him spreading the Madness. Your warning, Dobell?"

"How can we trust what he's saying?" Alice asked.

Toby reached into his pocket and pulled out a leather flask. It might have been brown at one point, but as he held it towards them, it dripped blood onto the floor. He uncorked the top and held it in the air.

"I don't have long left. Please. Your promise, that's all I ask," Toby said.

"What's in the bottle?" Ash shouted down, a lump rising in his throat.

Toby smirked, though it came across as a weak effort. "The blood of my enemies." He cocked his arm back and set it ready to throw. "If I throw this, anyone who ingests or finds the tiniest bit of blood in their system will join me in the quick descent into Madness. Please"—he seemed desperate now, his hands shaking, and eyes streaming—"your promise is all I ask."

Ash looked at the guards on either side. When he looked back down at Toby, he nodded as if he'd read the honesty in his eyes.

"I promise," he said.

Toby let out a hollow chuckle and fell once more to his knees. When he looked back up, it was with a mixture of peace and loss. His words were cracked and dry. "Beware of the Firestarters…they're…they're coming…"

"The Firestarters?" Ash asked. But before he could question him further, an arrow whistled through the air and struck Toby in the throat. He pawed weakly, gasping for breath as more blood leaked down his front.

Alice twisted in rage. "What the—"

The greasy-haired guard looked at his hands. "Oops! It must have slipped."

Alice flew at him, but Ash caught her. He held her back as she flailed, attempting to calm her down, and twisted her around to stare into her eyes as he spoke. "It doesn't matter. He was as good as dead anyway. He was beyond saving."

Alice took a few deep breaths, feeling her heart rate slow. She rested her head on Ash's chest and let a single tear fall.

Ash addressed the guards. "Watch out for the others. See that they make it here in one piece. We wouldn't want all of this to be for nothing."

They left the parapet and made their way into the throngs in the streets of the town. Alice replayed the incident in her head, seeing the moment when Toby's throat had become a pin cushion over and over until her thoughts drifted in a different direction.

She wondered where Toby had come from and where he had expected to go. The surprise in the man's face at finding the walls of Silver Creek was unmistakable and, to the best of her knowledge, Silver Creek was as unknown to the world as New Leaf had been to them.

What the hell have they really been running from? What forces a group of five to stroll through Mad-infested woods with no real protection?

"Firestarters," she said. "That's what Toby said. 'They're coming.'"

Ash stopped short and fixed her with a hard look. The fixed expression in his eyes made it clear that, like her, he thought back to the thin ribbon of smoke in the distance.

Psycho Joe's Garbage Lot, Silver Creek Forest, Toronto

Caitlin awoke with a start.

It was dark inside Joe's living space—it felt too pretentious to call it a house—and the torches and candles had all burned down to their wick. Mary-Anne was still dozing beside her. Over the far side, leaning a little lopsidedly against the wall, Kain was fast asleep, his chin tucked into his chest.

Caitlin felt annoyance bubble inside her. She had given Kain *one* job to do, and he had failed her. Her instructions were simple—stay awake and watch their backs, make sure no funny business happened, and wake Mary-Anne so that she could have a shift on watch. That's all she needed from him—*one thing*—and he had fallen asleep.

She reached out to wake Mary-Anne, then paused.

It suddenly occurred to her that she had never had to

wake a vampire before, putting aside the time Caitlin had gatecrashed Mary-Anne's manor with a horde of Mad behind her. Was it like waking a human? Just nudge them until their eyes opened?

Only one way to find out.

"Ma?" Caitlin whispered. "Ma, wake up."

The instant Caitlin touched her arm, her eyes snapped open. She turned with vampire speed and was on her feet. Jaxon rumbled deep in his chest, a threat to bark, then stopped once he saw they were all okay.

Mary-Anne looked around, her eyes a dull red in the dark. It took a second or two before she saw her friend on the floor and remembered where she was.

Caitlin put a finger over her lips. She pointed to Kain and rolled her eyes theatrically.

Mary-Anne grinned, already knowing what Caitlin had in mind.

They snuck across the room until they were both inches from his face. Mary-Anne took center stage, and Caitlin provided backup.

"One," Caitlin mouthed.

"Two."

"*Wake up maggot!*"

"*Get your ass up, soldier!*"

Kain's eyes snapped open and met Mary-Anne's blazing red ones. His mouth fell open and he tried to push himself further back against the wall, scrambling madly as if he thought that with enough pressure, he could sink through the metal and disappear. Jaxon barked happily and leaped up at Kain, his paws padding on his chest and tongue reaching for his neck.

Mary-Anne and Caitlin fell about laughing.

"You should've seen your face," Mary-Anne said, doing a cheap impression of Kain scrambling in fear. "Now you know how it feels."

Caitlin doubled over, unable to remember the last time she had laughed so hard. The noise echoed around the room, sounding like several more people had joined in.

Kain's brow furrowed and he stood up, brushing himself down. "Very funny. But you should know you've picked a powerful enemy, friends."

But neither woman paid him any heed, too lost in their laughter to respond.

It took a few minutes for them to recover, and when they eventually did, they wiped their eyes and gathered their clothes.

"Is it already time to leave?" Mary-Anne asked, stretching and rubbing her eyes.

"I'm not sure. Hold on." Caitlin stepped through the doorway and returned a minute later. "Sun is just setting. The colors really are beautiful."

"Way to rub it in," Mary-Anne teased.

"We should say goodbye to Joe before we go," Caitlin suggested, strapping her sword around her waist and bending to look through the tiny entrance to their room.

"Y'know, I'm surprised he didn't poke his head into the room and tell us to keep it down," Mary-Anne said, looking at Kain and Caitlin. "Wouldn't want to wake his 'Violet.'"

"Yeah, who the hell is that?" Kain asked. "Hope it's not some flower he keeps in a jar, waiting until the last petal falls."

"You mean like Beauty and the Beast?" Mary-Anne

asked.

"Beauty and the what?" Kain replied.

"Never mind," Mary-Anne said.

"Still, that is strange," Caitlin muttered, holding onto the notion that Joe surely would have admonished them for the rowdy way they'd woken Kain.

The truth was that Joe was nowhere to be found. They crawled through the doorway and out the front. Caitlin didn't realize how claustrophobic it felt inside the house until they found themselves back in the fresh air. It was dark now, the stars shining above. A crescent moon climbed into the sky, shining a ghostly glow over the trash piles which made them look more and more like the skeletal remains of relics from the old world.

"It feels wrong to leave without saying goodbye," Caitlin said.

Kain raised his eyebrows.

"What?" Caitlin said. "Manners count for something. If we can't be nice to those who help us, what the hell are we fighting for?"

"Fun?" Kain grinned.

They crawled back inside and searched the rooms. There were several, each with purposes they simply couldn't identify. Every room looked like the one they had slept in, only with a different array of sordid junk. A dozen or so rooms linked together made Caitlin think of an insect hive.

Eventually, they crawled into a room almost triple the size of any they had seen. An awful stink hit their noses.

"Jee-sus Christ," Kain said, his nose wrinkling.

Piled up against the far wall were the skins and

carcasses of various fruits and forest creatures. A thick black pot stood above a stack of charred logs in the center of the room. Steady embers cracked and popped. Gunk and crusted food had dried around its rim. Maybe at one point, the food had smelled nice, but now it was stale, with a slight smell of burning lingering in the air. Above them was a small hole in the roof so smoke and steam could escape as Joe cooked.

"Well, I'm not hungry anymore," Kain said, ready to turn and leave.

"That makes a first," Mary-Anne said.

Jaxon bent low and began to growl.

"What is it, boy?" Caitlin asked.

"If it smells bad for you, imagine what it's like for us. Dogs' and Weres' noses are much more powerful than yours."

"And mine," Mary-Anne said, moving closer to investigate the pile of rotting food. "Joe's quite the huntsman, isn't he? Look. Rabbits, foxes…is that a deer?"

"I suppose you have to get good at hunting when you're by yourself in the forest." Caitlin pondered the incongruity of Joe and his odd home. She reached into her pocket and pulled out her map. Frowning, she traced along the route she believed they were heading and saw no reference to where they were. No sketch or illustrations of an enormous pile of trash. "I wonder why Trisk doesn't help out more? Maybe send food packages or something?"

"Maybe because the governor is a prick?" Kain suggested.

Joe appeared in the entranceway behind them. "Ise haven't seens the guv'nor in nigh on ten years, for sure." He looked tired, holding his shotgun by his side with three mice hanging by their tails in his fist. "That mans don'ts want no ones to know about his junkyard, no siree."

"What? Why?" Kain asked, clearly unable to help himself. Then he scowled as he answered his own question. "Because he wants those under his rule to believe that he has the world under control. He wants to remove the mess of the towns and villages to keep things tidy and make it look like he's actually contributing. Taking care of something." Kain looked at Joe. "Am I close?"

"How do you know this?" Caitlin asked.

Mary-Anne looked down her nose. "You think this is the first evil dictator we've come across?"

Jaxon continued growling. Caitlin bent and stroked down his scruff, trying to tickle beneath his neck. "Easy, boy. It's okay, we're safe here."

Joe eyed Jaxon uneasily as he walked to the pot in the center of the room and threw the mice in. One of them struggled and squealed, but the other two were as dead as a doornail.

"The luna womans is right. Ol' Joe 'ere came abouts this way when there was nothin's more than a few mounds of trash. Now, they piled up so highs I can'ts hardly 'member what the forest look like." He fanned the embers beneath the pot and a fire began to spring to life. "Yous hungry? Wants some chow before you goes on your journeys?"

They shrugged, Kain pulling a face. "Does it taste better than it smells?"

They took a seat around the pot, reveling in its warmth.

Joe was fascinating to watch as he pulled herbs and mushrooms out of his pocket, tearing and crumbling, working the pot like a witch around a cauldron. Despite the disgusting pile of crap in the corner, they had to admit that what he was cooking actually smelled half-decent.

"Joe?" Caitlin said when she was handed a bowl with questionable chunks stuck to the side. The warmth of the food in her hands lit her senses. How had she not realized she was *this* hungry?

"Hmmm?"

"I don't mean to bring this up again, but I can't help wondering. Who's Violet?" Caitlin felt guilty the instant Joe froze.

"Oh, that's my ol' lady, yes she is," he said, his eyes glancing at a crudely cut door at the far side of the room. The same place Jaxon seemed unable to take his attention off. "She sleeps a lot these days, but I does what I can to keeps her happy, I sure do. Y'know, this year will be thirty years we's been together, and I can't imagines what I'd does if she weren't around, no sirree."

Caitlin smiled, looking at Mary-Anne and Kain and already feeling the same way. Even in a world where dictators ruled and the Mad roamed, there was still a little bit of humanity in everyone.

"I'd love to meet her before we leave," Caitlin said, tutting at Jaxon and bringing a mouthful of stew to her lips. The flavor was divine, the meat melting on her tongue. She relished the taste for a moment before returning her attention to their host. "You think we could?"

Joe looked at Caitlin for a long while, his eyes unblinking. He turned again to the door. "I'd have ta asks her, yes I would. No sense disturbin' her now for no small reasons. She likes her sleep now, yes she do."

"Ah, come on, it'll be fun," Kain said as he stood and marched to the door.

"Kain," Caitlin called, feeling ever more sorry for Joe as he rushed to his feet and chased after the Were, nearly spilling the pot along the way. Jaxon leaped out of Caitlin's grasp and followed, bounding speedily to catch up with Kain. He danced and barked around his legs, his eyes trained on the doorway.

"See, Jaxon gets it. Why wouldn't anyone want to meet new people? They've been cooped up here for thirty years, so let's say hi. Make this shindig a party."

Caitlin looked at Mary-Anne for help. She shrugged and returned to her stew. "He's a big kid, Cat. Just try to stop him."

"No, no, no, no, no," Joe called as he stumbled and fell. He rose again but didn't make it in time to stop Kain from opening the door.

Jaxon exploded into barks.

The room beyond was no larger than a broom cupboard. There were spider webs in the corner and bones on the floor. A fetid stink burst forth in a thick puff of air, and they gasped.

In the center of the room stood a decrepit old woman. A thick chain around her neck was fixed to the wall. The moment she saw them all her eyes lit up, and she gnashed and chomped in their direction, her hands reaching for them all.

Caitlin instantly lost her appetite as she studied the sores and marks over the woman's body.

Joe turned ashamedly to the others. "Evry'ones. Meet Violet."

CHAPTER FOUR

Psycho Joe's Garbage Lot, Silver Creek Forest, Old Ontario

Violet gnashed and growled, fighting against her restraints.

She was haunting to look at. Caitlin had no idea how long she had been infected by the Madness, but they could take a guess and say a fair while.

"Er...Joe. Fancy explaining what the fuck I'm looking at here?" Kain said, recoiling in disgust. He reached automatically for his blade but was stopped by Joe before he could get it out.

"No! Please, I asks ya. Please!" Joe shouted.

Violet reached for Kain, her arms inches from his chest. Kain turned to Mary-Anne and Caitlin and said, "What do you reckon, girls? Go for the kiss? She seems pretty into me."

Kain tugged for his sword, fighting against Joe. Caitlin could see the intent in his eyes.

"Kain, no. *Wait*," Caitlin said, already running to help.

But it was Mary-Anne who sped to his side and now separated Joe and Kain. Her eyes glowed like Violet's, though hers displayed sense. She pulled them apart and held them at arm's length, her nose wrinkling at the smell coming from the cupboard. Caitlin caught up at last, tugging Jaxon by his collar and pulling him back.

"Oh, come on," Kain said, wriggling in Mary-Anne's grasp. "At least let's put her out of her misery."

"I can explains..." Joe said, spinning around like a Christmas tree decoration in Mary-Anne's grip.

Mary-Anne let Joe free. He stumbled as he was dropped on his feet, rubbing the scruff of his neck where Mary-Anne had held him. She turned to Kain. "Let's not do anything rash, huh? Hear him out."

"Thanks, ma'am," Joe groveled. "Thankings you so much."

Mary-Anne flashed her eyes at him. "You better have a good explanation for this, because if you don't, I'm going to let him end her misery."

Joe nodded, looking miserably at the floor.

When Kain calmed down, Joe led everyone back to the fire. He sat with his shoulders slumped and his head hanging down as he told them about Violet. Slowly, with halts and stuttering, he explained how they had been romantic partners in a world gone Mad, fighting in each other's corner, always having each other's back. He said it was amazing how easy it was to take the Mad down once you got them stuck in a maze of trash and separated them from the others. They'd set booby traps, then they'd pair up and hunt them down, clearing the junkyard and making it a safer place for Trisk's visits.

"But the guv'nor never tolds us he ain'ts comin' no more," Joe said, his voice cracked and blue. "Just stopped appearin' ones day." He stirred the stew as the smoke turned from white to black.

It seemed the governor had grown bored of his visits and left them both to their own devices. Joe and Violet had carried on the work they had been assigned to do without question. They simply continued to exist in the only way they knew how. The only way that gave them purpose.

"That is, until a few weeks agoes. Me and Violets had a big arguments about whether to keeps on keepin' on." Violet snapped away in her room as if trying to contribute to the conversation. Choked and gurgling sounds issued from her throat. "I tol' her, I says, 'We've got a job ta do. Now, it migh' not be the prettiest. But it's ours, ands our owns. If we don't keep ta world cleans, then who wills? There's a whole lotta folks doin' somethin' and it's on us to do our part'."

He heaved a sigh and looked at Violet with nothing but love and sorrow. "But she was tired o' it all. Wents for a walk ta clear her heads. Foun' herselfs fightin' off three lunas with nothin' more than her bare hands. By the times I heard them, I was too lates to help her."

"How long did it take her to change?" Mary-Anne asked.

"'Bout three days," Joe said gloomily. "At firs' we cleans them wounds good an' proper. Lots an' lots o' hot water making' her scream like a loon in the night 'til the bleedin' stopped. Then the sores came. Then...well..."

Caitlin looked up at the woman trapped in a recycled broom cupboard, never resting, constantly reaching forward for them the entire time but held back by the chain around her neck.

The whole thing was awful. For Violet to have been attacked and survive but still lose her life...

Where was the justice in that?

"And you don't know of any cure?" Caitlin said, hearing her heart's soft melancholy in her voice.

"No one do!" Joe said.

Caitlin looked at Mary-Anne, who shook her head, then to Kain.

Kain thought for a moment. "I've wandered enough to have heard tell of folks who think that they've found the cure. But you can't trust nobody these days. Let's just say I've never seen it happen myself, and I've seen a lot of people suffer. Whatever it was that brought this... monstrosity to the world, the answers aren't going to be in a junkyard dog's house, or along the lonely roads. You'll want cities. You'll want larger societies with medics and doctors."

"And they still exist?" Caitlin asked.

Kain shrugged. "I've heard of some that do but haven't seen them myself in years. Again, when a world falls to pieces and everyone in it is looking for hope, people don't stop to check the facts or question the rumors. They'll just blindly follow where strangers tell them hope is. It's the way of it. Human nature."

Mary-Anne scoffed. "Pah. Humans."

"Tell me about it," Kain agreed.

Caitlin closed her eyes for a moment and thought it through. A city like the ones she'd heard the older folks tell her about in her youth, like the ones she'd seen in books and drawings with buildings taller than the trees and people wherever you looked.

Were there any left out there in the world?

She thought again of the governor and wondered what he'd really been hiding of the world outside. All the people of Silver Creek had trusted him with their lives, and he had hidden the truth from them all. Trisk kept them locked up like animals with no knowledge of what lay beyond the walls other than the very real danger of the Madness.

Violet thrashed against her chains. Jaxon's growls quietened but didn't cease.

Sure, the Madness was something awful and horrific, but there were plenty of scarier monsters out there.

And the governor was one.

Silver Creek, Silver Creek Forest, Old Ontario

Alice sat and waited for them all to finish their drinks.

Toby's wife was beautiful to look at. She had been the first to arrive, leading a group of two men and two women. All presented a complete contrast to the man who had sprinted through the woods, covered in blood with his hair shaggy and clumped. Toby's wife, with piercing blue eyes and blonde hair that spilled down to her breasts, now sat on a chair. The others sat beside her in undisguised shock as if not quite believing what had happened out there in the forest.

They each slurped and drained large cups which Alice and Ash had provided them, water spilling down their chin and dampening their clothes.

"Thank you. So. Much," the woman said, wiping her

mouth with the back of her hand and standing up to hug Ash. Tears were hot in her eyes—of course, they were, her husband had just died—but she did her best to smile.

Alice offered her arms for a hug. The woman ignored her.

She scowled under her breath.

"Can we get you anything else? More water? Some food? We might have some plates left over from last night," Ash offered.

"Some food would be great…" The woman paused, providing Ash with a chance to say his name.

"Ash. Deputy captain here at Silver Creek. This is Alice." He pointed Alice's way, and she gave a strained smile. "She's—"

"His girlfriend," Alice said sharply.

She already didn't like the way that Ash eyed the woman.

"I'm Laurie," the woman said, sweeping her hair behind her shoulder and turning to her children. "And these good folks here are Harry, Nina, Maria, and Damon."

The others waved a hand but didn't look up from their cups.

"We're awfully sorry about your husband, Laurie," Alice said. "It sounds like you've all had one hell of a journey. We know from experience that the forests out there are awful for anyone to travel through, much less a family of five with young children. I'm from a small village just west of here, myself. Where did you come from?"

Laurie pulled her hair into her hands and began to plait it as she spoke. Alice couldn't help but notice her hands were visibly shaking. "That doesn't really matter, I suppose. What matters is we're safe."

"That's right, for now," Ash said. "Silver Creek is the safest town around. We'll get you set up somewhere nice and warm and ensure you have plenty of food and water. We made a promise to your husband, and we intend to keep it."

Laurie smiled warmly then stood up.

"Thank you so much," Laurie said, approaching Ash and kissing his cheek. He flushed instantly, and Alice imaged the warmth he must feel with her against his body.

Laurie then moved to Alice, who reluctantly offered her cheek, realizing a moment later that this was one of the strangers' customs. They all rose and kissed both their cheeks.

Alice and Ash glanced at each other as the final newcomer laid a wet kiss on Alice.

"Yeah, yeah, all the thanks," Alice said. "Let's get you guys cleaned up."

Psycho Joe's Garbage Lot, Silver Creek Forest, Toronto

Joe stood at the doorway to his trash house and waved the three of them off.

They had tried to convince him to join them—well, Mary-Anne and Caitlin had. Kain was a little less sure about the 'psycho' who kept his zombie wife around and locked in a cupboard.

"The best thing he can do for her is to stab her in the heart," he had said under his breath, receiving a walloping from Caitlin as she shushed him.

Sure, it would have been nice to have him accompany them, but Caitlin understood his dilemma. This life was all he could remember. All he would ever really know. He'd continue to seek trash and bring it back to his piles until the day he died.

And that was okay.

Everybody had a purpose. That's what made the world go round.

They passed back the way they had come, aiming for the place where they had met Joe to continue their journey from there. Caitlin expected to find the bodies of the Mad she had killed, but instead, saw only dark patches of blood and tracks where the bodies had been dragged off. Maybe by some wild creature, she reasoned, or maybe by some other Mad.

Who knew?

Perhaps the Mad were growing intelligent, collecting their dead together to reanimate into—

No! Bad thought, bad thoughts, bad thoughts. Stop now.

They walked along in silence, all deep within their own thoughts. A couple of times, they heard creatures moving through the forest. An owl hooted as they passed beneath its tree. Somewhere up ahead, something rustled in the grass, a small creature by its non-threatening sound.

The trees grew noticeably thinner as they continued. Soon enough, Jaxon skipped ahead and whined, his nose pointing skyward. They all looked up and saw several ribbons of smoke spiral into the air in the distance.

"Over there," Caitlin said. "Look."

"Well, I'll be damned," Mary-Anne said. "Where there's smoke—"

"There's fire," Kain finished, a little more grimly.

"And people?" Caitlin asked. "Surely where there's fire, there's people?"

Mary-Anne nodded. "Unless there's a forest fire ahead. But judging by the fact the trees are thinning and the ground is getting grassier, I'd say that we're probably in the clear. If I didn't know any better, I'd say we're looking at the result of domestic fires. Except maybe that one there." She pointed at a particularly thick and blackened column of smoke. "That looks more like some sort of bonfire to me."

"What's a bonfire doing burning in the early hours of the morning?" Kain muttered and scratched his chin in a telltale sign of disquiet. "Don't suppose it's a load of naked vamps doing their dance around the flames?"

"You need to sort out your fantasies, Pooch," Mary-Anne replied.

"Why don't we go investigate?" Caitlin suggested.

Eventually, the trees disappeared, and they came to the edge of a large field, the grass so high that it tickled their chests. It felt funny for Caitlin to feel real grass like that. Most of the grass in Silver Creek had been trampled and destroyed through years of footfalls. Even the grass in the forest was little more than short patches struggling to fight for sunlight.

"Look here," Caitlin said, holding the map out in front of her to catch the moon's glow. "Edge of the forest. We're not far now. I'm guessing that means we're here, near..." She leaned in closer, bringing the map to her nose. "I can't make out the name."

"Here, let me try," Kain said, snatching the map.

"Oh, because your eyesight will be so much better with smudgy words—"

"Ashdale Pond."

Caitlin narrowed her eyes. "All right, then."

She folded the map and put it back in her pocket. They began walking through the grass and could soon see the rise of an old brick building off on the horizon. There was a spire on top with a small cross, the tiles either hanging off the roof or missing completely to reveal huge holes in its construction. Light flickered inside, and they could faintly make out the silhouettes of an undefined number of people inside.

"There, that looks promising," Caitlin said, doubling her speed.

"Here's an idea," Mary-Anne said, placing a hand on Caitlin's shoulder and pulling her back. "Before you go crashing about in a town where you have no idea whether the people will skin you or fuck you, why don't you and Kain hold back, and I'll do some investigatory work?"

"What are you going to do? Taste their blood and see if they're the good guys?" Kain said.

"If that's what it takes." Mary-Anne licked her lips.

Kain shuddered.

Caitlin thought a moment. It made sense. Mary-Anne was fast and would likely be quieter than a human and a werewolf stomping through the brush and announcing their arrival. At least this way, they could get the lay of the land and work out a game plan together.

"Go ahead." Caitlin smiled. "We'll hold back, but not for long. And if you need to find yourself a snack," she looked at Mary-Anne and winked, "at least be subtle about it, please."

Mary-Anne's eyes blazed red and her fangs extended. She bent low and sped off through the grass.

"Y'know, it's all well and good being on that bitch's good side, but what happens if she turns on us and goes *Maaaaad?*" Kain held his arms in front, and his voice shook as he said that last part.

Mary-Anne reappeared. "Call me a bitch again, and you'll find out," she said and slapped him before disappearing once more.

"I guess just stay on her good side and you won't have to find out." Caitlin chuckled.

They took a seat in the grass and waited. Jaxon sniffed at the ground, found interest in a butterfly that took the air, and gave chase. Kain kicked off one of his boots and began shaking it, angling its opening to the ground.

"What are you doing?" Caitlin asked.

"I've had something in here since we set off from Silver Creek. It's been driving me mad." He paused. "Bad choice of words?"

"Maybe a little." Caitlin smiled. She thought for a moment, staring at the stars as her mind boiled and bubbled. "Do you think they're real? Those big cities that you mentioned back at Joe's? Do you really think there's civilization out there somewhere?"

Kain shrugged, digging his hands into his boot. "I don't know. Maybe. Can't be impossible, can it? There was a time when it was nothing more than a quick run down the road before you found one. People everywhere. Claustrophobic things, those cities. Though, ironically, super easy to hide in plain sight... Ah!" His eyes widened, and he pulled out a thorn that had lodged itself into the sole of his shoe. "Aha. Gotcha, you little shit."

"But you've not seen any recently?" Caitlin asked, ignoring the boot comment.

Kain placed his shoe back on, his tongue sticking out of his mouth. When he looked at Caitlin, his shoulders dropped. "Look, I've been around a fair while in this fucked up era, and all I've seen are ruins. The old towns and cities I used to visit before my pack and I went off to find our own salvation were desolate aside from the Mad. Think about it, would you rather be out in the country to risk running into a couple dozen Mad, or slap-bang in the center of the city where there might be several thousand? That was the way of things when it all happened. When the shit went down. Some people just...turned."

Caitlin sighed, staring at the sky. She could see the constellations swirl above her, gleaming orbs and planets dotted out in space. Surely, somewhere, there was a group of folks living better than this?

Kain put his shoe back on. He looked at Caitlin, noting how deflated she looked in that moment. "Cat, I like to hold on to hope and say that somewhere out there is something bigger and better where people can live safely. Maybe even with tech and electricity. But, kid..." He leaned closer and placed a hand on her shoulder. "When the Madness came, no one saw it coming. I saw people change in an instant, as though suddenly struck by lightning. I can't explain it, but it was like something in humanity just snapped. Some people were unaffected, others went batshit. That's all there is to it. Do *you* think a city would survive something like that?"

Caitlin went quiet, pondering Kain's words.

They both sat in silent thought, watching Jaxon frolic as they waited for Mary-Anne to return.

CHAPTER FIVE

Silver Creek, Silver Creek Forest, Old Ontario

Dylan stood on the level ground near the gates and watched as the heavy wooden doors swung open. There was a large, clumsily boarded patch over the hole where Mary-Anne had smashed through with nothing more than her bare fists.

The doors protested and then clunked into place. A woman, wrapped in a shawl, walked through with a man at her side. There, they met a guard who spoke to them at arm's reach and informed them of the process of new arrivals.

Dylan shook his head, watching them limp away, escorted by a pair of guards instructed to keep one hand on their weapons at all times.

"That's the fifth set of stragglers we've had arrive today," Sullivan said, standing proudly at his side.

"How many is that in total, now?" Dylan watched the couple disappear around the corner.

Sullivan counted on his fingers, his face screwed up in thought. "Nineteen in three days."

"What the hell is happening out there?" Dylan muttered, more to himself than to Sullivan. "It's been years since any strangers have come through our gates, and now we've had *nineteen* in three days? Something's going on out there, Sully. Something's going on out there in the woods. Maybe even beyond—and I don't like it."

"Maybe a bear?" Sullivan offered.

Dylan ignored the comment and stroked his chin, taking a second to try to understand what could be behind the sudden influx of refugees. It wasn't like the strangers could have *aimed* for Silver Creek. To the best of his knowledge, Silver Creek was a mystery, surrounded by trees and invisible from afar. There were only four people out there who knew where Silver Creek was, and three of them were occupied chasing the governor.

The other one…well, that *was* the governor.

"Maybe a bear?" Sullivan asked, a little louder.

"Probably not a bear," Dylan said. "But definitely something." He placed his hands on his hips and wondered whether this was a good or bad omen. "Gather the CoR. I think this warrants a discussion."

Sullivan nodded and headed off into the town, his heavy footsteps loud enough to hear even once he vanished around the corner.

Dylan made his way up the steps and to the top of the gates, nodding at each guard he passed. It felt strange, now, being on the other side of it all. Just a few weeks ago, he had felt the divide between guards and scouts. Guards would look down their noses or make snide comments as he passed by in his cloak to head out on patrol, but now, everyone was friendly, smiling, eager to say hello—well, mostly everyone.

Maybe that's what happened when you took down an evil dictator.

Or maybe that's just how everyone treated the man in charge of it all.

Either way, Dylan wasn't completely sure he liked it.

He looked out over the treetops, deep in thought. Stirred by some quiet inner instinct, he squinted into the distance and saw something wobbling on the horizon, just above the trees. A gray ribbon of...smoke, it seemed. Though he couldn't be certain. If he wanted to be sure, he'd need someone with better eyes like—

A vampire?

Dylan chuckled to himself and made his way back down the stairs, thinking of the new arrivals. All nineteen strangers had now been offered the basic amenities.

Food, water, shelter.

That was the golden three, right?

Well...and the occasional good romp in the sack, Dylan thought. *A chance to empty the pipes and release some hormones.* When was the last time he'd had that?

As he made his way along the street, it was impossible not to notice that the atmosphere was different these days. Calmer. Folks smiled, and people waved. There seemed to be more color in the world, and Dylan couldn't help but join in the smiles.

It had been messy, though, and the fight had been hard, but it had all been for the betterment of Silver Creek. The liberation was the turning point the town had so desperately needed.

My sister, the hero. Who'd have thought it?

When Mother Wendy's Tavern came into view, Dylan shaded his eyes from the sun and looked ahead to where a buxom woman stood in the doorway, with breasts so large that they drooped and hung over her waist. She was a pretty woman, about the size of a small house. Her dark hair was pigtailed over each shoulder, and her lips shone bright red against her pale face. She wore her signature dark tunic over a white dress and held a pan in her hand.

"Mother Wendy," Dylan said, doffing his hood.

"Cut that out right now, Dylan. You know my friends call me 'Wen.'" She bounded forward and squeezed Dylan so tightly that his breath caught. With a broad smile, she leaned back, clutched his face in her hands, and said, "Now give me some sugar."

She placed a large wet, red kiss on Dylan's face, leaving a mark. Nobody knew how she created her signature lipstick. What with the world falling to bits, it was hardly high on people's agenda to doll themselves up with makeup. Though many people had asked Mother Wendy her secret, she'd always repeat that that was, "a trick I'm taking to the grave."

"I still can't believe it," she said, finally releasing Dylan. "Dylan Harrison, the brand-new governor of Silver Creek."

"Erm, captain of the guards," Dylan corrected her. "I'm *nothing* like the governor."

"That's true. But you're also much more than just the captain, now. Especially with your sister gone, too. You've got the whole town to be looking after. I swear, I've never heard anyone's names brought up so much these days as you and your sweet sister. It's all people talk about." She shot a knowing look his way. "I'm thinking maybe that's why there's a table of darlings waiting for you in the back room, now?"

"I'd hardly call them darlings." He grinned. "They're all here, then?"

"That's right. Your little pet, Sully, came by not too long ago and said to set up for their arrival. Is there anything I should be worried about? Not planning a conspiracy or anything unlawful in the back of my humble abode, now, are you?" She fanned herself with a towel and started walking back inside. "That's all I need, for my tavern to turn into a political boardroom of mayhem."

She paused when she reached the door. "Actually, that might not be bad for business... Well? You're coming in, aren't you?"

Mother Wendy busied herself preparing a tray of varying frothy drinks for Dylan's company. He couldn't believe how speedily she did it either. For a woman her size, he figured it would be something of a challenge to maneuver around the bar and get everything ready.

But lickety-split, she was done.

"This way, now, sugar," she cooed, opening the door with one arm and allowing him entrance.

Five faces turned to look when Dylan walked in. He watched Mother Wendy fuss with people's drinks, her large frame hardly able to navigate around the large table in the center of the room without knocking into people's chairs.

When she finished her round, she stopped at the door

and yelled, "Drinks are on the governor," winked, and laughed heartily before closing the door behind her.

Dylan flushed. "She's kidding."

"Yeah, the governor hasn't got two cents to rub together," Sullivan joked, then shut up quick when Dylan shot him daggers.

Dylan took his place at the table next to Sullivan. To his left sat Ash, then Alice, Vex, and Belle. He took a swig of his drink, then said, "Thank you all for coming on such short notice. I know that we haven't all had a chance to gather properly since—"

"Since we kicked ass and scared Trisk to high heaven?"

There was a chorus of laughs and 'Hear, hear!'

Dylan couldn't stop his own smile. "Exactly. But I believe we all know why we're here, today?"

"Because Caitlin's a friggin' rock star and loves us enough to put us in charge?" Vex said, whacking Belle on the arm as if waiting for her to laugh. "Nothing?" She rolled her eyes, grinned, and waited patiently for Dylan to continue speaking.

"In a manner of speaking," Dylan continued. "Truth is that my sister believes in you all. Which means I believe in you all. We spoke at great length before she left about how this town should run—*would* run. What changes we could make to ensure that this town would never again fall into a dictatorship and would instead be led by the people. I believe that this is the beginning of that. You five, the traveling three, and I are the new council."

Sullivan bounced excitedly on his chair. "The CoR, right?"

"What the hell is the CoR?" Alice leaned forward.

"Sounds like the middle of an apple or some shit. Who the hell wants to be named after a fruit?"

"It's the Council of Revolutionaries." Ash remained composed and calm. His former guard training had taught him manners in situations such as these. "Am I right, oh captain, my captain?"

Dylan nodded. "That's right. It's our job to work together and lead the people. It's our duty to keep the people of Silver Creek safe from what's going on out there." He pointed out the window. "I'm not sure how many of you will have noticed—with more than half of you being new to this town—but we've had a steady stream of stragglers filtering through our gates ever since the governor's departure."

Quietly, Dylan filled them all in on the numbers. He told them how people arrived with nothing more than the clothes on their back, unwilling to tell their tales. They listened in silence as he added that they had empty rooms available in the town, at Mother Wendy's, and in people's houses, but these were filling up quickly.

"It's got to be Trisk, right?" Belle said when he ceased his explanation. She was considerably younger than the rest, not long out of her teens, but the fire inside her shone brightly. "That's got to be the only explanation."

"Does it?" Ash said. "There are all sorts of dangers out there. What's the likelihood that one man would disrupt something enough to send a whole town fleeing? The Madness is still very much the biggest cause of suffering and despair around. Who's to say that a horde or fleet of Mad-riddled fuckers hasn't swept through and taken out a town? We now know that vampires and Werewolves are real, though their numbers are small. Have we ever thought about what happens if one of those goes Mad? The destruction that could cause?"

Everyone nodded solemnly.

"You might be on to something there," Alice said. "Just this morning, we saw a man appear at the gates, begging to be shot in exchange for the safety of his family. He had the sores and the telltale signs of the Madness and said it was from defending his family in the woods."

"Are you suggesting he lied?" Ash asked.

"Those sores were several days old. He told us he was *recently* attacked by the Mad. Either the incubation period of the Madness is getting shorter, or the man was lying." Without conscious thought, Alice reached for Ash's hand and held it under the table.

The room fell silent for a while as everyone fell into thought, evidently considering this new insight with the seriousness it deserved. Outside, they could hear a few birds chirping, and from the other side of the door came the mumbles of Mother Wendy's patrons as they chattered and drank their day away.

"That wasn't all he said," Ash added. "He mentioned that something was coming. He spoke of something called the Firestarters. Does that ring a bell with anyone?"

The group shook their heads as one.

"Sounds like some kind of music band to me," Sullivan said.

"Did he say anything else?" Dylan asked.

Ash shrugged a denial. "Not before one of our men lost his grip and sent an arrow into his throat."

Alice closed her eyes as if to blink the memory away.

Dylan sat back and ran a hand through his hair. He wasn't sure why, but he felt restless. No matter what day he woke up, there were threats. Threats from the Madness, threats from the governor, and now, threats from the Firestarters—whatever they were. He hadn't long been appointed as captain of the guard, and already, he felt constricted, like he was attacked from every side.

"I say we send out a party of rangers and see what's going on out there," Vex suggested. "If something is happening, isn't attack the best form of defense? Wouldn't it be best to know if it is the Madness, or the gov, or the firecrackers?"

"Fire*starters*," Alice corrected.

"Yeah, them."

Dylan thought back to the Mad he had seen over the years. Then he thought of the people who had filed through his gates, and an awful thought suddenly crossed his mind. Had they even checked them all? What was the likelihood that someone had come through with early signs of the Madness already on them and was now sleeping in Silver Creek, the Madness slowly taking hold, already putting everyone at risk of infection?

"We need to tighten our protocol," Dylan said suddenly. "If something is going on out there, we need to work from the inside out. Make sure Silver Creek is solid and safe before we send anyone out there to die."

"What do you suggest, boss?" Sullivan asked.

"We need to assess each and every individual who has come through the gates in the last week. Anyone else new who comes through, we check them, head to foot. If people don't like it, we throw them out."

"That seems a bit harsh," Vex said. "I thought Silver Creek was a town of safety and community?"

Before Dylan could speak, Ash jumped in. "It is. That's why we have to be stricter than everywhere else. You know what it's like out there. You've seen the Mad on a daily basis. If one person in Silver Creek is infected, it puts us all at risk. Who wins then? One case is all it could take before it spreads like wildfire." He turned to Dylan. "I'll gather several of my men, have them dress top-to-bottom in protective clothing, and round up those who have come through. We'll strip and search everyone."

Alice rolled her eyes, remembering the sideways glances Ash had given to Laurie—the pretty blonde, now newly single—earlier that day. "I bet you will," she mumbled.

"Perfect. Sullivan, you spread the word to the men on the gates that nobody else comes through without a thorough inspection. If they want in, we search them, and they tell us what they know."

Sullivan nodded at Dylan.

"What about what's happening out there?" Vex asked. "We need to find out what the hell is going on. If we suddenly get a wave of the Mad, it doesn't matter how thick our gate is. Enough of them pushing against it and they'll get through. If it's something else. Then...well..."

Dylan stroked his chin. "Okay, well argued. You." He pointed at Vex.

"It's Vex, sir."

Sir? Dylan thought, remembering his role in all this now. It still felt strange to be given a title.

"And," he said, pointing at Belle.

"Belle."

"Right. Vex and Belle, I need you to partner up and tag along with Ash and his team. See what you can get out of the newcomers. Find out their story. See if there's any correlation between their arrival at the town and any Mad attacks. Any stories. What the links connecting everyone are, and is there anything we should worry about?" Dylan stood up, kicking his chair back. "Revolutionaries," he said, raising his glass. "Silver Creek is very much our town now, and it's our duty to protect it. Let's not allow the governor's downfall to also be the downfall of Silver Creek. We're better than that. Stronger together. We are the revolution."

They all raised their glasses and drank deeply.

Except for Alice. "What about me? What do I do?"

"You lead the rest of the Revolutionaries with their training. Have them work with the guards to improve their swordsmanship. If something is going on out there, we're going to need a group who can travel together and tackle it. We'll need the Revolutionaries." Dylan looked at Alice with a determined expression. "We won't hide behind these walls forever. We make our base strong, we train our men, then, should the call come, we'll be ready to come out from hiding behind these walls. If Caitlin and the others are out there, fighting for sanity, then we sure as hell will be ready to, too."

Alice beamed, squeezed Ash's hand, and drank her drink in one. "Huzzah!"

CHAPTER SIX

Ashdale Pond, Old Ontario

Mary-Anne couldn't believe it. The church was *full*.

She knew it was a church, of course. They'd been around before the Madness came, remnants of a forgotten religion which fell apart during the great fall. She'd heard that people used to flock to church every Sunday to pray to their deity, a savior who would protect them when times got hard.

Yeah, because that worked out so well when the nukes hit Earth.

Still, never in a thousand years could she have imagined she'd see what she now saw.

Rows upon rows of seats. Dozens. *Hundreds,* even. Around two hundred people sat there, all facing the front where a man in a dark black robe addressed them animatedly. Candles lined the aisles. Several people nodded their heads repeatedly as he spoke. From somewhere in the throng came the tinny whine of a baby crying.

Mary-Anne licked her lips. It would be easy pickings for her if she were a bestial Nosferatu or Forsaken—vampires who had chosen against integration with civilization and instead, saw humans as nothing more than a food source. Luckily, the Queen Bitch had seen to most of them. There wasn't a gun in sight. No weapon, no nothing.

How stupid were these folks?

She made her way around the church to get a better look and took a deep sniff when something caught her attention. At the front of the church was a large arch where a door had once been. A woman in dark clothing stood watch, her tattooed arms crossed over her chest. Mary-Anne clung to the shadows until she was a few feet away then, in a click of the fingers, she pounced, her hand going over the woman's mouth as she dragged her away.

Working at speed, Mary-Anne created a gag out of the cloth of the woman's shirt. She ripped spare material and bound her hands and feet together, leaving her next to an old, cracked gravestone.

Would she hurt her?

Probably not. Not unless the woman decided to do something stupid.

"Felicity?" a man's voice came from around the corner. "Flick? Where'd you go?"

Shit.

"I'm here...darling?" Mary-Anne said in a voice that came out with a clumsy British accent.

What the hell are you thinking? Since when was the last time you heard a British accent?

"Darling?" the voice replied.

Mary-Anne moved quickly, and a second later, the man

joined the woman on the floor. They both looked at Mary-Anne with wide eyes which went even wider when she revealed her fangs and placed a finger over her lips.

"Try screaming for help. See where that gets you," she said. The man stopped wriggling. "Now, who wants to spill *all* the beans and tell me what's going on in there?"

———

Caitlin looked at Kain in disgust as he picked his teeth clean with the stub of a stick he had found on the floor.

"Do you have any idea where that's been?"

Kain looked confused. "On the floor. Duh."

Caitlin rolled her eyes but couldn't help but grin. Sure, he didn't have table manners. But with the strength and the powers that he did have, she'd choose Kain over a weak-willed minion any day of the weak.

"Do you remember packs of playing cards?" Kain asked.

Caitlin raised an eyebrow and gave Kain a look as if to say, "Are you kidding me?"

"Ah. Yeah. You're probably too young." Kain sat back and looked at the sky. "My old man used to have a deck. Found them in a dilapidated house a few years before I was born. Used to play games with them. Matching colors. Matching numbers. Blackjack. Poker. Used to make some good money from doing tricks, too."

Caitlin couldn't help but laugh. "Why are you telling me this?"

Kain shrugged. "I don't know. I guess sometimes, it's nice to remember the way the world once was. The simpler things that made people happy. Before life became about hunting or being hunted. My old man never had a zombie break into his house and try to rip off his face. He just smoked, shit, and played cards."

"Not all at once, I hope."

Kain shrugged. "Who knows?"

Caitlin thought this over. That life sounded quaint. Peaceful. Nice. Sure, it seemed Kain had grown up in the days after the world went to shit and had to live in a post-apocalyptic world, but at least it had been before the Madness. At least he'd had a chance to see the world wiped clean.

"C'mon then, Kitty-Cat," Kain said, jumping to his feet. He scanned the ground nearby and found two moderate-sized sticks.

Caitlin laughed. "What are you doing?"

"Let's not just waste time, eh? Show us what you got." He tossed a stick to Caitlin.

She raised her eyebrows. "You think you've got what it takes to beat me?"

Kain smiled playfully. "She's a cocky one. The cute little village girl thinks she can outdo an experienced werewolf? You might be good against the zombs and the naughty humans, but let's see if we can't teach you a trick or two."

Caitlin lunged in for the strike. Immediately, Kain batted her stick, knocking it to the floor. She looked down at her stick, stunned.

Kain grinned. "Not so easy, huh? I meant it. Don't get cocky, kid." He winked.

Caitlin bent down, picked up her stick, and went in for round two.

The two hostages blabbed almost instantly. Well, maybe one spewed words a little bit faster than the other.

The man simply froze and forgot to breathe for a few seconds.

"If you're hoping to get mouth to mouth, I don't see that working out too well for you," Mary-Anne had said before his eyes refocused and he told her everything.

Now, Mary-Anne stood next to the doorway and listened. The sermon, led by Pastor Andrews, Mary-Anne had been told, was the town's weekly congregation in honor of the Lord, their God, and the governor who had supposedly been sent down to Earth from the stars to save them all in the time of the Mad.

Mary-Anne raised the corner of her lip in a mixture of confusion and anger. They had literally just deposed the governor from one town, and they'd made their way to a town in which he was virtually worshiped as some kind of higher being.

When Mary-Anne had taken refuge in her manor, she had figured that hibernation would be enough to sleep through the worst of the Madness. Of course, she hadn't taken into account that lack of *real* human blood for the best part of sixty years would have had such detrimental effect on her . But she figured that perhaps she'd wake up, and the worst would be over. Someone would maybe have fixed it all, and the nightmare would be gone.

But shit like this…

There came a chorus of "Amen" from the crowd. Mary-Anne let her curiosity get the better of her and took a seat beside an old woman cloaked in a shawl at the back of the church.

The woman flashed a toothless grin.

The pastor's voice droned on. "And it is from the darkness of the days that the light shall arise. Sent forth from Him above through the prophet, our governor, to deliver us through these times of trial and grant us our redemption."

When everyone repeated, "Amen," Mary-Anne noticed the old woman still staring at her with that same smile on her face.

"You're new to town, dear?" the old woman asked. Her skin was so wrinkled that Mary-Anne wondered what kind of treasures could be found in the folds of her flesh.

"Just arrived," she responded, doing her best not to engage. She faced away and pretended to devote her attention to the pastor.

"For when the Madness fell, it was He who said, 'and 'lo, for your sins the blessed shall suffer, until all that is righteous is equal—'"

"I'm ninety-six, you know."

That caught Mary-Anne's attention. "Excuse me?"

"Gary Nimbler was a friend of mine. Great sport. It's a shame he has to work on Wednesdays." The old woman's eyes turned dark as she turned her gaze to the floor in obvious confusion. "Nobody's got time for Mabel anymore."

A man with dark, slicked-back hair turned from the row in front and shushed them.

To Mary-Anne's horror, Mabel stood up and clobbered the man around the ear.

"Hey," he complained.

All heads turned to the back.

"Mabel, now, now. There's no need for violence in the Lord's house." The pastor spread his arms wide, his face a picture of kindness as he addressed the congregation. "That kind of behavior can wait until after." He stretched that last bit and chuckled the falsest laugh Mary-Anne had ever heard.

"But seriously," he continued. "Mabel, dearest, let's all get along now, shall we? What would the governor think if he were to see this kind of behavior in our church?"

Mabel's face melted from anger to regret. She shrank into her chair. "I'm awfully sorry, Pastor, I...I meant no offense to the governor." She crossed her hands over her chest. "Long may he live."

The congregation all crossed their chests and repeated, "Long may he live."

What the... Mary-Anne watched everyone's attention return to the front.

The pastor continued his sermon as if he hadn't been interrupted. Mary-Anne sat as long as she could, genuinely intrigued by the whole thing. The pastor was quite the entertainer, reeling off stories and proverbs that she had never heard before in her life, and which no one in the room—bar Mabel, maybe—would know held no relevance or truth in the real world. He was certainly a showman, and the people sitting with eager eyes drank it all up as though they'd been dying of thirst in the desert and he was a nice cool milkshake.

Mabel mumbled and tried to keep talking to Mary-Anne. It was actually as the sermon began to wrap up and she began to panic that she turned to leave, only to find that Mabel had grabbed her hand.

"Where are you going, dear?" Mabel said, a lot too loudly for her liking.

Once again, the congregation turned toward the disturbance.

Mary-Anne swallowed uncomfortably.

"What's the hurry?" the pastor added. Mary-Anne didn't like the way that he looked at her. Though outwardly, his face was kind, his eyes looked like he was scanning her. She felt him reading her, trying to work out what she was. "I assure you, we're near the end now, sister. There's no need to dash off into the night, especially for newcomers such as yourself. Please, stay awhile." He gave a fake chuckle which made Mary-Anne's skin crawl. "What are you? A vampire?"

The congregation burst into laughter. Mary-Anne froze, then joined in.

"No, no," Mary-Anne said, doing her best to shrug off the pastor's comment. "I just needed to stretch my legs. Sorry for the disturbance."

She sat back down. Mabel shuffled along the seat until her legs were touching Mary-Anne's. "The secret ingredient is cinnamon. Just a dash, mind. No more, no less. That's how you end up giving people the chicken pox."

What the hell is this woman taking? Mary-Anne looked down her nose at the grinning old bat.

"What are you—" Mary-Anne began, but the question cut off as she snatched a breath.

Suddenly, Mabel's eyes snapped into focus. She looked around as though waking from a dream. She grabbed

Mary-Anne's thigh and looked into her eyes as though seeing her for the first time. "The sun will be rising soon, my dear," she said in a voice so quiet that Mary-Anne now had to lean in to listen. "You'll need some rest. Some sleep. There's a room at my place. It's dark in the daylight. It's yours if you require it."

The pastor's voice droned on as he paced toward the end of his sermon. Mary-Anne looked Mabel in the face, their eyes now locked onto each other.

"You...know?" she began, thinking how stupid it would be to say what she was out loud. That was not the kind of thing a room full of brainwashed, gullible individuals needed—to discover that a creature they believed extinct and reputedly drank blood currently sat in their midst. "You *know?*"

Mabel nodded, though with great effort.

"Meet me outside when the pastor is done," she instructed.

She turned her attention back to the preacher. Mary-Anne followed suit, her mind speeding at 120 miles per hour. Though she was eager to find out more about this woman and what she might or might not already know, she couldn't help but worry slightly that she had left two guards hogtied and dumped in the graveyard. Should someone find them, or should they free themselves, they would likely blab in an instant.

But who would believe that a vampire had appeared and taken them hostage?

No one, maybe.

Or perhaps everyone.

Mary-Anne knew she'd have to play this very carefully

if she didn't want to arouse the town's suspicions and pave the way for Caitlin to pursue Trisk without resistance.

The congregation was already batshit crazy. What would they say when a vampire and a werewolf appeared?

When the meeting finished, Mary-Anne was the first to leave. She moved fast—not as fast as she could have, but definitely faster than everyone else—and raced out the door to untie the man and woman she had left hidden behind a tombstone.

Her eyes blazed as red as she could manage. "Here's the deal," she began as they rubbed their wrists and watched her in fear. "You are free...for now. You haven't seen a vampire. No one will believe that you've seen a vampire. If you tell anyone what you saw, I will know. A vampire's hearing is tenfold what a human's is, and I will know. And if I know, I will hunt you down in seconds. You won't see me coming. You won't *hear* me coming. One minute you'll be breathing, the next, you'll know nothing but eternal darkness. Got it?"

They both nodded.

"Good. Because I'm going to be sticking around for a little while, and I'd like to not have to kill anyone in that time if I can help it."

When she was satisfied that her words had been heard, she made her way back to the front of the church. The grass was long, and the night was cold. She found Mabel waiting outside, looking around in confusion. The rest of the congregation filed out behind her, holding torches and walking in single file.

Creepy fuckers.

"Shall we?" Mary-Anne asked Mabel.

"Shall we what?" Mabel said, confused. "Oh!" She reached into her pocket and pulled out a turnip. "Here's my spare. Did you want it?"

Mary-Anne couldn't help but grin. The woman might be batshit insane, but there was something endearing about her for all that.

Besides, she was the only person Mary-Anne had met in years who even came close to her own age.

Other than Kain, maybe.

But Weres didn't count.

"You were going to show me to your house," she said, gently encouraging a revival of memory.

"Oh," Mabel said, though the word brought no further dawn of recognition on her face. "Of course. Very well. Very well." As they began to walk down the slope and towards a collection of houses, she added. "It's just as well really. The roaches are becoming too much for me to handle by myself. I just didn't think exterminators existed anymore."

Mary-Anne laughed and followed Mabel home. She only looked back for a second, her thoughts turning to Caitlin and Kain. She'd come back for them shortly—after she'd found out what she could from Mabel.

The sun was starting to come up, after all.

Caitlin grew restless, the wait wearing on her patience.

Kain had lain back, now, his hands laced behind his head as he stared at the stars. The same piece of grass stuck out of his mouth as he chewed upon it.

He was a handsome man beneath all the scars. When Kain wasn't looking, Caitlin would sneak a peek and wonder at each and every line and scar across his face. He was world-worn. His body told a story of the struggles and survival that it took simply to make it through each day in the wild.

She found herself curious, wanting to know where he had come from. From what she understood of Weres, during the age following the fall—and maybe even before that—Weres roamed in packs. Groups would band up, led by a single alpha, and that bond would be near unbreakable.

It was nature.

"Kain?"

"Hmm?"

Caitlin weighed her words. "Your pack...where are they?"

Kain tensed at that, glancing down at a long red scar on his arm which gleamed brighter than the rest. "What makes you think I had a pack?"

"It just makes sense. Weres roam in packs, right?"

"Some do," Kain said, avoiding her gaze. "Some Weres reject the brutal nature of their pack and go solo. Life is easier on your own."

"Is that what happened to you?"

He didn't answer. Instead, he leaned back, looked at the stars, and played with the grass hanging between his lips. "I bet that bitch is getting a stake dinner."

Caitlin studied Kain a moment, sensing the need to change the subject. She allowed it. *This time.*

"Do vampires eat steak?" she asked.

"If a sharpened two-by-four is hammered through their hearts, they do." He laughed. "Not that it ever really works. There's a lotta people don't know about how to kill Weres and vamps. Especially these days."

Caitlin pondered this, stroking the silver tip of her sword absently.

"You think she's okay?" she asked.

Kain rolled over onto his side and propped his head on his hand. "Sure. She's a vampire—and a badass one at that. Please don't tell her I said that. It's hardly like she's going to be held captive by some old lady, is it?"

They both laughed. It felt good to laugh, really. After she had lost Kiera and discovered the governor had imprisoned Dylan, there was a moment when she never thought she would laugh again. But now...

Caitlin looked at the sky, noting the black of the night beginning to fade. Birds tweeted in the forest behind them, and somewhere, a cockerel crowed.

"Still...she should be back by now, right?" Caitlin pointed at the church. "Look, the lights are going out."

Kain stood up, took a deep breath, and closed his eyes. "I can hardly smell her at all, now." He raised his nose to the sky. "I can smell *lots* of people, though."

"What does that mean?" Caitlin asked.

"It means we're standing up-wind," Kain replied as if it were the most obvious thing in the world. "Come on," he said, moving forward through the grass. "Enough waiting for sweet-fangs. Let's go see what crazy fuckery this town has to offer."

They both headed towards the church which, only an hour ago, had been packed to the walls. With their dark cloaks pulled close and careful steps, they moved as swiftly as shadows. Caitlin thought of the little red circle she had seen on her map next to Ashdale Pond, and her heart fluttered with excitement as she thought of Trisk and how satisfying it would feel to slide her steel across his neck.

CHAPTER SEVEN

Silver Creek, Silver Creek Forest, Old Ontario

The Revolutionaries rounded up those who had arrived over the last few days, and the newcomers didn't take too kindly to being prodded and probed. Ash had to admit that he didn't like it too much either.

Still, when it came down to a choice between forcing folks to get naked so they could be examined for any signs of the Madness, or having the disease spread town-wide in a matter of days, the choice was simple.

"Here, you're clean," Sid, a former high-security prison guard who had watched over Kain during his stay at hotel Iron Bar, said as he threw a pile of clothes back at a man with a scraggly beard and a shaven head.

"That's what I told you, fuckwits. I've been here three days. You think if I had the Madness I wouldn't have turned already?"

Ash placed a hand on the hilt of his sword. He wasn't going to cut the man, oh no. But even the movement alone was enough to suggest that the guy needed to watch his tone.

The man backed down instantly. "I meant no offense."

"What about on-fence?" Ash asked. Then, when the man only looked confused, added, "*Off*-fence? *On*-fence? No? Ah, just forget it."

The man skulked away with a scowl.

"Next," Sid called.

Over the following few hours, they made their way through a fair majority of the newcomers. They each filed in slowly, making their way to the inspection room as soon as they had been found and identified.

Still, they hadn't found them all yet. Out of the nineteen or so they knew to be in Silver Creek, they had dealt with six, and now another six were lined up and waiting. That left seven somewhere else in town that Sullivan had either missed, or they were deliberately hiding.

That didn't bode well.

Sullivan entered the room, his bulk filling most of the doorway. As he took his place by Ash's side, Laurie stepped up to the plate. The guards, now cloaked from head to foot in protective clothing, had taken great pleasure in undressing her, and now Ash sat leaning back in his chair, doing his best not to stare at her.

Instead, he counted the remaining newcomers.

"What are you doing back here? That's not all of them," Ash said.

"I've found as many as I can. I've also sent several other men to find the ones who are missing." Sullivan was slightly breathless, his forehead peppered with sweat from running around all day.

Ash raised an eyebrow as Laurie took a seat, her body statuesque in the glow of the guard's lantern. Her eyes found his. "They're hiding?"

"Not hiding, I don't think. Rather, either asleep in other people's homes, or just around the town. We'll find them all and bring them in, I promise." Sullivan hung his head, almost expecting to be reprimanded for his failure.

Ash waved him away, watching as the examiner raised Laurie's arm to a right angle and looked in the crook of her armpit. As her arms lowered, he couldn't help but notice her breasts wobble delicately. Her gaze did not leave his. "No problem. As you say, we'll get them all in the end. Keep up the good work."

Sullivan followed Ash's eyes and finally realized where he was looking. He seemed to grow suddenly uncomfortable. "Oh, and...er...I was asked by *Miss Alice* to let you know that the Revolutionaries have been briefed on their new training regime."

At the sound of Alice's name, Ash looked up at Sullivan, breaking eye contact with Laurie.

"Oh. Yes. Good," he said, shifting uncomfortably. "Good."

―――

Vex had grown fond of Belle a lot more quickly than he ever imagined he would. As a guy in his mid-thirties, he'd had a group of his own friends at New Leaf. Most had been the sad fucks who stayed behind when the Revolutionaries formed and moved on to Silver Creek.

Idiots with more pride than sense.

Ha. Suckers.

But he had never really bothered with anyone outside his own gender or age. Belle was the polar opposite of everything he had ever known, and he was learning to love her.

Not in a romantic way.

Fuck, no.

More in a brotherly way.

He'd had her back during the battle at Silver Creek gates, leaping over defending guards and helping her out of tight spots—not that she really needed it. Belle certainly knew her way around her daggers. Her small and nimble frame was enough to help her wriggle out of any situation like a slippery fish in the bare hands of a fisherman. And now, he was glad that they had paired up and been given the same duties.

"Take your time. We're in no rush. Just tell us what you know when you're ready." Belle's soft voice spoke encouragement as they sat across from a weary-looking woman and her son, who was about eight years of age.

Belle was perfect for this. Vex mostly sat quietly, letting Belle do most of the talking. Though he believed he had his own charm when it came to getting information out of people, Belle's method was certainly a lot more kind.

And a lot less invasive.

Though even that hadn't really helped them, Vex thought as the tired woman refused to speak and simply shook her head. Belle dismissed her and exhaled.

"What is with these people?" She scowled and leaned back with her head against the wall. It was their job to interview those who had already been marked as clean by

Ash and his group. "We take them in. We give them a home. We provide them with security which, by any means and measure, is damn near impossible these days, and they won't talk."

Vex nodded glumly. "Someone will, I'm sure of it. Whatever it is that's got them spooked enough to run here won't have affected them all. We'll get to the bottom of it, one way or the other."

Vex flexed his biceps, then cracked his knuckles.

"Not like that we won't," Belle said sharply. "Interrogation won't get us anywhere."

It felt strange being told what not to do by a girl, much less a girl of Belle's age and size. Vex supposed he was okay with it, considering he had already taken orders from Caitlin when they left New Leaf.

What a world to live in. One minute, the men held the power. The next...

"You've clearly never been tortured," Vex said playfully, prodding Belle in the arm. "You've never had your toenails peeled up from the skin. You've never had fire held to your open eyeball. I bet you've never even had a thorn stuck in your side." He watched her shudder. "You don't even know what pain is, do you?"

Belle pinched her nose and waved her hand. "Pain is sitting here and getting a waft of your stinking breath every time you open your mouth. C'mon, man. I know we're busy these days, but that shouldn't stop basic personal hygiene."

Vex's face dropped. He cupped his mouth, exhaled, then sniffed.

Not bad, but not great.

Still, not bad was better than bad.

"Yeah, well..." Vex said, trying to regain some face. "Real pain is facing the rest of the apocalypse with you. Talk about a thorn in my side? I think I've got one."

She feigned offense and slapped him on the chest.

"A-hem," came a cough from behind. They turned and saw a man waiting patiently. He wore an eyepatch, and his left arm was studded with crudely drawn and badly finished tattoos.

Where the hell he had found the ink, Vex had no idea. The last time he had seen anything that closely resembled a tattoo was a girl who had turned Mad as she ran at the barbed wire surrounding his old village and caught her legs in the trap. The scratches had been created like zig-zags in parallel, but that hadn't slowed her down. She kept running and running as pieces of skin tore off, the Madness fueling her forward against common sense until all that was left were shreds of skin and a torso crawling on the floor.

When he had clubbed her head, she had fallen on her face. On the back of her neck was a symbol of a skull with leering red eyes.

"I heard you want to ask some questions?" the man said.

Belle and Vex looked at each other. This was the first person who had stepped up to the plate who seemed even remotely happy to talk.

"Sure, sure. Take a seat," Belle instructed.

The man obliged. When he sat comfortably, he looked up and nodded. "Sergeant Hitchcock at your service, though my friends call me Tom."

Vex and Belle introduced themselves.

"Wow, a sergeant?" Belle said, impressed. "What does that mean?"

"It means that the world is dead and I can call myself whatever the hell I want," Tom said with a grin that brightened his face. "My mother told me my great-great-grandfather was one of the armed forces. Fought for the country. Died for the country. One of the lost ones who fell when the world did. Though there's no real organization these days to defend us—or none that I know, anyway—I figured I'd take the title myself. Who knows? One day, it might come in handy."

"I like your spunk," Vex said, admiring the man's bravado.

"I bet you do," Belle said with a sidelong look.

"Hey, your tastes are your tastes, my friend. But I'll keep my tongue on the carpet rather than the broom handle, if you know what I mean?" Tom said, making a crude gesture with his hand and mouth.

"No, no. That's not what I meant!" Vex said, burning red. "I meant I appreciate your gusto. You're the first newcomer through these doors today who has had any kind of interest in talking to us."

"Well, I'll tell you what I can. Your man, Sullivan, has told me that this is some serious shit. Whatever I can do to help, I will."

Vex sat forward in his chair. "Well, why don't we start with where the hell everyone has come from. Why are so many people wandering through the forest to get to our humble little abode?"

At that, Tom's eyebrows raised. "Wow, straight to it, huh?"

Vex and Belle waited patiently.

"It's like this, my friend. Folks are refusing to talk to you because they're scared of what might happen to them if they do. Some of them are scared that you won't believe them if they told you. I don't know if you've noticed, but it ain't all sunshine and rainbows out there these days. There are some nasty things in the world—some things worse than the Mad. And those things sometimes use fire to make a point."

"What things are you talking about?" Belle asked, putting aside her nice girl routine as curiosity got the better of her. "What could be worse than the Mad?"

"People." Tom said it without hesitation. "People who have been corrupted by the world. People who have been molded by fear and hate and hurt. People with an unresolved strength like I've never seen and a belief in the Lord that borders on psychotic. People with the power to influence and brainwash."

Tom looked around the room then. He glanced out the window to where a couple of children giggled and played, chasing some insect through the air.

"We ain't all half as lucky as you guys to have built a town like this. A place that's safe. My guess is that the people you've spoken to are scared that if they tell you where they've come from, then this—Silver Creek—will disappear too. They've already lost their homes, their place in the world, their identity. They're clinging on to whatever the hell they've now got left. They've been lucky enough to stumble across this place in the middle of a friggin' forest, and now, they're holding on." Tom scratched the back of his neck and reclined in his chair. "I feel sorry for the poor bastards still wandering aimlessly out there in the woods," he added under his breath.

"There are still people out there?" Belle gasped, turning to Vex. "We have to do something. They're sitting ducks out there in the forest."

Vex sat in thought a moment. "Who are these people? Why are they doing this?"

"Nothing more than bullies under a spell," Tom said. "Though they have a name for themselves. Firestarters."

"Firestarters?" Belle repeated, catching Vex's eye. They were both clearly thinking the same thing, that there was maybe something in what Ash had told the CoR of the Mad man at the wall.

"Yeah, like an old song or some shit. Their mission is to convert all to their way of thinking, to worship the Lord and the prophet, and to burn any who stand in their way." Tom lifted the bottom of his trousers and revealed a patch of skin that was sore and blistered. The skin was warped and stretched from the burn. "I fought against them. They burned my home while I slept. Our village is shrinking day by day as more people flee in fear, fancying their chances of survival in the forest over the medieval witch-burning that's happening at home."

"That sounds awful," Belle said, trying to imagine it. Her mind easily conjured wooden houses turned white and orange in flame and a faceless group terrorizing a town and setting fire to all who stood in their way.

"Where is this town?" Vex asked, wishing Caitlin had made a copy of that map of hers. "What's its name?"

Tom raised his eyepatch and revealed nothing but skin and a small divot where his eye had been before the flesh had reclaimed his face. He reached a finger and scratched around the edges, then lowered it back in place. "I'm not sure I could tell you *where* it is. That forest is like a fucking labyrinth. But I'm sure it wouldn't be too hard to find once they start burning again. Just look out for the black smoke pluming into the sky, head that way, and you'll soon reach Ashdale Pond." He paused, letting out a shallow chuckle. "Our little piece of heaven."

CHAPTER EIGHT

Ashdale Pond, Old Ontario

Caitlin peeked out from behind the shed, suppressing her impatience with a strong instinct for caution.

Not too far away, a man with a wide-brimmed hat and a grease-stained vest top worked a plot of land. It seemed the outskirts of Ashdale pond were bordered with a checkerboard of miscellaneous allotments, though this was the first man they'd seen since they arrived.

She watched him with a quiet fascination. He seemed at peace as he turned the soil, occasionally crouching to remove a handful of weeds. Behind him, a rusted wheelbarrow was piled high with misshapen spuds.

"What do we think? Is he a threat?" Kain whispered into Caitlin's ear. Jaxon waited patiently between them, resting on his hindquarters.

Caitlin scanned the rest of the area. Just beyond the allotments many houses sprawled in the first light of the day. Big wooden constructions, each with their own unique shape, meant a town. Though the sun was rising, she figured that it would be a while still before most of the townspeople came out and greeted the day. This solitary farmer seemed to be the odd exception, already taking on his tasks despite the late night the congregation had spent in the church.

"I don't think so. Let's check."

She picked up a rock and threw it a little way ahead. It landed squarely between the shed and the man.

"Huh?" he said, taking a second to stretch his back and wipe his forehead. "Who goes there?"

Caitlin and Kain remained silent, waiting for curiosity to kill the cat. To Caitlin's satisfaction, the man wandered over to where the rock had landed. He turned it over in his hand, looked around him as if thinking things through, then decided to continue forward in their direction.

Caitlin revealed herself when he reached the shadow of the shed, stepping out with her hands in the air and a smile on her face.

The man jumped. He grabbed the handle of his hoe and raised it, ready to strike, until his eyes caught Caitlin's and he calmed. "Praise be! You scared the ba-jeesus out of me, miss. I thought you might be Mad. What are you doing back there?"

"Not having sex outdoors, I can assure you," Kain said, stepping out from behind Caitlin. She rolled her eyes.

The man raised his hoe again.

"Ignore him," Caitlin said, taking a step forward and smiling. Jaxon followed from behind, sniffed the ground, and made his way over to the man. He paused at his feet, then began licking the toes of his boots. "Please."

The stranger watched Jaxon, and his face softened.

"Who are you folks? You know it doesn't do well to sneak around and jump out on people like that. Not these days." A shadow crossed his face as he looked back at the town and into the sky where a trail of smoke wound into the clouds. "Especially not these days."

"A truth we know only too well," Caitlin said. "So, let's get to know one another. My name is Caitlin Harrison of Silver Creek, and this here is Kain Sudeikis."

"How do you do?" Kain said, doffing his hood.

"Jamie Crawley. Pleased to meet you." He leaned down to stroke Jaxon. "And who is this wonderful little ball of fluff down here? I haven't seen anything as cute as him since the day my mama birthed me."

"Oh, that's Jaxon," Caitlin said, joining Jamie in giving the pooch a good pet. "He's our star player." Jaxon flopped onto the ground and showed his belly, panting and rolling as the two laughed. Kain leaned against the shed, his arms folded.

"Erm... Cat?" Kain coughed.

"Oh, right," Caitlin stood. "We're sorry to disturb you, Jamie, but we were actually wondering if we could ask a few questions. We're new around here and, to put it bluntly, we're looking for someone. Could you maybe point us in the direction of your tavern or somewhere we could ask for answers?"

"Sure thing," Jamie said. "Which tavern would you like to go to?"

"There's more than one?" Caitlin asked, incredulous.

Jamie laughed. "Aye, three to be exact. You've got the Spit & Bucket on the south side of town—that's just a ways over there where the roof peaks high." They followed his finger to where a dark wooden roof zigzagged higher than the rest of the houses. "There's the Horse & Master across on the east side, then we've got the Cloak & Dagger down in the suburbs." He leaned in conspiratorially. "Though I'd recommend you stay back from that one if I were you. A lot of...unsavory folk take to the Cloak. If you fancy yourselves honorable, you'd do best to stay clear."

"And what's over that way?" Caitlin said, pointing at the gray column of smoke. It came in thick bursts, rising like a ribbon then dispelling into the atmosphere. Beyond it, several smaller plumes rose like visible echoes.

"Oh, that? That's over near the Cloak. As I say, a lot of unsavory folks... *Shit*. Hide. Quick." Jamie stopped talking, but his abrupt silence did nothing to hide the sudden wariness that defined him, his eyes alert now as he looked around. At first, Caitlin could see nothing to explain his behavior, but she believed his urgency. She grabbed Jaxon and disappeared behind the shed with Kain. Jamie returned to the patch where he had been digging before he had been interrupted.

"What the fuck was that about?" Kain whispered into Caitlin's ear.

"No idea—"

"There he is!" came a gruff, mocking voice. "Morning Jay-Jay."

"Good morning to you both, and what a beautiful one at that," Jamie replied.

Caitlin leaned cautiously around the corner. Approaching Jamie was a man and a woman, each wearing dark shirts with rips and tears. The man sported a thick beard which spilled to his chest, the woman a shorn head.

Their arms were slick with what appeared to be a mixture of sweat and soot. On their right biceps, they each had a tattoo of a church in flames.

"We didn't see you at last night's congregation," the woman said.

"Yeah. You think you're too good for Pastor Andrews' sermons? Not ready to yield with the other sheep, yet?" the other jibed.

Jamie shuffled nervously. "Oh, come now, Christy, you know I don't think like that." Caitlin felt a twang of pity as Jamie looked imploringly at the girl. "Someone's got to be bright-eyed and ready to nourish the crop while the town sleeps."

"What do you think, Christy? Is that a good enough excuse?" the man asked.

Christy crossed her arms and stroked her chin. "I don't know, Yusuf. I'm not sure the pastor would agree with it. Way I see it, you could always attend congregation, then get straight out into farming. Go all nocturnal-like and sleep in the daytime."

Caitlin watched, then, as Yusuf strutted forward and bashed deliberately into Jamie's shoulder as he passed. He strode over to the wheelbarrow, pulled down the front part of his trousers, and began pissing on the potatoes.

"This is what I think of your excuses," Yusuf said as he let out an extraordinarily loud moan of relief.

"You know they're for everyone, right?" Jamie said. "Those spuds are going to make their way around the town and could very well end up on your own plate."

Yusuf's face dropped. He shook his pecker, pulled his trousers up, and squared up to Jamie. "I'll just know to avoid spuds for the next few weeks." He tapped the side of his head. "See...outsmarted. How does that feel?"

When Jamie opened his mouth to speak, he saw Christy shaking her head as if to say "Say no more idiot, this isn't going to end well for you."

"I don't really feel any different, to be hones—*argh!*"

Yusuf threw his head forward, catching Jamie squarely in the face. Caitlin winced from her vantage spot, imagining the pain and the white lights that must have bloomed and sparked in Jamie's vision. From where she stood, the thug's forehead looked like a boulder, and now, great globs of blood spilled from his victim's nose onto the soil below.

"Pastor wants everyone at congregation. No excuses," Yusuf said, grabbing the scruffy neckline of Jamie's top with his left hand. In his right hand, he now held a dagger. "There's a change coming, *Jay-jay*. A new order. Salvation for this shit-heap of a town which is *looong* overdue. Anyone left behind will be burned and forgotten, and we know you don't want *that* now, do you? Especially not when you're looking after that nana of yours."

Jamie shook his head. Caitlin noticed Christy look away as Yusuf threw another headbutt. The sound was like stone cracking on stone.

"I suppose that's your handiwork, too?" Jamie said, struggling to nod towards the smoke in the distance. "Burn those who disobey?"

Caitlin half-expected Yusuf to rock another bash to his skull, but instead, he lowered Jamie to his feet and grinned. His biceps were thick, veins bulging out from the muscle in silent evidence of his strength. Yusuf nodded.

Jamie looked helplessly at Christy. There was an unmistakable note of something in their glance. Recognition? Kinship? Romance?

Christy's face hardened. "That's right. Governor's orders."

And with that, they walked away, Yusuf deliberately making his footsteps heavier to leave thick track marks in the soil. Jamie watched them until they were out of sight. Once they were gone, his knees buckled, and he fell to the ground, his face in his hands. Caitlin ran to his side, careful to keep her face hidden by her cloak in case the pair returned.

"Come, let's go someplace safe," she said, helping him to his feet. Kain came round the other side and added his support.

"If you wanted safe, you should have stayed in the forest," Jamie retorted. He words were slow as if he was still dazed and disoriented. When neither Caitlin nor Kain commented further, he added, "I know a place. I wouldn't say it's safe, but it's home."

As they wandered into town, Caitlin noted how quiet it was for early morning. The streets were empty, meaning their journey was fast and unencumbered. Only once did they have to duck out of the way of some more people in black clothing. She assumed that most of the town was still asleep after their late-night congregation—the church had been empty when they checked, after all—although she couldn't help but feel the eyes on her from all directions.

When they finally entered through the doorway of Jamie's home, she thought of Mary-Anne. She could only hope and pray that, wherever she was, she was okay.

Pastor Ray Andrews, for the most part, slept soundly in his bed. When his wife awoke and got herself ready, heading downstairs to potter around and perform her womanly chores, he hardly moved at all. These days, he found he slept more deeply than he ever had before in his life—and he had only one person to thank for that.

Times are a-changing, he thought to himself after he awoke around midday. He folded his arms across his naked torso and looked out his window on Ashdale's streets. The town itself was of moderate size. If he had seen Silver Creek before, he might have compared the two, noting that the only difference was where Silver Creek's walls stood tall and proud around every inch of the town, while Ashdale Pond had none.

Not that it didn't have *any* protection, of course. There were alarms posted at intersections around the perimeter, as well as within a short running distance of key facilities in the town. Tall beams of wood with bells on top, connected to long pieces of rope that could be tugged in an emergency and summon assistance. There was safety in numbers, it was said, and that motto had served them well for the most part so far.

"I didn't hear you wake." Lynne Andrews, a slight woman with a gaunt face and prematurely graying hair tightly ponytailed, stood in the doorway, holding a tray of various crockery and biscuits.

Ray beamed at his wife, practically floating across the room to greet her. Her eyes widened, and she backed away —just a step, but it was enough for him to notice.

"Why so afraid?" he asked, taking the tray and placing it on the floor beside her. He took her hands in his. "It's yet another glorious day in paradise. And, what's more, I get to share it with you."

He placed a kiss on Lynne's cheek. She closed her eyes tightly before coughing into her hand.

"Is it so glorious when the air is constantly filled with a spicing of smoke—"

She cut off when his hand met her cheek. Her mouth opened, and no sound came out, a response that had been trained into Lynne over the years. Suffer in silence, that was Pastor Ray Andrews' motto. She brought her hand up to her cheek, cradling the warmth left by his slap though she avoided looking at him.

Ray's eyes flashed, just for a second, before his gaze melted into a softer glow of sympathy. "Oh, my dear wife. Still with this? You'd think after years of suffering and living on the bottom rungs of the ladder that maybe, just maybe, you'd be happy for me. Happy for *us*. The winds are changing, my dear. The winds to bring us good fortune, and they come from Him above who sent forth the governor. For once, we hold the cards. Can't you see that?"

Lynne stared vacantly at the floor.

"*Can't you see that?*" Ray said, suddenly angry as he grabbed his wife and threw her onto the bed.

A short while later, Ray blinked as the sun greeted his doorstep. His clothing was pristine, his white collar standing out amidst the black, making him instantly identifiable from afar. It was his badge of honor, a symbol of his stature and pride.

Not a soul he passed didn't greet him as he made his

way through town. The last few weeks had been a whirl-wind for Ray. A firework explosion of luck and joy as he rose in ranks from nothing more than a simple believer, into the beacon of communication and hope for all of Ashdale's citizens.

Well, give or take a few stubborn fuckers who had yet to bow, or those who had run away. In the end, the fire should see to them.

But mostly, he still couldn't believe his luck. That *he* had been the one to find him on the edge of the forest. That *he* had been the one to offer the governor aid and nourishment after an arduous journey through the forest. That *he* had been blessed by Him above to be privy to the governor's plan and made the lynchpin for the whole damn operation.

Oh, yes. Very lucky indeed.

Ray made his way towards the smoke—something that several folks he'd passed seemed keen to do the opposite of. He was glad to see that his followers had become obedient. A sly grin crept back into his face as he saw another thin column of smoke join the several others now pluming into the sky above the far reaches of town. In the distance, screams punctuated the early morning stillness.

He put a skip in his step, waved at an elderly gentleman holding hands with a young girl, and turned down a side street.

When the sign for the Cloak & Dagger came into view, Ray raised his hood. He knocked three times on the door—loud, quiet, then loud again—before a face appeared between the slats. Silently, the door swung open and allowed him passage.

He nodded to the doorman, keeping his hood tight about his face. Inside the tavern, a couple of dozen citizens huddled in the dim gloom, barely distinguishable in the low light that seeped through the cracks and holes in the roof. There were several tables and a man who was only tall enough for Ray to see the tops of his eyes above the counter stood behind a long bar lining one wall.

"Is he here?" Ray asked the man known commonly as Stump. "Has he come?"

Stump busied himself cleaning a glass with a rag that looked far too dirty to do anything other than smear more dirt on it. He grunted, his eyes never leaving the glass.

"Room number?" Ray asked, casting a furtive glance around the room to make sure no one was eavesdropping.

Stump dug a misshapen hand into his pocket and threw the key on the counter. Ray examined the number fifteen carved crudely into one side. He tossed a rough-forged coin onto the countertop and walked to the stairs at the far side of the room, his heart fluttering a little with the excitement of what was to come.

Although Ray had the key, he knocked twice on the door. When he heard the sharp acknowledgment from the other side, he placed the key in the lock, twisted it, and entered.

The room was dark, the curtains were drawn. An overwhelming stench of body odor and decay spilled into the closed space.

"Ah, my favorite of all our pastors," came Halrod Trisk's sickly-sweet voice. "Come in, come in. We have much to discuss."

CHAPTER NINE

Ashdale Pond, Old Ontario

Jamie dabbed the cloth to his nose. Most of the blood had dried now, but the beating he had taken already looked nasty. Around the area where Yusuf's head had connected, the skin was beginning to turn dark.

"That's going to leave a mark," Kain, sitting on a wide wooden bench across the room, said without much compassion. "You might want to put some ice on that to slow the swelling."

Jamie looked incredulously at Kain, then at Caitlin. When was the last time anyone had *seen* ice? Over the years, the climate had grown steadily muggier, and fridges and freezers had all stopped working when the power died.

"Ignore him," Caitlin said. "He thinks he's funny. Some-times, he contributes useful stuff to a conversation, but for all intents and purposes, focus your words at me." She grinned as Kain's mouth flapped open and closed.

"Charming," he managed.

Jamie chuckled. "Noted."

"So, you were saying?" Caitlin encouraged him to continue. "You know those two out there who did this to you?"

"*Knew* them, I think is more exact. Well, Christy at least, anyway." Jamie removed the cloth and, satisfied there was no more fresh blood, placed it on his lap. "Christy used to be a friend of mine—a good one, actually. We grew up together as our moms were friends. While they pottered around the house or went to visit neighbors, me and Christy would do everything together. After my parents died, she was there for me, like a surrogate mother and sister all wrapped into one. That is...until a few weeks ago."

"What happened?" Kain asked, leaning forward with interest. Caitlin raised her eyebrows. "*What*? I can't show a little intrigue in a man's tale?"

Jamie explained to them how, one day, there had been a commotion in the center of town. The sun had been high, and spirits were particularly low—years of loss, pain, and misery did that to a place. The alarm in the center of town had rung. Citizens flocked towards the sound, bringing anything that could be used as a weapon with them— brooms, rakes, knives. "It's the way of survival, here. If there's any threat of danger, ring the bell, and the town will band together. Safety in numbers, and all that."

When everyone congregated in the center of town, though, it wasn't a Mad attack they had found—or any kind of attack, really. What they had found was a man standing on a podium in the middle of the main square, his arms spread as wide as his grin.

"We all recognized him, of course. Ray Andrews. He had been a weedy guy for most of his life. The town's garbage man. He spent most of his days collecting people's buckets of piss and shit and burying them in pits on the outskirts of town. There had actually been a few rumors about him collaring and harassing girls throughout the years. And then, suddenly, there he was, standing there in a dark coverall with a white dog collar."

Jaxon whined and pawed at Caitlin's lap. "Not that kind of collar, buddy."

Jamie told them how Ray Andrews, or Pastor Andrews as he had suddenly re-labeled himself, then spent a good deal of time explaining to the gathered crowd how he had seen the light. How change was coming, and the world was about to move on to a new age.

"There was a lot of talk about coin tossing and standing on the precipice of a blade. 'Which side will you fall on,' blah, blah, blah."

"Sounds like a bunch of preachy bullshit to me," Kain said.

"And to me, too," Jamie continued. "In fact, throughout the talk, several groups of people peeled away with eyes rolling and went about their day.

"It was when Ray began closing his speech and started asking questions that I felt a change in the winds. He asked who would be willing to join him on this journey, now that he had a figure of power standing beside him." Jamie pointed skyward then. "And at first, I thought no one would put their hands up. Who in their right mind would listen to this mad raving from some nobody who spent his days clearing up skid marks and dumps?"

"But people did," Caitlin said flatly. "Show anybody a sign of hope, a change in this miserable age, and people will flock. No sense required. People just need a leader."

Jamie nodded solemnly. He rubbed his tired eyes, then winced as if a jolt of pain had surged from the bruises on his face. "One by one, people raised their hands. The smile wiped clean off my face. I couldn't believe it. Neither could Christy. It wasn't until a few days later that she changed her mind."

"Why?" Kain asked.

"She never said. Just did." Jamie took a deep breath and looked solemnly at the floor.

"But that doesn't explain such a change in attitude," Kain said, breaking the silence. "People can't seriously believe that a man could talk to God and everything would be okay? There's more to it, right? No one's *that* deluded."

Jamie nodded.

"Christy mentioned the governor," Caitlin probed. "Out by the allotment. 'Governor's' orders?' What did that mean?"

"You know him?" Jamie asked.

Caitlin grinned. "You could say that."

The governor had always been somewhat of an enigma, Jamie explained. He only appeared once in a blue moon to take the same podium Ray Andrews had used to issue a short speech and show his face. He would be flanked by his entourage and would disappear before questions were asked, and those in the town lived in a shadow of fear that, at any point, Trisk and his men could come and change their lives forever.

"It would never be him directly, but rumors spread of

guards appearing in the middle of the night to take men away from families who had disobeyed or spoken ill of the governor and his name. Often, you'd hear the screams at night, and that would be it. You'd never see them again."

"Sounds awful," Caitlin said.

"Mmhmm," Jamie agreed. "So, when Ray then dropped the man's name into his sermon, explaining that he had announced to him that he was to take permanent residence in Ashdale, that he was looking for a new task force, and that Ray would be the messenger through which all orders would consequently come, there was a ripple of fear from many. But, also, a few who delighted at the news."

"Why would that make people excited?" Caitlin asked. "If people feared the man as much as you say?"

"Because it's safer sitting on Trisk's good side," Kain replied. "Who wouldn't choose to sit on the safe side of the street if given the choice?"

"That's about the size of it," Jamie said, a shadow crossing his face. "Though some people are just assholes."

"Beardy McFuckface?" Kain said.

"Yusuf? You got it."

Caitlin thought for a moment, absorbing it all. How far-reaching was the governor's terror that he could simply click his fingers and draw a new band of protection to himself? She thought back to Yusuf and Christy. Yusuf had been blatantly eager to enforce the rules and put Jamie in his place with no indication of remorse. How many more of them were in the town? Folks with clothing as dark as their hearts. Folks with—

"They had tattoos," Caitlin said. "On their arms. Dark churches roaring with flames."

"You've got good eyes," Jamie said. "That's the mark of the Firestarters. Fire is their weapon and smoke is their cover. I don't know whose great idea that was, but everyone fears it. A visit from the Firestarters usually means one thing and one thing only. That your world, and everything you know, is going to burn."

They sat for some time with Jamie answering their questions about the Firestarters, these brave new bandits gathering together to serve under Pastor Andrews as the governor's puppets. Jamie told them stories of homes being burned to a crisp, of attacks and flames in the middle of the night, trapping people while they slept. For the last few weeks, there had been a steady stream of burning across town, and it was a wonder that the rest of Ashdale hadn't caught on fire.

"The whole damn place is wood. How are the flames controlled?" Kain exclaimed disbelievingly.

"There are gaps between the houses," Caitlin answered, remembering what she had seen on the way over. "Far enough away that it's difficult for the flames to jump."

"But not impossible. Just last week, the town banded together to stop the spread of a fire in the west quarter."

"Fuck, this is twisted," Kain said. "Cat, what mess have we walked into?"

In the streets outside, they could hear people now, footsteps and murmuring voices as Ashdale citizens went about their day. From inside the house, it all seemed normal—or as normal as anything could be these days. Caitlin wandered towards the window and peeked out, noting the rapid pace with which people walked and the glum looks on faces. When she saw a group of three women walking side-by-side with an assortment of bats and blades by their hips, torn black clothing, and surly expressions on their faces, she ducked away from the glass.

Jaxon whined and found a seat next to Kain. He stroked the dog's head idly, his eyes fixed on Caitlin.

"This is what we signed up for," Caitlin said. "We've come to stop Trisk. If we need to pull together to stop a rogue group of fire-starting bandits who think they're serving a higher purpose in the name of the fat lard-ass who oppressed Silver Creek for years, then that's what we're going to do."

There came the sound of footsteps from upstairs. Caitlin's hand moved instinctively to her sword. Kain sniffed the air.

"Who else is here?" he whispered.

"Show yourself," Caitlin called. "Or thank your Lord for the final breath you'll ever take."

"*No.*" Jamie stood and tried to calm them both with furious hand signals. Jaxon lay down lazily and rolled over.

A shadow appeared, then an old woman, wrinkled and lined beyond anything Kain or Caitlin had ever seen. She paused at the railing upstairs, looking down at them all through milk-bottle spectacles which magnified her eyes to two huge discs.

"If I'd known we had visitors, I'd have made myself more presentable. Been a while since the Harpers came around." The old woman hiked up her nightdress, flashing an undesirable amount of leg which caused Kain to look away sharply. "What? No rosé? What are we, on a budget?"

Kain raised an eyebrow as the woman disappeared into a room, emerging a moment later with a tankard in one hand and a half-melted candle in the other. "Er...Jamie? Want to explain this one to us?"

The woman moved down the stairs with surprising speed. She glided over to Caitlin, threw her arms around her, and planted a wet, prickly kiss on her cheek. "Ah, Julie." When she turned to Kain, he held his hands in front of him to keep her at bay, but it was no use. She took his right hand in a firm handshake and pulled him in for a squeeze. "Robert." She beamed at them. "I can't remember the last time we butted heads and played castles. I'll crack out the moonshine, and you dim the lights, Jackie. Let's make this palooza a party."

Jamie's cheeks flushed with color. "It's Jamie, Nana. You know that."

Caitlin laughed, shrugged her shoulders at Kain, then waited for an explanation.

"Caitlin. Kain. Meet my nana, Mabel. She's feisty, proud, and a little bit..." Jamie twirled a finger near his ear and crossed his eyes.

"I got that impression," Kain said. He cupped his mouth and raised his volume as he said, "Mabel, collect your bags dear, you need to be in the home by six."

Surprisingly, Jamie laughed at that. "She's not deaf, just a little bit forgetful." He moved closer to her on his chair and wrapped an arm around her. "Ain't that right, Nana?"

Mabel didn't say anything but sucked her gums and nodded without pause. Her hair was wispy, floating like cotton puffs on the wind. She wore a thin dress that revealed a little too much of what was going on under-neath. Her skin had settled into a series of folds and lines, making it almost impossible for Caitlin to tell how old she was.

Very, she supposed.

After a short round of conversation, in which Mabel offered very little in the way of sense but a great deal in the amount of amusement she seemed to bring Kain, Caitlin asked a question that made Jamie's mirthful demeanor drop as reality set back in.

"You said that Pastor Ray wants everyone in town to join his cause. That the Firestarters are his recruits, enforcing his law. They said it themselves out on the allotment. They want you to come around and join them. How long do you think you have?"

"Thirty minutes, I'd say," Mabel chipped in. "Fan the flame, keep it steady, and watch that pastry rise."

Jamie's eyes were glazed with wetness. "A couple of days, if that. I'm running out of excuses to not attend the congregation, and every day, they get harder on me. I send Nana out to attend every night just to keep her safe. She hasn't got a clue what's going on in there, not really. They won't hurt her if she's a part of the crowd, and they won't exactly use an old woman for dark purposes."

"I should hope not," Caitlin said. "Who else is left who is resisting?"

"Hard to say. I've kept myself to myself the best I can over the last few weeks. Many who have resisted have left, preferring their chances out in the woods or over the wolds beyond than stay here. I guess the only way to be absolutely certain is to wait until nightfall and search the town. Take a headcount on who's still in their right mind. Are you guys okay with the dark?"

Caitlin and Kain grinned at each other. "We've got some experience working at night."

Their faces both dropped as the same thought hit them. Just where exactly *was* Mary-Anne? If they could find her —or if she could find them—that might make everything a whole shitload easier when the sun fell and the moon rose.

Caitlin tried to fight off a yawn and failed. Jamie caught this, offering a room upstairs for them to both sleep in if they wished.

"Together?" Kain asked. "My dreams are coming true."

Caitlin rolled her eyes, looking at Jamie for help.

"Sorry." He shrugged. "It's Ma and Pa's old room from way back when. It's a double or nothing."

Jamie led them both upstairs and showed them the way. Mabel stayed downstairs, fussing over Jaxon and muttering gibberish beneath her breath. They passed a room which, Caitlin guessed, was Mabel's, based on the decor and the state the room was in, as well as a room with the door firmly closed. She couldn't be certain, but she thought she could hear deep breathing through the wooden door. Finally, they came to a small room with a bed that could hardly be described as a double. Much more like a single, and then some.

Before Jamie moved away and headed to his own room, Caitlin said, "Thanks so much for your hospitality, Jamie. It might not seem like it, yet, but things will get better. Trust us. This is what we do."

Jamie smiled. "I look forward to seeing you at work, but we're going to need a miracle to shake this town."

"Miracles are what we do, babycakes." Kain grunted his particular sound of amusement.

"One more question?" Caitlin asked.

"Sure."

"Has anyone actually *seen* the governor since his glorious arrival from the stars?"

Jamie considered this a moment. "Not that I know of, except for those odd occasions where he appears from nowhere, makes his speech, and vanishes again. He wasn't there on the day Ray started it all, and unless he attends the congregations—which I'm pretty sure he doesn't—then, no. At least, Nana has never mentioned him during her rare lucid moments. If I were to guess, I'd say he'll be hiding somewhere near the Cloak & Dagger, but with everything so strange these days it's hard to know if that's true."

When Jamie had gone, Caitlin lay for a while next to Kain, her head filled with thoughts. He fell to sleep almost instantly, and the room quickly filled with the sound of gentle snores.

Caitlin thought about the Firestarters, about Trisk and this Pastor Andrews. But most of all, she thought of Mary-Anne, wondering where she might be right now, and how much they would need her in all of this if they were to track down the governor and take a stand to bring peace and order back to the town.

But, most importantly, she thought of Jamie and his Nana and the others who tried to resist Trisk's evil.

CHAPTER TEN

Silver Creek, Silver Creek Forest, Old Ontario

The sky spread a ceiling of blue above the town, with only a few wisps of cloud marring its perfection. The sun had already sunk low, preparing to set beyond the trees.

And still, Alice refused to speak.

Ash walked beside her, a strange knot in his stomach. Around them, townsfolk went about their lives, talking to friends, carrying wares and purchases from a day at the market, beginning to make their way home for the evening. He looked at Alice, trying to catch her eye, then looked away when she did not yield.

It was a far cry from how she had treated him previously. If he closed his eyes for a moment, he could see her lying in her bed, the silky sheets falling off her body.

Sullivan's fault. It was all his fault, with his queer side look and telltale flush.

But was it, though?

After the searches and the interviews, Ash and the rest of the Revolutionaries had been called back together by

Dylan. They had revealed their findings—which, besides from Tom's tales, had been pretty much zero—taking it in turns around the circle to report.

Alice told them how the Revolutionaries were already growing restless. "Don't get me wrong, they appreciate the safe, quiet life of Silver Creek far more than they ever did at New Leaf. But they know something's up. They're not stupid."

Dylan smiled. "No. They're most certainly not."

Vex and Belle spoke next, telling the CoR about Sergeant Tom and what he had told them of his own experiences walking through the forest. How he had fled with the others after a group called the Firestarters had taken to burning down houses. The group stirred at that as they no doubt remembered what Ash had told them of the man who had been shot at the wall—Laurie's husband. Dylan fell into thought, listening intently to every detail. They all did, remembering the faint veil of smoke they'd seen from afar.

"Do we think it's got anything to do with the governor?" Vex asked the group.

"If it hasn't, it's a pretty strange coincidence," Dylan answered. "Trisk's gone for a couple of weeks, and suddenly, there are people arriving at our door and talk of burning? Where is this place?"

"Ashdale Pond," Belle replied.

Dylan's face dropped, the name shouting out to him like the call of an alarm. He instantly remembered the governor's map with the small villages circled around the paper. Ashdale Pond—the town which had been marked by Trisk himself. The exact same place where Caitlin,

Mary-Anne, Kain, and Jaxon had set out to just a few days ago.

"Shit," he muttered.

"What's wrong, boss?" Sullivan asked.

Dylan told them, watching realization dawn on all their faces. He stood and paced around the room a while, running a hand through his hair, while the others talked in disbelief, noting that no one else they had interviewed that day had mentioned Ashdale Pond or anything similar.

"We didn't get a chance to interview everyone, though," Sullivan said, his face glowing red as it always did with suppressed emotion.

Dylan turned. "Excuse me?"

Despite his massive size, Sullivan seemed to shrink. "We still have seven to find, sir. I tried to gather them all, but some are...missing. I'm sure they're just sleeping or keeping themselves to themselves. We managed to bring in the bulk of them. The woman with the frizzy hair—"

"Gail," Ash added.

"Yes, Gail. And Laurie and her clan." Sullivan's eyes flicked to Ash, then to Alice who watched him intently. Ash squirmed slightly and looked at the table.

"So, you're telling me that, despite our concerns that we expressed in our last meeting over strangers coming into our town potentially harboring diseases—you remember the Madness, right, Sullivan?—that they're still not all accounted for?"

"I'm sure it'll be fine, Dill," Vex said, leaning on the table. "We'll find them."

Dylan took a deep breath, feeling his initial anger begin to subside. A slight wave of embarrassment washed over him as his mind reeled back to the day the governor had roared at himself and Caitlin for letting him down in not catching Mary-Anne. Was that the type of leader he wanted to be? His anger switching to life at the touch of a button? Where had that even come from?

The responsibility rests on your shoulders now, buddy boy.

No, not on Dylan's shoulders. On the CoR's.

But who's the man who leads the CoR in Caitlin's absence?

Dylan rubbed his eyes and sat back down. He took a long draught of the amber nectar Mother Wendy had provided. "We find them before nightfall. We can't have unchecked civilians loose in Silver Creek. Even if they are fine, we need to know for sure—especially if we want to leave this place safe and get to Ashdale. The last thing we need is for the Madness to take home base while we gallivant around the forests."

Vex suddenly looked up excitedly. "You mean—"

Dylan nodded. "Yes. If things really are as bad as I think they are, Caitlin's going to need all the help she can get."

And now, as Ash and Alice turned down the side street they had been assigned by Dylan, she grabbed his arm and pulled him to a stop. The street was so narrow that dark shadows encroached where the sun couldn't reach. It was empty, though that wasn't unusual for this side of Silver Creek at this time of day when most folks were inside doing chores.

For a moment, Alice lingered, her eyes shimmering as she weighed her words. "You like her, don't you?"

"Who?" Ash dumbly replied.

"That woman. The wife of the man whom we shot at the gates. Laurie. You like her. I can see it every time you look at her. Every time her name is mentioned, you glow red. Don't think I can't see it."

Ash opened his mouth to speak, then closed it.

Truth was, he found her attractive, yes. But more than Alice? Did he have the same connection as he had with the girl from New Leaf? The one he had fallen for on their travels back through the woods?

"That's crazy," he said, moving in close and placing his hands on her hips.

Alice pulled away, folding her arms tight about her.

"Hey, leave that bitch alone," came a voice.

Ash turned, only now noticing the man leaning coolly against the wall. He had one foot on the wood behind him and one hand near the hilt of his sword. The other held a leather head guard under the crook of his arm.

Alice's expression said she'd recognized him at once, and Ash scowled the same disgust. That no-good greasy fuck who had let loose his arrow on Laurie's husband on the parapet walls.

"You're a little bit out of your zone, don't you think?" Ash replied, his demeanor one of friendly inquiry but his hand poised and ready for his sword, should he need it. "If I remember rightly, shouldn't you be down by the paddocks on the east side?"

The man grinned. "I suppose that depends on who's giving the orders."

"Your *captain* is giving the orders, Greeb."

"*Captain*, he says." Greeb chuckled, looking around as if addressing a crowd. "Captain, indeed. What do we think, fellas? Are we taking orders from the captain?"

As if melting out of the shadows, several more men

joined Greeb in the street. They walked with dark purpose, hardened stares on their faces. Ash felt his heart drop. These were men he remembered had been advocates of the former captain of the guard, Hank Newman, for as long as Ash had been on the guard force. They had all actively sought ways to satiate their twisted desires by abusing their power and taking what they wanted.

And they outnumbered himself and Alice three-to-one.

Ash nudged Alice slowly behind him.

"I suppose we would take orders from the captain—if he were still alive," one of the men croaked. He walked with a slight limp. His hair was slimed back, and he sported a particularly large mole on his neck. "Not the best example to set, now, eh?"

"Oh no," Greeb said patronizingly. "Not good at all. How does this so-called captain expect us not to over-throw the leader, when that's exactly what he and his reductionaries did?"

"I think you'll find we're called 'Revolutionaries,'" Alice said, leaning around Ash. "Is he deaf as well as ugly?"

Ash closed his eyes, wishing Alice would be quiet. He heard movement behind him, turned, and saw another two men with smiles on their faces.

Great. Four to one.

The chorus of choking laughter stirred a burning hatred in Ash's stomach. He had expected this on some level. After Caitlin had taken the town back from Trisk and killed the madman who had been Silver Creek's captain of the guard, he knew there might be some backlash. In the last couple of weeks, he had worked hard with the guards, making sure that he earned their respect while also protecting the town. There had been a few who resisted, at first, ignoring orders and only putting in half-effort. But he thought he'd overcome it.

Apparently not.

"How do you think you're going to go about this?" Ash asked. "You...what? Kill us? Then what happens? You think you're going to take down the Revolutionaries? You think the town will fall in line behind you all, and that you'll have the power you've hungered for while hiding in your master's shadow for all these years?"

Greeb's smile faded. He drew his sword and examined the tip nonchalantly. "Maybe. Maybe not. To be honest, I've not thought past this part. But, then again, this has always been my favorite part of the plan. And, since your bitch-tits leader is out exploring the wilds with the fanged bitch, why not take a chance when we get it? Right, boys?"

Nodding and grunts of agreement all around emphasized the danger they were in. Ash did his best to look for a way to escape but could see none. He heard Alice whisper behind him, "We can take them," but he wasn't so sure. He was a good fighter—one of the best in the guards' cohort—and he knew that Alice was skilled beyond comparison with twin blades. But two against eight? That left something to be desired.

"Let's see how your Residuaries react when we hand over your corpse," Greeb said, raising his sword and coming for Ash. "Sic 'em, boys."

They moved quickly, coming at them from all angles. Instinctively, Ash and Alice moved so they were back to back. In a movement so fast it could have been missed by anyone caught unawares, their weapons were in their hands as they grunted and huffed with defensive parries.

Ash blocked a two-by-four with nails sticking out the end, cutting it clean in half with his sword—a piece of craftsmanship Mary-Anne had given the Revolutionaries from the old world. The blade made all their attackers' weapons pale in comparison. He followed through the chop, bashing his head into the man's skull. There was an audible crack, and the man fell on his ass.

"Humpty Dumpty had a great fall—" Ash mocked, stopping quickly as a blade darted for his face. He twisted his face away just in time to duck—luckily, Alice was a foot shorter than himself—and hooked his foot around the guard's ankle. Off-balance from his strike, he was swept to the floor, landing clumsily on top of the thug still rubbing his forehead.

Alice, meanwhile, roared as she used Ash's back to lift herself off the ground and booted the man with slick-backed hair with both feet. He grunted as the air was knocked out of him, then came back for another attempt. She sliced at him, now, launching toward her left, and caught his throat. His face melted from enthusiasm to horror in a millisecond, his fingers clutched at his neck in a useless attempt to stem the blood that stained them.

"Stupid bitch," he croaked, unable to stem the flow, and fell to the floor.

Somewhere out of sight, they heard Greeb cry in anger.

"What's the matter with you? Get them, you shit-eating-assholes!"

"If you're going to eat shit, the asshole is the best place to go," Ash muttered between blocks and attacks. Somewhere nearby, he heard a door open and close. "How you holding up, babycakes?"

"Really?" Alice replied between breaths. "Pet names, at a time like this?"

"If we're to die, I'd have at least liked to have given it a go."

Alice blocked old slick-back but took a mean right hook to her jaw. Her face half-turned toward Ash. "Well, don't," she said, turned back, and drove a dagger up into the underside of Slick-back's jaw. She saw the metal cut through the skin, driving through his tongue and tickling the roof of his mouth where the tip of the blade stopped. "Or at least find something better than babycakes, okay?"

"Deal," Ash replied.

Alice watched slick-back as comprehension dawned. A moment later, he ran from the fray, disappearing around the corner with a muffled cry.

She had no time to cheer as two more men came at her. Both she and Ash fought well, taking the occasional nick and managing to keep them at bay. It wasn't until Ash took a fist to the stomach—narrowly avoiding a blade driving into his hip—that he saw Greeb watching from a safe distance. Only, now, he held a bow and arrow.

Whether he had hidden it in the alley and grabbed it while the two of them had been distracted, Ash had no idea. But there it was. Greeb's one eye closed as the other trained down the line of sight, directly at his face.

He could see the assassin release a deep breath. Ash reached behind him with one hand and pulled Alice down, but not before he heard the arrow whistling through the air.

He closed his eyes, waiting for the lightning bolt of pain to take them both. It did not come. What he did hear was the grunt of a body falling to the floor beside him, and the gurgled grunts of choking.

Alice...no. Please! his mind protested. But when he opened his eyes, he was looking into the vacant, glassy stares of a guard lying dead next to him.

"Ash! Look!" Alice urged from behind.

Lying dead on the floor with an arrow protruding from his chest, lay Greeb. His eyes were closed, and a growing pool of blood collected beneath his body. Chatters of confusion and disbelief sounded around them as a face Ash and Alice recognized moved into view.

"Take another step towards them and you're next," Laurie said, shaking her long blonde hair behind her. She held another arrow knocked in her bow, ready to fire. When one of the guards shouted, "Fuck this!" and dove at Alice, she loosed the arrow to find its mark deep in the guard's skull, dropping him to the ground.

"Who's next?" she said. "Drop your weapons if you want to live."

The remaining guards did so, some a little more quickly than others. Laurie approached Ash and Alice with her weapon still drawn and handed them a coil of rope. They hurried to bind the guards until they all sat back-to-back, their eyes doing everything possible to avoid Greeb's bleeding corpse some ten feet away.

"Thanks," Ash said once the guards were secure. He flushed red, trying his best not to look at Laurie directly, conscious of Alice's eyes on him, too.

There was an awkward silence before Alice said, "Yeah, thanks. You really saved our asses back there."

"It's the least I could do. You saved mine and my kin by letting us stay here. I couldn't give enough thanks for that. Hopefully, this will go some way to repaying that debt."

Alice looked around at the street which stood empty aside from themselves and the guards. "What were you doing down here?"

Ash saw a dark suspicion cross her face and, for a second, he wondered the same thing. Had she been *following* them?

"Visiting a friend," Laurie replied, not meeting their eyes. "I'd heard they had come through the gates, also. I wanted to see how they were faring."

Taking a breath, Ash looked directly at Laurie. She truly was beautiful. Her eyes reminded Ash of summer skies, and her hair flowed like a golden waterfall. His feelings, of course, were with Alice. But still…

"Your friend. What's their name?"

A shadow crossed Laurie's face. "He didn't come to your investigatory meeting, huh?"

They both shook their heads.

"Can you take us to him?" Ash asked. He almost jumped when he felt someone beside him. A moment later, he realized it was Alice, and the tension left him. They wiped their blades on the hems of their clothing and put their weapons away. Alice's hand found his.

Laurie looked down at their hands, then back to their eyes as if studying them. "Very well," she said at last. "Though I'm going to warn you, it isn't pretty."

CHAPTER ELEVEN

Silver Creek, Silver Creek Forest, Old Ontario

Laurie wasn't kidding. It wasn't pretty at all.

The curtains were partly drawn, leaving thin strips of dying light to illuminate the room. Laurie had led them through a house which made Alice think more of a hovel than anywhere a person would live. A pile of blankets had been gathered in the corner of the room, bundled and grimy. From within this pile came a series of coughs.

Laurie had pulled back a blanket to reveal a head. Chester—the man they were hoping to find. Only they had hoped they wouldn't find him like this.

"Is it bad, Doc? Is it *terrrrrible?*" Chester croaked, his words barely more than a whisper.

"These aren't doctors," Laurie replied, a shimmer in her eyes as she took a step back and looked at the specimen before them, her eyes soft with pity.

Chester's condition was appalling. His fiery red hair looked greasy and clumps stuck out at all angles, except for those places where there was no hair at all. Patches of bald skin looked as though he must've yanked out fistfuls of his own hair at some point. His skin was a mix of weeping sores and red patches as if blood had boiled to the surface and stopped. His eye twitched as he spoke, and occasionally, his hands would jerk out at them before a mask of surprise grew on his face and he tucked them into the crook of his arms.

"C'mon, Doc. Just give it to me straight," Chester begged.

Alice moved closer to Ash. "How long do you think he has?" Her whisper emerged as barely a sound.

Ash stepped up beside Chester and went down to one knee. "It's not good," he said flatly.

A strange yelp escaped the patient's mouth. He put a fist to his lips and bit into the skin, seemingly unaware of the pain as droplets of blood broke through the flesh.

"Listen, I will try to help you," Ash continued. "But first, I need you to answer a few questions for me, okay?"

Chester hesitated, then nodded.

"Have you put anyone else at risk, anyone at all? Hugged, kissed, bitten, spread the sores to anyone you might know of?"

Chester shook his head. "No. It's just been me. I was scared of what it might do to people if I let them too close."

"When you arrived at Silver Creek, who did you arrive with?"

Chester told them he had arrived alone. His two companions had been attacked in the forest, and he had managed to escape—but not before receiving what he thought to be a minor scratch. His face grew shameful, perhaps at the memory of leaving his friends behind.

"What do we do?" Laurie asked.

"There's only one cure for the Madness," Ash said.

He moved so fast that Laurie's protestations only came after Chester's throat was sliced and the blankets turned dark from his blood. She folded to her knees, tears running unchecked. Though it was an inevitable decision, Ash understood the emotion that came from losing someone close.

He stood up, torn between hugging Laurie or leaving her to grieve. She was beautiful even when she cried. He felt Alice at his side and looked down into her eyes.

She looked sad. Though, if he wasn't mistaken, there was a slight hint of something else there. A satisfaction that it had been Ash who had had to play the bad guy in front of Laurie.

"Come. We'll need to relay this to the CoR," Ash said, looking at Laurie now. "Maybe on the way, you can explain more about where the fuck you learned to shoot like that."

Ashdale Pond, Old Ontario

Caitlin's dreams were filled with fire. Of wood and smoke and flame. She saw Silver Creek alight in a wash of orange and yellow, wooden structures fodder to hungry flames that surged with every breath of the wind.

Everywhere she looked, people ran. Grime and ash clung to tears. Somewhere amidst it all, he came—her own version of the man she had yet to see, Pastor Andrews. Walking slowly through the chaos with the steady grace of a doe, his face wore a mask of pleasure and delight.

Caitlin ran at him, but as she struck him down, he fizzled into nothingness, disappearing with the smoke.

"Coward!" she roared above the crackles of the flames.

And there, above it all, sounded a deep, steady chuckle she recognized immediately. Governor Halrod Trisk. The Firestarter. The twisted Firestarter.

A series of bangs shook Caitlin from her dream. She sat up, her face clammy with sweat. Kain was already alert, fully dressed and his weapon drawn. Outside, all was dark, yet a faint smell of smoke still lingered in the air.

Kain placed a finger to his lips and creaked the door open. Caitlin could hear someone walking down the stairs —Jamie, judging by his pace. A moment later, her thoughts were confirmed as he spoke.

"All right, all right. I'm coming," he moaned. "Hold your horses."

Another aggressive burst of knocks sounded before they heard the door open, and Yusuf's voice rang deep and clear. "It's time. Get your shit. Grab your Nana. No excuses."

Jamie's voice carried up the stairs. "Nana. Time for communion."

"Tell them I'm at work. These spuds aren't going to plow themselves," Mabel's croaked reply came.

"Nana, I—"

"Not *just* her, Jay-Jay," Yusuf admonished in hard tones. There was malice in his voice as if he had said those words before but now had the conviction to follow through.

"I've told Pastor Andrews before, the crops need attention. Someone's got to stay up while the town sleeps—"

"No. More. Excuses, fuck-face," Yusuf said. Caitlin could hear the glee in his voice. *"Governor's* orders."

There was a pause. Jamie stumbled over his words. "Christy...please...you must surely understand?"

Another pause dragged out a long silence before Christy repeated, "Governor's orders, Jay."

"Good, then it's settled." Yusuf clapped. "Now, get your geriatric side-bitch downstairs and let's be on our way. Plenty more folks to drag from their safe little cocoons before the service starts."

"You mean—" Jamie said.

"You think you're the only resistant twat we need to lug out? Come on, *Jay-Jay*, you're better than that."

Kain's face creased as he snarled. He looked ready to run out and mow them both down until Caitlin caught his wrist and shook her head.

"Wait," she mouthed.

Caitlin peeked around the door, certain she could still hear Mabel in her room down the hall. As the old girl came out of her room, she caught Caitlin's gaze and, for the first time since Caitlin had arrived at the house, something like recognition flashed across them.

An icy shiver ran down Caitlin's spine as she began to panic, wondering if Mabel would rat them both out. *"You've forgotten these ones, too. We've got two stowaways up here who the governor would probably* love *to meet. Now, carry my bags for me, dear, because my back can't take much more."*

But that's not what happened.

Mabel brought a shaking finger to her lips, then half-turned to point at the room behind her, still closed from when they passed the door on their way to bed.

"What?" Caitlin mouthed.

Mabel didn't reply, but she gestured with two fingers pointing downwards from each corner of her mouth, like a child attempting to pretend they had fangs A strange gesture, really.

"Nana, come on," Jamie called again, all strength faded from his voice.

"I'm coming, I'm coming," Mabel said, winking at Caitlin before heading down the stairs. "Try to stop me. That Pastor Andrews is quite the looker. Strange that he only comes out at night, though. If I didn't know better"— Mabel raised her voice so that Kain and Caitlin could hear her without even trying—"I'd say he was a *vampire*."

Mabel shrieked with laughter. Yusuf said something which Caitlin assumed had been derogatory, but she didn't hear the words. The door closed behind them, and Mabel's cackles faded down the street a moment later.

"What in the name of Sam Hill was all that about?" Kain asked, putting his sword back. "That bitch really does have a screw loose, huh?"

Caitlin shook her head. "Not this time, Kain. There was something there. Something in her eyes which changed, as though she was *seeing* properly for the first time."

"And jabbering about potatoes? Yeah…because that's *real* normal."

Caitlin told Kain that she had seen Mabel make a visible pretense of fangs, no accident given the mention of the vampire before she left. "You don't think she's seen Mary-Anne, do you?"

"Oh yes, definitely. And pixies, and trolls, and goblins,

dwarves, and dragons." Kain whirled a finger next to his temple. "That bitch has seen *everything*."

"C'mon, pooch. Get real," Caitlin snapped.

Kain turned to Jaxon who had been snoozing for most of the encounter. He raised his head, whined, then lowered it again. "You hear that, Jax? Kitty Cat hates it when you fantasize."

"*Kain*," Caitlin growled.

"Fine. Maybe she has seen Ma. But what are we going to do about it here and now? The plan is to follow *them*, right? Sneak up to the church and check out what's going down? Y'know, the exact same shit that Ma was supposed to do before she—oh…what happened again? Oh, that's right. Before she disappeared?"

The creaking of a door opening punctuated his sarcasm. Caitlin stared intensely at Kain, wrestling with her response to his scorn.

Jaxon stood up lazily, shook off his sleep, slipped between their legs, and headed out of the room. Caitlin ignored him and focused instead on how to proceed. They needed a plan that went beyond simply trying their luck.

"We'll find her," Caitlin said as the only answer to Kain's sarcasm. "I'm sure we will." She didn't say what she was truly thinking at that moment. *If we don't, we're more fucked than a greased-up whore left to sleep naked in Wendy's Tavern.*

"Come. Get your shit together," Caitlin said. "Let's go find them."

It was as they were set to leave the room that she realized Jaxon had not returned. "Jax?" Kain called, having obviously noticed the dog's absence as well.

"Where's he gone?"

"If I knew that, I wouldn't have called for him, would I?"

"Jaaaaax?" Caitlin said, clicking side-mouthed to call Jaxon back. But she needn't have bothered. As she stepped out into the landing, she saw Jaxon lying on his back on the floor as Mary-Anne scratched his belly.

"I wondered how long it would take you to realize," Mary-Anne said, a grin on her face. "And you, Kain. How bad must your sense be if you couldn't detect a vampire napping in the spare room?"

Caitlin laughed and ran forward, embracing Mary-Anne in a hug which knocked her back and almost off her feet.

"I'm starting to think I can't tell who's worse. The governor, or this so-called pastor," Caitlin said.

They had each swapped news of what they'd discovered. Mary-Anne detailed her strange experience sitting as part of the congregation and the absurd way they had spoken about the governor, as though he were some kind of prophet come to deliver them all from evil. Caitlin and Kain shared their story of Jamie and what he had told them about that fateful day, just a few weeks before, out in the town square when the pastor had announced his duties on behalf of Trisk and the town itself.

"He sounds like a real scrote-bag," Kain said, crunching on a biscuit he had found in another room.

"That's one way to put it," Mary-Anne chuckled. "Yet, despite everything, he does hold a certain charm."

"Easy now, Ma. Now's not the time to go googly-eyed for the vicar."

"*Pastor*," Mary-Anne retorted.

"What's the difference?"

"A pastor is someone who is in charge of a church. A reverend is anyone who is a member of the clergy—"

"*Snore!*" Kain interrupted, closing his eyes and throwing his head back.

"Enough," Caitlin snapped, rousing from her thoughts. "It doesn't really matter what he says he is. We just need to decide what the fuck we're going to do."

They looked at each other for a moment, Jaxon weaving between them all, vying for their attention.

"Well, the town's empty, right?" Kain asked.

"Your point?" Mary-Anne said.

"I say we take a look around."

And that's exactly what they did. As the half-moon cloaked itself behind thin wisps of cloud, they prowled the silent streets. It was eerie, the dust kicking beneath their feet like phantom puffs of murky fog. The dim light of the moon cast spectral shadows all around. They had never experienced anything so quiet. It was as though the town had been entirely abandoned, though they knew that wasn't exactly true.

"I've got to say, it's a hell of a defense mechanism," Kain whispered as they rounded a corner and saw the creaking sign for the Horse & Master pub. The windows were boarded. Only a couple of windows with cracked glass remained unobscured.

"What is?" Caitlin asked.

"Pack mentality," Kain replied. "Ring a bell and

everyone flocks to your side to protect you. Go to church, and the entire freakin' town goes, too. No walls. No fences. Just reliance on your fellow man. I've not seen anything like it before."

"You should know all about pack mentality, eh, Were?" Mary-Anne sniffed.

Caitlin tensed.

Kain snorted the remark away, walking ahead without a word.

Caitlin thought about it. Pack mentality certainly seemed like an effective method. She thought of Silver Creek and her life hidden behind the wooden walls which surrounded the entire town. The more she thought about it, the more it seemed less like a town than a fortress. A cage. She began to wonder if the walls were more to keep the monsters out or to lock the people in.

No wonder a coward like the governor would make his residence at the Creek rather than a town like this.

They made a right and were met with another short row of houses—and what looked like an old apothecary store selling a variety of elixirs and wares—but Mary-Anne held the group back. She sniffed the air and, a moment later, Jaxon confirmed her suspicions as his head bent low, his haunches raised as he bared his teeth in a snarl.

"What? What is it?" Caitlin asked, reaching automatically for her sword.

But there was no need for Mary-Anne to answer. From the end of the street, two figures stumbled and hobbled towards them. By the demeanor of the Mad, they hadn't yet spotted the four of them.

"There you go, pooch. She can be your prom date,"

Mary-Anne chided, pointing at the one on the left who still sported the shredded remains of a dress. Blood and grime had coagulated into the weavings of the fiber. One of her arms looked as if someone had tried to cut it off at the elbow but only managed part of the job.

"I thought vampires were supposed to have good taste in women," Kain whispered back. "Not interested in the fella?"

The man by the girl's side looked to have once been a fairly large man. Now, however, his fat had sagged through his time suffering from the Madness, and his skin hung down in long flaps which almost reached his knees. His mouth drooped in the corner, and his beard sported a mesh of twigs, leaves, and various other debris.

"Not really my type," Mary-Anne replied. "I prefer my men less…"

"Dead man walking-looking?" Caitlin offered.

"You got it."

As the two Mad drew closer, Caitlin, Mary-Anne, and Kain exchanged glances. They nodded their confirmation, then sprinted towards them. The girl was down in seconds, Mary-Anne using her vampire speed to dash ahead. In one fluid motion, she ducked low, avoided the girl's grasp, and skidded along the floor as she held out her blade and sliced at the girl's leg.

As the Mad girl fell to her knee, Mary-Anne spun and plunged the blade into her back.

The light extinguished from her eyes almost immediately, but that didn't stifle her scream. The noise reminded Caitlin of the gunshot she had fired into the sky back at Silver Creek. A clap of thunder.

"Save one for us," Kain said, grinning at Caitlin as they ran side-by-side. The formerly obese man reached for them both, his nails long and sharp. They each took a side, Caitlin using all her strength to match Kain's as they attempted to slice off his arms.

Caitlin winced as the blade cut through the degenerating muscle and tissue with ease, clunking against the bone. Kain grunted, pushing his strength in his effort to hack the arm. The bone splintered with an awful cracking sound.

Caitlin used one foot to steady herself on the fat man as she withdrew the sword and went in for another attack. This time, she managed it, though she felt Mary-Anne's hands wrap around her waist and pull her back just in time to stop the man taking a chomp out of her flesh.

"Thanks." Caitlin breathed heavily, as much from the awareness of her narrow escape as from the effort of the fight.

"Don't mention it."

"Aw, how lovely," Kain said sarcastically. "Why don't we save it until Tubs is down, eh?"

"Right," Caitlin agreed, bringing her sword back as far as she could. Effort stretched her features into determination. "Stand back."

She tore the sword through the air, swinging the blade in a triumphant arc aimed at Tubs' neck. He turned in surprise at the whistling sound, only adding more power to her swing. The blade ate through the skin as though it were water, emerging on the other side in a thick spray of blood.

A moment later, the man's head thudded onto the

ground, rolling a few feet before stopping to stare at the sky in horror.

"I did it," Caitlin said in surprise. "One swing, and he's down."

Kain and Mary-Anne exchanged a knowing glance as if they were both thinking the same thing. With their Were and vamp strength, taking off heads wasn't that difficult. Yet, Caitlin decided, even they would have to agree it was still impressive to finally watch her take one down in a single stroke. She didn't have their abilities or strength, after all.

"Humans. Cute, ain't they?" Kain said.

Caitlin beamed, holding her sword up before her. She would've kissed the blade had it not been covered in zombie blood.

Jaxon barked and hopped around her legs.

"I know. Mummy's got the strength of ten thousand men," Caitlin said, degenerating to baby talk as she stroked Jaxon's fur and pulled his face to hers. "The wittle zombies need to be very scared, don't they? Yes, they do."

But Jaxon pulled away, turning once more to the end of the street where at least another dozen Mad had emerged from around the corner, their numbers increasing as they filed towards them.

"It must've been the girl's scream," Mary-Anne said. "The sound of it drew the others."

"Where have they even come from?" Caitlin asked as close to another dozen joined. Those at the front noticed the four of them standing out in the open, and a high-pitched keening resounded through their ranks.

"Does it matter?" Kain remarked.

Caitlin sighed. "Not really. Think we can take"—she began to count by pointing as the Mad at the front screamed and began to run towards them—"two dozen and counting?"

"Perhaps. But is it worth the risk?" Kain said, already turning to run.

"Probably not," Caitlin said, turning to join him. "Maybe it's time we tested the town's defense?" She clicked at Jaxon to follow, and he streaked alongside them, a blur of brown and black. "See what the herd mentality works like when faced with a threat?"

They turned right, several of the Mad hot on their heels —those who had clearly been recent victims of the Madness and hadn't suffered from as much degeneration as the others. They passed the shadows of empty houses, doing their best to remember their way through town.

Caitlin half-turned as she ran, catching the eyes of a man who, at one time, might have been considered handsome. He was around her age, with a physique built for running and fucking. She was surprised to see him gaining on them.

She suddenly remembered the belt Ash had given her before she left Silver Creek. Without slowing her stride, she reached down and pulled out one of the throwing knives. It felt good in her hand. Light. Powerful.

She turned, took aim as she ran, and threw it.

The blade spun through the air, narrowly avoiding the man's face and landing impotently on the floor behind him. He growled, his eyes blazing red.

Caitlin reached for blade number two, took aim, and threw.

This time, the aim was true, but the handle thumped squarely on the man's forehead.

"Shit," she exclaimed.

Two more blades remained. Kain and Mary-Anne took a turn which Caitlin followed without a thought. She stopped for just long enough to take aim once more, aware that this was one of her last chances with the blades.

"Eat metal, shitbag," Caitlin whispered, grunting as she released the knife.

The blade hit its target, spinning furiously through the air and finding entry into the man's skull. The knife embedded all the way to the hilt, immediately extinguishing the light from his eyes.

"Bullseye," Caitlin said.

"Nice one," Kain called from some way ahead. "Now, unless you got enough knives for the lot of them, get that skinny ass in gear and haul it!"

Caitlin sprinted after them, Jaxon's barks a beacon in the dark. They were not far from the edge of town now. By her reckoning, they couldn't be far from the church. She wondered how much of the chaos the congregants would have heard inside the building and if they were at all prepared for the horde now being led straight to the residents of Ashdale Pond.

CHAPTER TWELVE

Silver Creek, Silver Creek Forest, Old Ontario

Dylan and Ash sat in the corner of Mother Wendy's tavern, taking refuge in the shadows. It was quiet, with only a few groups of revelers lingering as Mother Wendy cleaned up after a long night.

Dylan took a long drag of his pipe. It was a habit he hadn't particularly had before, but after finding the object in the governor's room with a decent stash of dried herbs beside it, he thought he'd give it a try.

If the rest of the world is looking to set fires, might as well start a mini one of my own.

He coughed gently, his lungs almost used to the gritty texture of the smoke through his airways. Beside him, Ash took a deep draught from his drink and set it back on the table, his eyes wandering to Mother Wendy's mammoth behind as she bent to pick something off the floor.

"You ought to watch that," Dylan said.

"What do you think I'm trying to do?" Ash replied with a grin. When Dylan's face remained straight, he added, "I know. I can't help it. I've never been tied down before, and it's difficult to keep myself under control."

Dylan mulled this over. It made sense, really. Ash had been one of Trisk's goons until recently. Even if he had the moral heart of a unicorn, he had always hung around with bad types. Some of that would have rubbed off on him over the years.

That didn't stop Dylan feeling bad for Alice, though.

"Try harder. The CoR is unstable enough as it is, let alone the damn town. I hardly think a domestic between you love birds is going to help our cause, do you?" Dylan took a deep puff of the pipe, closed his eyes and reveled in the warmth of the smoke. "The last thing we need is for anyone to fall out or for word of a fracture to spread beyond our group. It's all about confidence and the illusion that we've got everything under control."

"We have, now. Haven't we?" Ash asked. "We've got them all—the missing ones. Everyone is accounted for and dealt with."

"That doesn't mean we trust them. One of them tried to hide and sat in one of *our* houses, suffering from the friggin' Madness. How can we be sure that no one else is at stage zero?"

"Stage zero?" Ash asked.

Across the bar, two gentlemen with thick mustaches and well-worn clothing chatted frantically, their heads so close to each other it looked like they were making out. A few tables behind them, a woman not much older than Belle sat, her body wracked with tears and a filthy cloth to her face.

"It's what we call the beginning stages of the Madness.

Before the outward signs show. When it's nothing more than a parasite swimming in your bloodstream, waiting for its chance to attack you from the inside out. Stage zero, by all accounts, is the worst."

"Which is why you're so uneasy?" Ash said.

Dylan side-eyed his companion for a moment, studying his face. Ash's stubble had begun to sprout into the makings of a beard, and his eyes were tired and heavy. Though he still wasn't sure how much he liked a man who eyeballed every woman within a five-mile radius—even within sight of his partner—he had to admit that he enjoyed the male company. Ash added something to the conversation which Sullivan could never manage, as hard as he'd tried.

Dylan nodded. "Yeah. That, amongst other things."

They sat and drank together as the night wore on, sharing idle chatter, as well as thoughts and proceedings of the meeting they had shared with the CoR just a few hours before.

Laurie and Tom had joined the six and had been questioned further about everything from Ashdale Pond to the Firestarters, to why the hell Laurie was able to shoot a bow with the best of them.

It seemed that she had been something of a hunter and gatherer at Ashdale, risking her life around the forest's edge, collecting meat and foods. She boasted of her skill in taking down elk and, in particular, the speed with which she could skewer a rabbit or a stoat.

"The minute their legs quiver, they know they're dead," she bragged.

"Surely that would've come in incredibly useful in saving your husband's life?" Alice had prodded.

Laurie had retorted with similar venom. "Did you *see* my bow when I got here?"

"Do you see me ramming a fist up your—"

"Okay, ladies," Dylan interjected. Vex looked disappointed at the break up of what could have been a rather tasty argument to watch.

They hastened to formulate a plan of action before the arguing started again and spoke with Tom at length over what he knew of the town and the Firestarters. Though he wouldn't say much, he did say he'd be more than happy to lead the way for anyone wanting to go and claim back what had once been a peaceful town.

"Peaceful? Under Trisk's rule?" Dylan had choked.

Though neither Tom nor Laurie responded to the governor's name, Dylan saw something in their eyes which told him more than he wanted to know. Something was afoot, and their old enemy was somehow behind it all.

When Ash's glass was down to its final dregs, he stood and headed to the bathroom. Dylan chuckled to himself as his companion stumbled away, knocking into a couple of tables along the way.

Dylan closed his eyes, feeling his own warmth from his beer and smoke. It had been a long day, and it hardly looked like he would get much sleep that night, either. If it wasn't one thing in this town, it was another.

He thought back to the thief he had caught earlier in the day. While on his way to see the Revolutionaries in training, he had watched the girl—no more than thirteen summers old—grab the trinket off a market stall and begin running before the owner even noticed.

Dylan chased the girl, managing to catch her as she tried to climb through an open window in an old building down a side street. After talking her down and threatening several days in jail—though secretly knowing he would never do that to someone so young—he managed to retrieve the trinket and hand it back to the stall holder.

"Thank you so much, Governor," the woman had beamed.

Dylan thought about correcting the woman but knew there would be no point. That was his role now, really. As much as he denied it, that was how people would see him. The governor of Silver Creek, the one *anyone* could turn to at all times, night and day.

Sigh.

He felt someone sit next to him. When he opened his eyes, he looked into the dark eyepatch of Sergeant Tom Hitchcock.

"You're not Ash."

"Observant, fucker, aren't we?" Tom grumbled, a grin on his face.

Despite Tom's cursing, Dylan couldn't help but enjoy the man's crass approach. It was refreshing to have someone speak to him like any other person, not as a reluctant leader of a town in the absence of his sister.

"What are you doing here?" Dylan asked. "Meeting finished hours ago. You should be at home by now."

"Home?" Tom replied. "I don't have a home anymore. You watch your world go up in flames, and it's hard to call any place home. Even one strike of a match in this town and, *poof*, the whole damn thing goes up in flames. Bricks. Mortar. That's what's missing from this world. Craftsmanship and integrity. Everything we build these days is temporary. A small fix. A field dressing on a wound that hasn't stopped pouring blood for years."

"That's a cheery change of conversation," Ash said, returning from the bathroom. "Who invited Bobo the Clown?"

Dylan laughed—the first genuine laugh he could remember for days. He signaled for Mother Wendy to bring them three more drinks. "It's only temporary if we stop trying to find a permanent solution. You, me, Ash, and even Mother Wendy all carry on because that's what we do. It's called survival. My sister is out there fighting to bring freedom and peace to this world again one town at a time because we know that there is good in this world. No amount of fire or flames is going to take that away. As long as we're all together, fighting on the same side, that's enough."

"And if the town burns? If the forest and the world catch fire?"

"We'll build the whole damn thing up again," Ash replied.

Tom nodded his head and took a big gulp of his drink. He held the goblet in towards the center of the table, and the other two clinked their drinks. "Cheers."

"Only one question, though." Tom wiped away the froth that had collected in the hairs on his upper lip. "Why are you leaving all the fighting to a *girl*?"

Dylan and Ash exchanged glances and smiled.

"Because we have a plan," Dylan said.

"And because she's one bitch who you don't want to get on the wrong side of," Ash added, chuckling into his drink.

Ashdale Pond, Old Ontario

Pastor Andrews had never felt so *alive*.

The church was so warm that he found himself sweating. He moved animatedly, the candlelight flickering and casting dramatic shadows as he preached, the body heat of nearly two hundred Ashdale folks making the church feel more like home than he'd ever experienced.

Nearly two hundred pairs of attentive eyes and not one of them seemed to blink.

This was what it was all for, and he couldn't thank the governor enough. He was a shepherd, and this was his flock. His word in this sacred room of light was law. With the power Trisk had granted him, he would never be at the bottom of the ladder again. He'd never be without a soul to love or to listen.

And it had been so damn *easy*. He wondered why he'd never thought of it before.

A few times during the ceremony, he took questions, impressed with the speed of his lies and how easily people bought them. When asked, "What day will the reckoning come?" or "What will happen on that fateful day that will deliver us from evil?" Pastor Andrews shared some bullshit about a holy crew with guns and holy water who would take down the Mad one-by-one until the world was cleaner than it had ever been.

A sacred trio. A *Holy Trinity*.

And Ashdale would be Eden reborn.

Still, he wasn't entirely convinced that the church was as full as it could've been. Not every single person in the town had yielded to his cause. His Firestarters had been tasked with the duty to convert everyone.

Every. Single. Person.

Yet, though he couldn't name names, he was certain that goal was yet to be achieved. It was a feeling in his stomach, like when you knew you were being watched but couldn't find the eyes. You just...*knew*.

They stood at the back now, his sacred guardians of light. A row of a dozen of his men and women, dressed in black cloth. Each now had their sigil emblazoned in black ink on their arms, the sign of a church in flames.

He smiled, sweeping his arms in enthusiastic showmanship as he looked to the back and nodded at a man in the middle. He resembled a Neanderthal character with no hair, a thick frown line on his head, and tattoos which bled up the entirety of the left side of his body—as far as the pastor could see, anyway. A guy affectionately called "the Clobberer," or Clob for short. His mountainous arms were barely contained by his dark sleeves. His reputation, far from savory, made him the perfect enforcer.

The bells were a simple construction, really. A large wooden pole embedded in the ground with a thick coil of wire wrapped around its beam like a snake poised and ready to constrict. These had been dotted around Ashdale, and all anyone had to do to grab attention was pull and leave.

Yet somehow, Kain had caught his wrist around the rope. He could tug, but he could not go.

"Come *on*," Caitlin roared, rolling her eyes as she slashed at the rope and freed the Were. Kain rubbed his wrist, then looked back at the swollen horde of Mad, their numbers now closer to fifty than the two dozen they had been when they started running. There was no telling where they had come from. And, to be honest, that wasn't at the front of anyone's mind.

They raced across the remaining distance towards the church, the lights spilling from the broken windows now a beacon to guide them to the others. The clanging bells pealed a melody for their flight.

Caitlin felt a pang of guilt, knowing that she had brought the threat to the masses. But if there was one way to make an entrance, this was it. Even heroes had to know when they were outnumbered.

When the doors to the church opened, it was with a bang so hard they nearly fell off their hinges. Silhouetted in the doorway was what Caitlin could only describe as a gargoyle. A giant. A mammoth of a man who looked like he'd been hewn from the thickest branch of the forest's oldest tree.

The man gritted his teeth, held a thick club in the air, and charged like a raging bull. He lowered his head, gathered speed, and streamed straight past Caitlin, Kain, and Mary-Anne towards the horde. With a single swing of his club, he caved in a skull. Another swing sent someone flying back into three of their comrades.

Caitlin watched in fascination, only mildly aware that several Mad were coming for her now.

"Kitty-Cat, eyes up front," Kain bellowed, drawing his own blade and standing firm. Caitlin searched for Mary-Anne, seeing then that she, too, was already in the throes of the attack. With her usual dexterity and strength, she dealt with several Mad in succession and eliminated them with a mere twist of their heads.

Caitlin couldn't help but notice her eyes weren't glowing.

Probably for the best. The last thing we need is to alert the town that we've got a vampire, too.

When she heard growls to her right, she drew her sword and went on the offensive. Her blade connected with an old man's face—blister-covered and raw, looking like the skin had been held to a flame—making its way first through one cheek, then out the other. The man gurgled and screamed with the metal between his teeth before Caitlin booted him in the chest, knocking him to the floor, and delivered the final blow.

Jaxon barked. Caitlin ordered him back, not knowing what exactly might happen to a dog who ingested the Madness.

A mixture of panic and alarm sounded inside the church. Above the growls, grunts, and screeches of the Mad, they could hear Pastor Andrews' voice bellowing, roaring instructions, and summoning the town together for the attack.

Like ants spilling from a hole filled with boiling water, the residents of Ashdale came, some faster than others. Each person carried some form of weapon, be it a stick, a shoe, a pan, or a knife. Their cries were deafening. Their herd mentality filled Caitlin with a sense of empowerment.

This was what the world should be—a banded force of people fighting for the same cause. Ready and willing to come together to protect the world they knew, not cowering behind walls, relying on distance and cover to keep them safe.

They were everywhere in seconds. Each zombie now battled with at least three men and women. There were cries, screams, calls, tears, and blood.

Lots of blood.

Caitlin crippled several Mad as she ran through the field, taking out their hamstrings and sending them to the ground where they crawled and chomped, aiming for legs, ankles, and anything they could grab in their frenzy. She watched Kain use a Mad's back to launch himself high into the air, coming back down with his blade in another Mad's head. She saw Mary-Anne trip and stab several Mad before they were bludgeoned by townsfolk.

But when she heard a small girl's scream, her blood ran cold.

She turned her head in all directions, searching the melee in silent desperation. Finally, she identified two zombies reaching and clawing at the underside of the remains of an abandoned car. Its tires sagged, the rubber shredded and much of the metal carcass had melted into the ground. The scream came again, and Caitlin ran without hesitation.

"Jaxon, *get!*" Caitlin called. The dog sprinted past them all, ducking under the car and taking a position in front of the girl, a furry bodyguard.

The Mad were so focused on the girl that they didn't see her coming. Caitlin stomped on the back of one of their necks, forcing it to the ground. When it raised itself back up, she'd already yanked open the car door and now slammed it shut against the side of its face. There was a delicious squelching sound of a melon dropped from a height. Skin stripped from the cheek to reveal bone before the zombie collapsed.

The other was already halfway under the car, now. A heavy woman, she scratched and clawed at the earth like an animal digging.

Caitlin looked down at the bare flesh of the Mad's leg. She wrapped her sleeve around her hand to avoid skin-to-skin contact and pulled it back into the open. The woman half-rolled onto her back and screeched in her direction.

"Not today," Caitlin muttered through gritted teeth, oblivious now to the battle behind her as the townspeople started to decimate the horde's numbers.

The Mad woman reached for her, sitting up with impressive speed. Caitlin stumbled backward, found her footing, and stabbed forward, wounding the woman in the gut. As she pulled her sword back, thick blood pooled in the woman's lap.

With another well-placed stab, Caitlin found the heart and thrust her blade home. The woman choked, the light fading from her eyes, then lay back, her hand stretching out underneath the car where the young girl cowered.

"It must be tiring work to smell and look that bad," Caitlin muttered.

Cautiously, she kneeled between the corpses. The girl was sweet, her dark hair spilling over her face as she shivered and shuddered beneath the car.

"It's okay," Caitlin said. "They're gone now. Come with me. I'll keep you safe."

Behind her, a Mad-infected man began to charge, alerting her with a bloodcurdling yell. Caitlin scrambled aside, caught on the defensive and unable to gain her feet. Not a second later, Kain appeared, knocked the man sideways, and cut furiously into his body. "You ought to watch your six, Kitty Cat. No telling what kind of freaks will take you from behind."

Caitlin raised her eyebrows.

"Tell me you're not tempted." Kain winked before throwing himself at another Mad.

Jaxon licked the young girl's face, circling behind her and nudging her with his nose. The girl giggled, wiped her eyes, and crawled out, never taking her eyes off the zombies lying on the floor.

"That's it," Caitlin said, scooping her up.

"Clarissa...Clara! Oh, my dear baby," a woman called, running from the throng towards them both, her tunic splattered with blood. Behind her, Caitlin could see the battle winding down as the town dealt with the few remaining Mad.

"Safe and sound," Caitlin said, handing Clarissa over. "Not a bump or scratch to be seen."

Clarissa burst into tears in her mother's arms. A man ran over, his eyes wide and shimmering with unshed tears. His fingers tugged at the wiry mutton chops on his face. "You saved her?"

Caitlin blushed, then felt Jaxon rubbing his face on her leg. "It was a team effort, really."

Led by Clarissa's parents, Caitlin made her way back to

the others. After the last Mad had stopped moving, the congregation began to collect together, marveling at the gore on the field. A few of them noticed the new arrivals in their midst. Caitlin did her best to avoid their stares but could feel them everywhere. When they all turned to head back to the church, she felt her blood boil.

Standing in the doorway of the church, without a drop of blood on his person, was who Caitlin could only assume to be Pastor Andrews. A Cheshire Cat grin split his face.

"Welcome to Ashdale, newcomers," he said, spreading his arms wide. "Seems you've made quite the entrance." He looked at Mary-Anne. "And you. Welcome back."

Caitlin and Kain turned to Mary-Anne, hiding their grins.

Mary-Anne shrugged.

"The saviors," a woman called from the back. "The sacred trio," another woman added. "They've come."

A ripple of murmuring exploded into the silence, gaining volume.

CHAPTER THIRTEEN

Ashdale Pond, Old Ontario

They were suddenly swallowed by the crowd as people fought to get closer to them from all sides. Caitlin felt a little overwhelmed but laughed at it all.

"Not every day you get celebrated by a bunch of gullible simpletons, eh?" Kain whispered.

"Hush," Caitlin said as, a second later, a gap opened in the crowd. People moved out of the way as the brute with the club who had taken charge earlier pushed people aside and moved toward the trio.

"Inside. Pastor's orders," the man said.

"Hard to argue with that," Kain added.

They followed him—the one the others called "Clob"—and immediately felt the warmth of the church as they entered the doors.

There was an atmosphere of excitement as they walked the aisle to take a seat at the front next to the lectern where Pastor Andrews took his place. Townsfolk filed in to sit quietly on the long wooden benches. From the growing sense of discomfort, Caitlin guessed all eyes were fixed on the three companions up front.

She saw Jamie and Mabel seated at the back. The old woman waved, her hand quickly batted down by her grandson as he did his best to avoid attracting attention to them both. A couple of rows in front of them, Caitlin saw Clarissa snuggling into her mother's bosom.

"Well, that was a bit of excitement, wasn't it?" Pastor Andrews said, motioning to the trio. There was a rumble of laughter. "You think you're strapped in for a quiet evening of congregation and prayer and then, the next thing you know, you're out there fighting the Madness. Slaying a horde of the Devil's critters and stopping them from digesting and spewing your town in one whole gulp."

Pastor Andrews paused then, as if unsure how to carry on.

"Let us all take a moment to thank the Lord for our victory and to bless the passing of those who laid down their lives today." He cast his head down and closed his eyes.

"And for the arrival of the Trinity," a man called. "The Lord has blessed us with our saviors. The day of the reckoning has come."

"Has come," a voice repeated.

The pastor looked up, his eyes flashing with an anger which disappeared almost as quickly as it appeared. He ran a hand through his hair and said, "And under whose proclamation do we make such a hyperbolic statement?"

Caitlin sensed it now—an unease that settled in the man's mind. This was not his plan at all. If what Jamie had told them was true, this was the last thing Pastor Andrews would have wanted, for someone else to steal the limelight.

"*You* did!" the woman called again. "You said a trio of heroes would come, and here they are. Straight from the nothingness of night to deliver us from evil."

Pastor Andrews grew red in the face. "They *delivered* evil. Straight to our doorstep. A half-hundred Mad straight out of the—"

"Please!" Caitlin said, pushing to her feet. The voices quietened immediately. "Your pastor is right, we're not heroes. We're not even a three." She pointed at Jaxon, who now sat with his tongue out in front of Kain. "We merely came from afar and were looking for somewhere safe to reside. That's all. Nothing more. Nothing less." She noticed a few heads drop with disappointment. "Please, no more of this "trinity" talk. You're in the safe hands of your pastor." She cast a glance over and saw the man's face soften. "He is your hero."

The smile found its way back onto Andrews' face. "There. See? Nothing more. Nothing less."

"What are your names, great ones?" someone called from the crowd.

Caitlin froze, looking to Mary-Anne and Kain for reassurance. If the governor in found out they were there in the same town that he supposedly was in, it would ruin any chance of surprise they might have.

Mary-Anne saved Caitlin the trouble of answering. "I am Detta Slystock. This man on my right is Arthur Cornswaggle, and this woman is Moxie Curtis. We thank you for your warm welcome."

After a warm round of greetings, Pastor Andrews took

back the reins. For a few minutes, his delivery of the final parts of his sermon was clunky and unbalanced, though once his enthusiasm was up and running, he delighted and entertained the congregation as though there had been no interruption.

When he had finished and those gathered uttered their final prayers, the townspeople began to file out. The sun looked to soon be crowning, and Mary-Anne looked eager to leave.

"I think we've had enough excitement for one evening without revealing I'm a vampire by watching me turn to ash in a heap on the floor," she said, pitching her voice low.

"After you, Miss Slystock," Caitlin teased.

"Cornswaggle?" Kain grumbled. "You couldn't think of anything better than Cornswagggle?"

"It was either that or Nobgobbling," Mary-Anne winked.

"Why was it just between those two?"

Before they could reach the doorway, Pastor Andrews called to them. He was stood in the center of the aisle, then walked toward them so smoothly it looked like he was floating.

"Miss Slystock. Miss Curtis. *Mr.* Cornswaggle," he crooned, his voice as slick as his hair. "A moment before you leave?"

Caitlin fought back a chuckle as Kain's face dropped. Mary-Anne looked longingly out at the town, clearly wanting nothing more than to find the darkest corner of Mabel's house and lie down.

"What is it, Pastor?" Caitlin said in the most innocent tone she could manage. The man gave her the creeps. He was what she had imagined vampires looked like before she met Mary-Anne—pale skin and piercing eyes.

"I saw what you did out there," Pastor Andrews said. "You three fought bravely. Better than most I've seen. It must've required some skill and talent for the three of you to make it so far in the wilderness on your own."

"We do all right," Kain chirped.

If Pastor Andrews found any humor in that, he showed none. "I wouldn't usually suggest this to newcomers, but times are a-changing, and we need all hands on deck to ensure that change is *managed*."

"What are you suggesting," Caitlin asked.

Pastor Andrews nodded at Clob, who pulled the sleeve of his top up to reveal the tattoo Caitlin and company had seen on Yusuf and Christy upon their arrival. On Clob, it could only be differentiated from his other tattoos by the depth of its color, which indicated the freshness of the ink.

"I'd like you to join our elite force. The defenders of Ashdale. I call them the Firestarters."

"Sounds pretty sadistic," Kain blurted.

Caitlin's eyes widened, a silent warning which Kain either missed or avoided. The pastor simply smiled.

"Life is a game of balance, Mr. Cornswaggle. With freedom comes restraint. With life comes death. If you want protection, and to channel your...gifts...to a higher cause, then it's this offer that I extend to you. We could use some recruits of your...talents."

Mary-Anne's brow was now peppered with sweat. She looked like she might dash away at any moment. Caitlin knew the danger she faced as the sky turned ever lighter.

Pastor Andrews swept between them with Clob

stomping behind. "Think about it," he said and glided down the steps and set off into the town.

"No. No way," Kain grunted.

"Think about it," Caitlin said.

"What's there to think about?" Kain crossed his eyes and put on a goofy voice. "Oh, yeah, great idea, let's join a so-called elite group of fuckinators who get their kicks by smoking out the elderly and setting their possessions ablaze."

"He's got a point," Jamie chipped in, rubbing his eyes.

Caitlin threw her hands in the air, rolling her eyes. Mary-Anne had disappeared upstairs the minute they had come into the house, immersing herself in the safety of the darkness. Occasionally, though, she still chimed into their conversation.

"Look," Caitlin said, taking a breath to calm herself down. She hadn't anticipated Kain being so short-sighted. "If we join his elite force, we're already ten steps ahead of the game. We'll have immediate insiders' access to everything the pastor says, or knows, or does. He's our link to the governor. It's *perfect!*"

"Hide in plain sight," Mary-Anne called from upstairs. Her vampire hearing always impressed Caitlin.

"Exactly."

"I don't know," Jamie said. "You may be in the pastor's good books now, but what if he gets wind of what you're all up to?"

"And what if he doesn't?" Caitlin interjected.

"Exactly," Mary-Anne called.

Mabel sat quietly in the corner of the room, nursing a steaming mug of something which smelled sweet. She seemed to be at ease in her own mind, her thoughts keeping her occupied. Jaxon, meanwhile, sniffed around the room, taking great laps of water which had been placed in a bowl by the corner.

"So, what do you think Trisk will think when he is told that two women—one a skinny chick with brown hair and a *sword*, the other a dark chick with black hair who looks faintly like a vampire—have stumbled across the town with a dog and me? You don't think he's going to be suspicious?"

"That depends how much he knows," Caitlin said, thinking back to the fight at Silver Creek. "He had no way of knowing that you joined us before he fled. He had no way of knowing that Jaxon was there, too. If the odds work in our favor, we *could* get away with it."

"And if they don't?" Kain said.

"But what if they *do*?" Caitlin replied. "Let's try to look on the positive side, eh, Cornswaggle?"

Jamie burst into a fit of laughter. Upstairs, they could hear Mary-Anne snort.

A shadow passed over Kain's face. "Look, no matter what happens, I'm likely going to follow you two. It's been a long time since I've found people who I can trust and a cause I can get behind. But I'm going to make this clear. If we get found out and we're put in a situation where we have to choose between life, death, and a wall of flames, I'm choosing life. I've come too far to be turned into cinders."

"If I didn't know better, I'd say that Pooch was afraid of fire," Mary-Anne mumbled.

Kain snarled.

"So, we're agreed?" Caitlin said, flashing a cheeky grin at Kain. "FFL?"

"What's she talking about?" Jamie asked Kain.

"Firestarters for life," Caitlin replied.

They laughed together then. Even Kain couldn't help but grin.

"One question first," Kain said.

"Go on."

"What are we going to do when Detta Slystock is asked to go out in the daytime to perform her duties?"

The smile fell from Caitlin's face. Kain was right. Though it seemed that most of the congregation and cere-monies took place at night, they had seen Firestarters walking around in the daytime. How would they get Mary-Anne—a *vampire*—out and into the sunlight to join their plan?

"What's the problem?" Jamie asked. "Why can't Detta...I mean, Mary-Anne, go out in the daylight?"

"The answer's simple," Mabel said suddenly, her eyes comprehending and bright.

"Nana?" Jamie said. He crossed the room and took a seat beside her, one hand on her knee. "You're back?"

Mabel waved him away as if it were no big deal.

"If you want to get a nightwalker out in the daytime, you need to block the sun."

Mabel got shakily to her feet and crossed the room. She disappeared from sight, but a moment later, they heard her challenge. "Well, what are you waiting for?"

They made an odd picture as the four of them stood in Mary-Anne's doorway. She held the cloth limply in her hands. With its dark color, it looked like she held the flaccid shape of a corpse's shadow.

"What the shit is this?" Mary-Anne asked, holding the cloth to her nose. It smelled of dust and time.

"Try it on," Mabel encouraged. "Should be about the right fit for you."

Mary-Anne's nose wrinkled. "Are you calling me fat?"

"Of course not," Mabel said, laughing. "You've got a lovely hourglass figure, dear. Particularly for a…well…you know."

"Does someone mind telling me what's going on?" Jamie whined.

They ignored him.

Mary-Anne made them stand outside the room and closed the door while she changed. They heard her moving around, knocking over a couple of items on shelves as she squeezed into the cloth. After a minute of quiet, Mabel knocked on the door. "All ready, dear?"

Silence.

Caitlin and Kain exchanged glances. "Ma?"

Mabel turned the handle and creaked the door open. The room was dark and looked empty. Caitlin stepped in, squinting her eyes to attempt to catch a glimpse of Mary-Anne and could see nothing.

"Ma? Where d'ya go—"

"Boo!" Mary-Anne said suddenly, appearing at Caitlin's side. Caitlin could only see her because her eyes twinkled in the darkness. Every other part of her was clothed in black. The minute she closed them, she might as well have vanished.

"Oh, good idea, Mabes. Give the vampire camouflage, too," Kain said.

"V...vampire?" Jamie stuttered. "She's a v...v—"

"Vampire, dear. Yes," Mabel said matter-of-factly. "I knew it from the moment I saw her in that church. You vamps have a certain...*something* about you. Now, give me a twirl."

Mary-Anne did, looking the most feminine Caitlin had ever seen her when she moved. One minute, Mary-Anne was looking at them, and the next moment, she was gone. As she finished her turn, her eyes returned her normal slightly mocking stare to their mute amazement.

"It looks even better on you than it did on her," Mabel said, clapping.

"Better than who, now?" Kain asked.

"Oh, dear. You think I've been on this planet for over nine decades without coming across your types before? What do you take old Mabel for? Ripe as bunnies, you supernatural folk were when I was a wee sprout. Couldn't turn a corner without some vamp fight or Were brawl."

"Were?" Jamie mumbled. "Where?"

Mabel continued as though she hadn't heard her grandson. "Just because the Madness has forgotten you doesn't mean I have. I always held out hope that your kind would be back. That we'd see more of you along the way."

"This used to belong to a vampire?" Mary-Anne marveled. "Who? When? What happened to them?"

Mabel waved her words away. "A story for another time. In short, a town protector whose hubris got the best of her. They're long gone now to the void from which none can return." She clapped her hands, tears pricking the corners of her eyes. "I can't believe it *fits*."

Mary-Anne studied herself. Every inch of her was covered in cloth, thick black material reaching to the tips of her fingers and toes. "And this is thick enough to block the sun?"

"It might get a bit hot, but if a single ray of sun hits you, I'll eat my own grandson."

Jamie, who had been staring at the floor in thought, suddenly chimed in. "*Nana*."

"What about her eyes?" Caitlin asked, realizing that while the outfit might be a good sunblock, Mary-Anne could hardly do her vampire shit without her eyes to guide her.

"Easy," Mabel said and reached forward to tug what looked like a long flap of cloth behind the hood. It fell in front of Mary-Anne's face like a veil, blocking her eyes from sight.

"Ho-ly-shit," Mary-Anne said from nowhere.

"That'll never work," Kain said. She can't see through that shit."

"Try me," Mary-Anne said.

Kain stuck his middle finger in the air. "Okay. How many fingers am I holding up?"

"One."

"*Shit*. That was too easy." He held his hand in the air, showing four fingers.

"Four."

He changed them to two.

"Two."

Five.

"Five."

None.

"None."

"Fuck!" Kain exclaimed. "Okay, she's passed my test. Who's next?"

"I think that's enough playing for now," Mabel said, the grin still on her face. "If we don't get my grandson a seat soon, I'm sure he might pass out."

While Mabel took Jamie downstairs and gave him something cool to drink, Kain, Mary-Anne, and Caitlin sat and talked for a while about their plan of action. Shortly after, they each headed to their rooms to catch some rest, tiredness felling them like bricks as soon as their heads hit the pillow.

As Caitlin drifted to sleep, she couldn't believe how excited she was at the prospect of bringing Mary-Anne along with them during the day. How long had it been since her friend had truly seen the world in the light? Felt the warmth of the sun on her skin.

Okay, well, not quite.

Either way, her heart fluttered with excitement. When she dreamed that night, the flames stayed away. Her head filled with memories of her family and visions of a world beyond the Madness.

CHAPTER FOURTEEN

Ashdale Pond, Old Ontario

Jamie would take them no further than the end of the street. They could see, about a hundred yards away, what looked to be a dilapidated outhouse with several floors. A swinging sign which creaked read, The Cloak & Dagger.

"This is where we'll find him?" Caitlin asked, staring at the odd angles of the building's construction. It looked as though it had been made of plastic and had overheated in the sun. The scent of burning was stronger on this side of town, and several plumes of smoke rose steadily in thin ribbons into the sky not too far away. A slight haze hung over the street.

"Sure is." Jamie wouldn't even look at the building and instead, looked over his shoulder and in all directions. "Knock three times. Loud, quiet, loud, and someone will let you in. Now, if you don't mind, I'll take my leave."

"Thank you, Jamie," Caitlin said, surprising Jamie with a warm embrace. "For everything."

"My friends call me, Jay-Jay," he responded.

"But those two—Yusuf and Christy—didn't they call you—" Kain began.

"It doesn't matter," Jamie said sharply, looking abashed. He turned and began walking in the opposite direction. "Be careful, and avoid making eye contact if you can."

Before they could utter another word, he was gone.

Caitlin knocked as Jamie had instructed, and heard the door unlock from the other side. They waited a moment before they gave it a push.

The door was stiff and screeched on its hinges as it opened. They looked a picture, Caitlin wrapped up tight in her dark green cloak, Kain with his scarred and worn face, and Mary-Anne swooping after them like a noir ghost with not an inch of her body exposed.

Not that blocking her skin from the sun would matter for long. Her nemesis would set soon, and she'd be able to travel without her protective layer.

It was dark inside and smelled of body odor. Straw and dirt were strewn across the floor, and the used glasses and goblets left on the tables were covered in sticky grime. Caitlin couldn't believe it. Was this what this place called service?

They found standing room at the bar and waited for someone to appear. Jaxon stayed close, his ears down while he investigated the place with his nose.

A handful of customers milled about the place. A group of thugs over in the corner played a game of cards, capturing Kain's attention. "Caitlin, *look!*" he muttered excitedly as she held him back from joining them. Several couples lingered in ramshackle booths, though they looked like they were more ready to fight each other than to ever make love.

Over the far side, beside a set of stairs, Clob sat in a deep armchair, his chin to his chest, snoring gently.

"Yes?" a voice sounded, seemingly from nowhere.

Caitlin, Mary-Anne, and Kain looked in all directions, failing to find the source of the voice. A hand lifted above the bar and waved. Caitlin leaned over the counter and saw the tiny man, his head only an inch taller than the damned thing.

"Hi," she said in surprise.

"Got a problem, get the fuck out," the man grumbled.

Wow. Who taught you manners?

He was a strange creature, really, a regular human with stunted growth. One of his hands sported malformed fingers with which he held a cup, and the other hand held a cloth with which he wiped the inside of the glass.

Not that it did much good, Caitlin noted. The cloth looked filthier than the glass.

They told him who they were looking for. The man studied them for a moment, then disappeared again behind the bar. He came around the front and joined them, leading them over to where Clob sat, drool dribbling down his chin.

"Oi. Clob," the man grumbled. When no response was forthcoming, the dwarf pulled a coin from his pocket and lobbed it at Clob's face. It struck him squarely in the forehead, bounced off, then clinked as it landed in the brute's cup. His drink fizzled and bubbled as the coin sank to the bottom.

Clob sat up in a hurry, looking in all directions. He

reached for the squat man, who batted his hand away. It was absurd, really, that a mammoth could be thwarted by a fly.

"What d'you want, Stump?" Clob said, recognition dawning on his face as he saw Caitlin, Kain, and Jaxon. He barely registered Mary-Anne, likely assuming her to be one of the other's shadows.

"They want to see the pastor," Stump said. "Take them to him."

Stump threw a set of keys which the large man somehow managed to catch.

"Why can't you do it? It's your place," Clob argued, tossing the keys back.

"I've got people to serve," Stump said, and the keys ended up back in Clob's hand.

They all looked at the bar, emptier than the governor's heart and soul.

Clob grinned triumphantly. "I can't see them."

As he went to throw the keys back at Stump, a woman entered. She hobbled over to the bar, one leg dragging in a noticeable limp and her back hunched and knobby. She took a seat at the bar and waited.

Stump beamed at Clob, although with the shadows cast over his face, it presented as more of a leer. "As I was saying…"

Stump disappeared. Clob looked at them each in turn, then sighed. "Follow me."

Clob dragged his club behind him as they climbed, the heavy wood making a loud clunk with every step.

Clob jangled the keys as they stood outside room fifteen. He knocked on the door, then waited until they heard a reply a moment later. He placed the key in the lock, turned it, and let himself in ahead of the others. Mary-Anne removed her hood as they stepped inside.

The first thing to hit Caitlin was a strange feeling of disgusted nostalgia. A smell lingered, reminding her of something she couldn't quite place—sweat, grease, and oil, in the clammy inside of the room without fresh air. Distracted by the impending meeting, she sifted her memories, trying to pinpoint the odd familiarity but couldn't think of what it might be.

"Jesus, smells like someone slept with the piggies, ate them, then shit them back out," Kain muttered as they made their way through the large receiving room. Pastor Andrews sat at the far end, looking out the window.

"Nice of you to join me. I wondered if I'd be seeing you all again. Nice attire," he added, half-turning to Mary-Anne, "I see you already noticed that the Firestarters have a particular liking for black."

They took seats around the room, Mary-Anne keeping herself as far away from the window as possible. The sun was setting on the far side of the house, but even the sight of it without her hood had her nauseated.

Caitlin drew her hood back. "We'd like to join you, Pastor. We're in. We want to join the Firestarters."

"Very good," he responded, drawing out the vowels. "Very good, indeed. You hear that, Clob? We've got some new recruits."

"Great," Clob said simply.

They sat in silence a moment.

"So, what do we do now? Do you provide the uniforms,

slap on the tatts, and we get out there on the streets?" Kain asked.

The pastor chuckled. "Not exactly." He stood and began pacing the room. "You think it's as simple as that? That I'd let any old nomad join the team without some sort of test? I don't know you from Adam. For all I know, you could be vigilantes, here to murder me and take over the town."

He laughed, a hearty sound which sent a shiver running up Caitlin's spine. The sound of it made Jaxon howl.

Their host circled the room, pausing behind Caitlin's chair. She could feel his breath on the top of her head and taste the musty odor that emanated from him.

"Then what do you need us to do?" she asked.

"I never thought you'd ask, Miss Curtis." He paused. "It is, *Miss* Curtis, isn't it?"

Caitlin suddenly felt warm as he made his way back to his chair, scanning her from top to bottom. She didn't like the way he looked at her but noted that perhaps it was something she could play on. She might be able to use it to her advantage.

"It is," she said, shuffling in her chair and catching Mary-Anne's disapproving gaze.

Kain feigned a cough.

The pastor broke his scrutiny. "I've got a task that I need you to complete. I need it done tonight, and in utter secrecy. On the upper east side of town, there's a house with broken windows and a blue door. Inside are some—how do I put this?—*troublemakers* who need to be taken care of. Smoke them out. Send a message. Either they kneel, or they die."

"Seems a bit extreme," Kain said before he could stop himself.

Mary-Anne and Caitlin glared at him.

"Extreme? Maybe," Pastor Andrews said, unflinching. "Yet it takes a great deal of leadership and strength to do what is necessary to secure peace. If you can't hack the task, then fine. Clob can see to you from here on out."

Clob tapped his club against his open palm, his eyes menacing.

"But if you can," the pastor continued, "then we'll get you inked, clothed, and ready to join an elite force the likes of which the world hasn't seen in years. The best food. The best company. It's all in your hands."

Caitlin felt her anger boil just below the surface of her calm, not a fan of the idea of being threatened. But this was not the time to let her emotions get the best of her.

She grinned, crossing her legs one over the other, revealing her lower calf. The pastor's eyes were drawn down, and she suppressed a triumphant grin.

"You've got yourself a deal," she said.

He clapped his hands. "Very good."

"Who lives in the house?" Mary-Anne asked suddenly.

The pastor smiled, a knowing look on his face. "As I said…troublemakers."

Silver Creek, Silver Creek Forest, Old Ontario

"More burning," Dylan murmured, standing on the parapets.

Sullivan squinted beside him. "More burning means more fire, right?"

Dylan nodded. He had checked on the plumes regularly, his curiosity drawn over the canopy of the forest to the faint traces of smoke beyond. He figured that maybe the fires would stop burning after a few days, but that didn't seem to be the case.

Couple that with the fact that several more vagabonds had somehow found their way through the forest and requested entry into Silver Creek, and Dylan started to grow anxious. If there really was something happening out there, then was Caitlin okay? Sure, Dylan had also grown to care for Kain and Mary-Anne—despite the fact she really gave him the creeps—but his loyalties lay with his sister.

"I hate this," Dylan said, his face growing stern.

"What's that, sir?"

"Standing and waiting while they're out there fighting. The last time this happened, I was stuck in a prison without a choice, but now..."

"What about the town? If we leave, who will stand guard and protect Silver Creek?" Sullivan scratched his head, looking down at his captain.

Dylan smiled and clapped the guard on the shoulder. "I'm looking at him."

Sullivan's face melted into shock. "Do you mean it, sir?"

But Dylan wasn't listening. At that moment, he wasn't standing on the parapets of Silver Creek *watching* the action. He was out there, with his sister, *taking part* in the action. Whatever was going on in the distance, he wanted in. As long as they had the smoke to guide them, they'd find their way.

Sullivan continued babbling, only stopping when Dylan said, "Come. Let's rouse the others. It's time."

"But I don't want to arouse the others," Sully said.

Dylan looked at him incredulously. "No. Not a-rouse. Just rouse."

Sully returned a blank stare.

"Never mind, just follow me."

CHAPTER FIFTEEN

Ashdale Pond, Old Ontario

Night had fallen by the time they made it to the house on the upper east side.

It was right where Pastor Andrews said it would be, though the faded blue door appeared more like gray in the starlight. The broken windows looked more like the mouths of demons yawning in a pit of black, the remains of glass the last remnants of the monsters' teeth.

"Go on," Clob said, his club by his side.

Caitlin had been surprised to find Clob waiting at the bottom of the street when they arrived, though in hindsight she should've figured as much.

"You think you've earned the pastor's trust yet, maggots?" Clob said in his gruff voice. "You've got a long ways to go to prove yourself. Now, get."

As they had started towards the house, Clob had added. "Oh, and the pastor expects to see smoke and flame."

With Jaxon leading, the four of them made their way to the house. There was a set of stairs leading to a front porch. They climbed them and peeked through the windows. The house was silent. The only sounds to be heard were their own breath and footsteps—though, granted, Mary-Anne was so light on her feet that she hardly made a sound.

"See anything?" Caitlin whispered.

"Nope," Mary-Anne replied.

They circled the house under the watchful eye of Clob who stood statuesque across the street. If they hadn't have known he was there, they could be forgiven for thinking he was nothing more than a blip in the shadows.

The back door was shut, but there was no lock. Caitlin pushed it open cautiously until the gap was large enough for her to slide through, told Jaxon to stand guard, then made her way inside.

The room was clothed in shadow. On a table to the side of the room stood a wooden frame holding a sketch of a woman who looked to be in her thirties with a little blonde girl on her lap. The girl was smiling, her hair divided into pigtails. There was something oddly familiar about her that Caitlin couldn't quite place.

Kain sniffed the air as he moved up beside her. "Something's off here."

"Maybe that's your own breath," Mary-Anne retorted.

"Divide and conquer?" Caitlin suggested. She had been adamant on the way over here that they make sure the house was empty before they smoked it out. Although joining the Firestarters might be their key to reaching the governor, the last thing Caitlin wanted to do was actually hurt any innocents.

Kain and Mary-Anne nodded. He took the room to the

left, Mary-Anne dashed up the stairs as silently as the wind, and Caitlin explored the room directly in front—what looked like a kitchen and parlor of sorts.

Another sketch had been nailed to the wall. A man and woman sat side-by-side, laughing. A girl played on the floor between them.

Again, Caitlin sensed that she knew her somehow. Knew *them*.

When she reached the bottom of the stairs, Kain approached from the opposite direction.

"Anything?" she asked.

"Nothing. Though we ought to make a move before old clobber-brains outside gets suspicious. We were supposed to start a fire and leave, right?"

"Right."

"Guys," Mary-Anne said, appearing at the top of the stairs. "You might want to see this."

They made their way upstairs, making no effort to avoid the creaking of the stairs. If anyone were in the house, Caitlin thought, they'd know they weren't alone anymore anyway. What was the point in hiding?

They followed Mary-Anne down the hallway to where a door stood ajar. Caitlin could already hear muffled sounds as though someone's face was covered with a pillow. She raised a questioning eyebrow at Mary-Anne, who opened the door.

A man and woman, most likely in their fifties, sat in the center of the room. Each had gray hair, with a fading circle of bald on the man's. A length of cloth tied around their heads, gagging them both, and a coil of rope tied their hands, feet, and bodies together.

Caitlin recognized them instantly as the couple from the pictures.

Their eyes widened with fear as the three of them walked into the room. Caitlin held up her hands, looked down at Mary-Anne's black clothing, and instantly felt foolish.

Of course, they're terrified. We look like the fucking undertaker has come to drag them to hell.

"It's okay, it's okay," Caitlin whispered, approaching with careful calm. She knelt by their side. "I'm going to cut these free. Please don't squirm too much in case I nick you, and *please* remain calm. We're not here to hurt you."

She cut their bonds and removed their gag. They spent a second rubbing their wrists.

"Who are you?" they asked.

Caitlin turned to Mary-Anne, who shook her head. "Now's not the time for that. You're in danger, and we need to get you out of here."

"They're coming back, aren't they?" the woman said, struggling to hide her fear. "They said they would be, those fucking Firestarters. Back with flame, they said. Back with fire."

"Keep your voice down," Kain hissed as the woman grew more frantic. "Unless you want good ol' Clob to swing by and turn your heads into smashed fruit?"

"He's back?" the man said. "Clob is back?"

"What do you mean, he's back?" Caitlin asked.

Mary-Anne tutted and indicated they needed to hurry.

"Who do you think tied us up?" the woman said. "We were fast asleep when he came in. He took us by surprise, coming into our room and overpowering us both. My husband's strong, but he's no match for that…freak."

"Said he had a surprise for us, and for us to sit tight," the man said, tugging at the tufts of his hair. "If we don't go soon, those Firestarters will come. We need to hurry. Let's go."

Caitlin looked guiltily at the floor.

"What? What is it?" the woman asked.

"We're the Firestarters. The pastor sent *us* to start the fire."

"*You?*" the woman said.

"It's not like that," Mary-Anne cut in, interrupting whatever protest the woman seemed more than ready to spew. "We're not one of *them*. We don't have time to explain, but we're the *good* guys."

Outside, they heard Jaxon begin to bark.

"Quick, we need to get moving," Kain said, shoving the man forward and into the hallway. "Do you have a back passageway out of here?"

"What does this place look like? A haunted friggin' castle?" The old man was fiery now, finally awake and on the offensive.

"My Christy. You must know my Christy?" the woman said, pausing next to her husband in the hallway as Caitlin and Mary-Anne filed out from behind.

Caitlin froze. *That's* why that picture looked so familiar.

"You're Christy's parents?" Caitlin asked.

They nodded. "Patricia and Felix Cordery. Have you seen her? Where is she?"

"I really feel like this conversation could wait for another time," Mary-Anne said.

Jaxon's barks grew louder as he ran inside the house. A voice followed him. "Keep your noise down, you mangy mutt!"

Their eyes all widened in alarm, and they sprinted down the stairs, pausing halfway when they saw Clob's gigantic form waiting at the bottom. He weighed his club in one hand, hid biceps bulging silver in the moonlight which filtered through the window.

"It's not what it looks like," Kain said.

"Really?" Clob leered. "Because it looks like you're trying to help our friends escape, now, doesn't it?"

"If this is how you treat your friends, I'd hate to see how you treat your enemies," Kain said.

From behind Clob, two more figures appeared. Yusuf held a makeshift mace in his hands, while Christy sported a whip and a rusted, notched machete.

"*Christy,*" Patricia exclaimed before Mary-Anne's hand found her mouth and silenced her.

Christy remained silent, doing anything she could to avoid making eye contact with her parents.

"She's one of us, you stupid bitch," Clob grunted. "And you three. Pastor Andrews had such high hopes for you all. It's a shame I'll have to go back and tell him that I took care of you all."

"That's bullshit," Caitlin said. "If he had high hopes, then why did he send his goons to babysit?"

"Because you don't get anywhere without trust in this world. There was always a chance you were up to no good, and here's the proof. These two have caused the pastor a headache ever since Christy...*joined*...our cause, and all he asked was that you scare them a touch. Torch their house. Send a message."

"Set the fuckers on fire, you mean?" Kain said. "That's what you were hoping, right? That we'd set the place ablaze and kill them both."

If Caitlin weren't mistaken, she'd say Christy's eyes widened slightly.

Clob shrugged. "There's always collateral in war."

He took a step, his footsteps like thunder through the house. Caitlin, Kain, and Mary-Anne drew their weapons. Jaxon bared his teeth.

"Get them back," Caitlin ordered Kain. "Get them somewhere safe. *Now*."

"Safe?" Clob said, taking another step. "Darling, in a few seconds, there won't be a place for you that's safe."

As if on cue, Yusuf and Christy drew tinder and flint from their pockets. Yusuf knelt down, poured a clear, viscous liquid in a puddle on the floor, and chipped away to create a spark. Christy mirrored his actions reluctantly on the other side. The instant the first spark hit the puddle, it sprang to life, glowing a litany of blues, whites, oranges, and reds. It crackled as it burned, slowly spreading wider and wider until it reached the bottom of the stairs and began climbing the stairway.

"Best get running," Clob said, manic glee on his face.

Caitlin and the others turned and fled up the stairs. They dashed into a room filled with junk and clothing at the far side of the house and pulled a window open to look outside.

Behind them, they heard Clob shout, "Take positions outside. Wait for the birdies to drop."

"Quick," Caitlin said, poking her head out the window. The fresh air hit her and, as she looked down, her vision went blurry. They were at least twenty feet from the ground. She hadn't jumped from many heights in her life, but she figured that jumping from there wouldn't be fun for anyone.

Yeah, try running away with both your shins splintered.

"What do we do?" Patricia asked. Felix held her tight, as though he hoped if he squeezed her hard enough, he might be able to absorb her and keep her safe.

"Like clubbing fish in a barrel," Clob said. They could see him in the hallway as he swung the club in a wide arc, smashing through the wood of the banister. Behind him, thick black smoke began to stream upstairs.

"You two go," Kain said, pointing into the hallway. "I'll get these guys to safety."

"What are you going to do? Sprout wings and fly down?" Mary-Anne chided.

Kain looked around, spotting a pile of linen and clothes on the floor. "I've got an idea," he said. "Now, go."

Mary-Anne looked uncertain for a moment until Caitlin shouted, "C'mon Ma, help me hold him back."

Caitlin picked up speed, heading toward Clob. He swung, and she ducked, leaning backward and skidding on her knees until she was on the other side of his massive form.

"Nice one, Moxie," she heard Mary-Anne remark.

"Thanks, Detta." Caitlin grinned.

As the fire crackled and grew, they fought Clob from either side. Mary-Anne used her vampire strength to bat away his club as if it were nothing more than the soft stem of a plant. Caitlin blocked with great effort and weaved around his blows, doing her best to buy time as the others tried to escape.

"Enough of these games," Clob said, lashing out with the club and catching Mary-Anne in the stomach. She smacked against the wall, winded, and fell to the floor. Clob smiled. "Good."

"*No*," Caitlin shouted, kicking at the back of Clob's leg. He fell to one knee, his massive weight breaking the floor-boards. The wood splintered around him, biting into his skin. He struggled against the timber, but it bit deeper into his knee. The fire had all but swallowed the stairs now, the smoke thick. It burned Caitlin's eyes as she pulled her cloak over her face.

She took a few steps back and stepped on Clob's back, spring-boarding herself across the hallway. He clawed at her legs as she passed, but she was too fast. She coughed and spluttered, grabbed Mary-Anne's hand on the way past, and dragged her into the room where the others had been. The space was now filled with nothing more than smoke.

Caitlin leaned out the window, gasping for the fresh air. Below them, she saw the coil of cloth and a sight that made her heart stop.

Yusuf held his mace in one hand, a knife in the other, and his arm wrapped about Patricia's throat, the knife pressed against her skin. Kain stood a few feet away, his sword drawn. Felix had gone pale, looking around helplessly.

"Another move and she dies," Yusuf said, glee bright on his face in the glow of the flames.

"Patricia, *no*," Felix cried.

"Oh, come on. You wanted to kill her anyway," Kain said. "How do we know you'll keep her alive if we behave?"

Yusuf looked up at the window. "Where's Clob?"

Caitlin looked back inside the house but could only see smoke. "I don't know."

A flicker of panic crossed Yusuf's face. "No matter," he said without conviction. "Like we ever needed that brute in the first place. I don't know *what* Pastor Andrews saw in him."

A mighty crash from behind was followed by a roar of pain. Caitlin imagined the stairs caving in on themselves, the wood splintering and falling down in a rain of wood and fire until a shape emerged from the smoke.

Clob coughed into his fist, swaying drunkenly as he walked. He shoved Caitlin to the side and stuck his head out the window, taking in the crisp night-time air. "I heard you...shithead..." he managed to say, leering down at Yusuf. "You think if I'm out of the picture the pastor will make you his number two? Dream on, pal."

Yusuf tensed, and Patricia cried as the knife broke the skin. A small sprinkle of blood crawled lazily down her neck.

"Dream on, you big lubbock," Yusuf shouted. Across the way, Caitlin was sure she saw several curtains shift. By her reckoning, it wouldn't be long now before the town began to pour out for congregation.

"Why you shit-eating, pee-spraying, pussy piece of —*argh!*"

Clob cut off as the creature wound its way around his neck. The black snake had appeared in the breath of a second. Caitlin moved back, afraid it might move to her, until she followed its length and saw Christy standing in the doorway, the whip taut in her hand. Her face was smeared with ash, her hair singed and scorched.

"Enough of this shit," she said, her voice steady behind the collar of her shirt as she tugged with all her strength.

Clob choked and fell backward, reminding Caitlin of a felled tree. He crashed to the ground, clutching his throat and his face growing red. Christy immediately followed the fall by raising a chair over her head and smashing Clob in the face. His eyes closed as he was knocked out cold.

"Smooth," Caitlin said.

Christy coughed. "Enough talk. Let's get out of here."

"Just one problem. You might want to stay back for this," Caitlin said.

Christy ran to the window. "Dad? *Mum?*" she cried.

"Christy? What are you doing—" Yusuf started.

He cut off the minute the blade embedded into his throat. He looked up at the window in alarm, his eyes fixed on Caitlin where she stood frozen after tossing the knife.

Yusuf gurgled on his own blood, his grip on Patricia loosening as he crumpled to the floor.

"That was a risky move," Christy said, slapping Caitlin on the back.

"A thanks would do just fine." She grinned.

"Here!" Kain called from below, picking up the end of the cloth rope they had tied together. He bound the end around a rock to help the light cloth fly higher, and Caitlin caught it easily. She tied the end around the curtain pole, then eased herself down, Christy following shortly after.

The family embraced with something close to desperation as she exploded into tears.

"Gotta love a good family reunion," Kain said. "Of course, most of my family have been dead for years."

"Speak for yourself," Mary-Anne quipped.

Caitlin turned and watched the fire. The entire bottom floor of the house was now ablaze. Smoke plumed thick into the night sky. She imagined Clob's body on the landing, his skin melting like waxworks. His only blessing was that he would have been unconscious in his dying moments as the flames took him.

"We need to burn the body," Caitlin said, looking at Yusuf.

"Agreed," Mary-Anne said. "Destroy the evidence."

"What the fuck are we going to tell the pastor?" Kain asked. "You think he's not going to be suspicious that the fire we were sent to start also destroyed two of his men?"

"He may be powerful, but he's not that bright," Christy said, breaking away from her parents. "Tell him it was an accident. Tell him that you completed his task, but there were some complications. Mum and Dad got into a fight with them both, and they got caught in the flames. I'll testify to that."

"You think he won't know that we're lying when Patricia and Felix arrive at congregation later tonight?" Kain asked.

"They won't be going to congregation," Caitlin said. "As far as the pastor knows, they're dead. Gone. Buried in the fire with the others. We need to get you two out of town and into safety."

"Where are we going to go? We've never left this town, not in all the years we've lived here," Felix said.

"I know a place," Caitlin said as an idea sprang into her mind. A safe place, not too distant but far enough away that no one would ever think of looking. A place where two someones had lived a quiet life in solitude until fairly recently. "Though you'll need a guide to get there." She grinned at Kain.

"Excuse me?"

"What are you talking about?" Patricia asked. "Where are we going?"

"Let's just say that Joe will be getting a visit by more than just 'lunas before the night is through."

"Ah, man." Kain sighed.

CHAPTER SIXTEEN

<u>Ashdale Pond, Old Ontario</u>

If Pastor Andrews could pat himself on the back, he most certainly would.

Tonight had been an exceptional performance. Who would have thought that years of studying old textbooks and exercising his imagination would have given him the fuel he needed to preach so damn well?

He remembered the days when he had been nothing more than shit on the town's shoe. The weeks and months he had spent as nothing more than a glorified cesspit-filler still rankled in his memory.

And now they applauded. They sang. They hung on his every word.

When the governor had first told him his new purpose, he knew he would take a risk. He hadn't truly believed that he could preach and the flock would follow. But he had to hand it to the fat man. Trisk knew *people*. He knew how they ticked, and he knew the tricks to make them all fall at his feet.

Well, the *pastor's* feet.

If merely a dose of fear was enough to keep people in line, what would a whole bucketload do?

"And praise be unto our governor. Prophet and man of guidance. Deliverer and shepherd from the days of the Madness," he spewed, the words rolling so easily off his tongue it was almost comical. All attention focused on him.

The only real problem was, what did the governor plan next? The people had fallen in line, sure—well, most of them. But, then what? Pastor Andrews sensed a stage two up Trisk's sleeves—he wasn't stupid, after all—but the governor had been reluctant to share. He now refused, with increasing regularity, to meet. On the few occasions when Andrews did manage time with him, he looked increasingly strange, covering up more of his body and losing weight at a phenomenal pace.

After that night's congregation, the pastor waited until all had filed out before talking to Moxie, Detta and Christy —he had noticed Clob and Yusuf's absence the minute they had all arrived partway through his performance. They told him that, while their task had been a success, they had lost Clob, Yusuf, and Arthur Cornswaggle along the way after the residents of the house had gotten into a scrap with the three of them. They had tried to save them, but there was nothing they could do.

He grew white at the news of Clob and eyed Christy suspiciously. After a minute or two of silence, he muttered, "Sad tidings, indeed," and swept from the church.

Pastor Andrews ground his teeth the entire way to the Cloak & Dagger, milling over every word the newcomers had said. He knocked on the door, stormed over to Stump, and scribbled on a piece of parchment. Then, hating the necessity of trusting an intermediary, he handed it over and instructed the small man to pass it on to the governor.

With a murmur of thanks to Stump, Andrews returned home to take his anger out on his wife. With every blow of his hand and pump of his hips, he contemplated Moxie's words, wondering if she was telling the truth. It seemed a strange coincidence that the night he tried to burn Christy's parents—a loyalty test he had been particularly proud of—two of his best men died in the fire, and the girl was spared.

As he lay panting and sweating beside Lynn, he wondered what the likelihood would be that his message would make it to Governor Trisk's hands in time. He needed to talk to him. He needed to discuss the governor's plans.

It had been several days since they last talked, now, and the pastor was already generating some plans of his own.

Governor Halrod Trisk coughed heavily into the collar of his shirt. The greasy, sweat-stained thing that had become more of a part of his body than an item of clothing which could be removed.

"That's the ticket," he said, catching something thick and green in his palm as it ejected from his mouth. He studied it momentarily, observing the luminescent green shimmer as it wobbled in his hand before wiping it on the hem of his top.

Halrod laughed, fell into a fit of coughing again, then

skirted around the room to where several wooden boxes were stacked precariously in the corner.

"Good, good. Very good." He tore the lid off one of the boxes and clapped excitedly. The sores on his palms popped and exploded with pus, but he hardly noticed the pain anymore. It had become a part of him now, the source merely another decoration on his body.

"Oh, the fun I can have with you," he said as he picked up a clay orb and studied it. A simple thing, brown with no decoration and small entry point at the top plugged by a lid.

He placed it back in the box with the other orbs, moved the box to the floor—grunting with effort as he did so—and picked up the box beneath. Words had been carved into the side to read "Danger: Explosive."

Halrod laughed once more and moved the box to a small table in the center of the room. He struggled with its weight and had to place the box down twice along the way.

Footsteps thumped on the boards above.

Once, he had been a strong man and a virile—his words —bull, capable of many things. But over the past few weeks, he seemed to shrink. The weight which he had carried on his person through years of gluttony and indulgence had shed like skin from a snake, and anyone who once knew him could be forgiven for not recognizing the sad sap muttering to himself in the candlelit glow.

He clawed at the top of the box, struggling to get purchase this time. The wood left splinters in his fingers and red and yellow stains where he gripped the wood.

Halrod hobbled across the room and returned with a crowbar. He shoved it into the gap near the top and levered it off, nearly toppling to the floor as the lid sprang into the air, clattering somewhere across the room.

"Shhh. *Shhh!*" he urged, a finger to his lip. Somewhere inside, a frantic need for caution shifted to something resembling paranoia. "They mustn't hear. They *can't* hear." *Not yet.*

The contents of the box were beautiful. Halrod leaned over his prize, a grin cracking his face. His pleasure over-rode the reality that he'd lost a few more teeth and his tongue was now poxed with ulcers. Slowly, and with the tenderness of a lover, he scooped what looked like black sand into his hands. When he raised them into the air, the gunpowder filtering through his fingers, pouring back into the box. Some particles clung to the oozing sores in his palms as if reluctant to leave him.

"Excellent," he said, eyes turning back to the corner where the orbs and several more of the boxes of gunpowder lay. "Just excellent."

Stump had excelled himself, that was for sure. The tiny man had a hidden reach that stretched further than the town itself. Halrod hadn't asked where Stump had acquired the boxes, nor did he really need to know. He had simply asked for what he needed, and Stump had delivered.

On more than one occasion.

Trisk turned his hands over, looked at his slick, black-ened palms, and laughed. To his annoyance, it emerged as more of a wheeze. He shuffled to the grimy mirror leaned up in a corner and studied his shoulders, his stomach, and his legs. All were now marred with the dark yellow patches where the sores had taken hold. These oozing relentlessly, congealing into the material of his clothing and creating a makeshift bandage. A dressing he didn't dare change for fear of what he might see.

"Not to worry," he said to himself, though he found no real comfort in the assurance. "Slow the poison. That's all you've got to do, Halrod. Slow it down until it stops."

He shuffled to where a stack of blankets was bundled in the corner. A dip in the cloth left an impression of where he slept each night—and several times during the day, now. He looked for the flask but could find nothing.

"What? Where is it?" He hissed his frustration like a cat stuck in a corner. "Where *is* it?"

Blankets soared through the air. Wood clattered. In seconds, he forgot his own rule on quiet and secrecy as he hunted furiously for the thing he was sure had kept the Madness at bay since its first signs had appeared several weeks before. The elixir Stump had concocted which, he claimed, "slows the movement of the blood, calms the Madness." The elixir of Halrod's life itself.

"*Nooooo!*" He moaned his despair, tears pricking his eyes. An ice-cold douse of fear shot down his back.

He whirled, looking around the room in panic.

Finally, he saw it over by the bucket he now used as a lavatory, its contents thick and stinking. He remembered now, he had been doing his business when he last had a sip, multi-tasking as he cleared his bowels.

Some in, some out. He chuckled, taking a few deep gulps to finish the flask off.

Once every last drop hit his tongue, he threw the flask across the room, moved to where a rope hung down through a hole in the ceiling, and tugged twice. The tinkling of a bell could be heard overhead and, a few minutes later, Stump emerged through a small doorway at the far end of the room. Though big enough for Stump to walk through, it was small enough that the governor remembered having trouble making his way inside upon his arrival at Ashdale.

"You rang?" Stump croaked.

"More," Halrod said, pointing at the flask on the floor. "I need more."

Stump raised his eyebrows.

"Please."

Stump trotted over to the flask and pocketed it. He approached the governor, a hand outstretched. Trisk recoiled.

"Still," Stump said.

He watched as Stump took his wrist and turned his hand over. The tiny man circled him, inspecting him from all angles.

Stump took a step back, his face shadowed. "You need to get clean."

"I can't," Halrod said.

Stump grabbed his wrist and showed his palm again. "Dirt leads to further infection. Gunpowder leads to exploding hands when striking a light." He nodded to the flickering candle.

"I know, I know," he responded, defeated.

"I'll bring you water. You sponge yourself down. Get rid of the pus from the sores and remove some of the stink." He pulled a piece of parchment out of his pocket and placed it on the table. "For you. From the pastor."

Stump turned sharply and grabbed Halrod's bucket of waste as he left.

"Stump?" he called, and the stocky figure stopped in the doorway.

"Yes?"

"What is in that drink? What is it doing to the Madness? Will I be cured?"

Stump shook his head slowly, a shadow passing over his face. "It will slow the spread, but it will not stop the disease. There is nothing that can."

"How long do I have?" Halrod asked, hating himself for the plea he knew was in his eyes.

Stump shrugged, picked the bucket back up, and disappeared from the room.

CHAPTER SEVENTEEN

Ashdale Pond, Old Ontario

When Caitlin awoke, it was to the sound of several voices downstairs.

She sat up sharply, disorientated from dreaming. Panic pushed through for a moment as she looked around for Kain, used to him now sleeping near her side.

And then it all came back. The night before. The fire, the flames. The death. The lies. The hiding.

She wouldn't see Kain for a while.

Then who was that voice downstairs? It was certainly too deep for Mary-Anne and Mabel and much too slow and measured to be Jamie.

Caitlin dressed, eased Jaxon gently out of his slumber, and headed downstairs, meeting Mary-Anne along the hallway.

"We wondered when you'd be joining us," Pastor Andrews said. "We thought we were going to have to come up there and drag you down."

He sat in one of Jamie's chairs, his back straight, and a

huge smile on his face. Mabel and Jamie were squeezed onto a chair for one. Jamie looked around fearfully, as though waiting for something unpleasant to erupt. Mabel hummed to herself and busied her hands with a woolen jumper she was knitting. Her hands shook so much she missed every other loop.

"How did you know we were—"

"Here?" Pastor Andrews finished. "It's easy, really. From the moment you made your entrance in Ashdale, I've had my men following you, keeping tabs on your every move."

"You...what?"

The pastor exploded into a fit of laughter. "I'm only kidding."

A wave of relief washed over Caitlin. "Always thought you had the capacity to be a creepy stalker." She smiled and winked.

He smiled back, wiping a tear from the corner of his eye. "Of course I haven't. What a waste of manpower that would have been on my part. No. Truth is, it doesn't matter how I know. The fact is, I'm here."

Caitlin studied him. The smile never left his face. It was unsettling. She wondered what his game was, whether he had already worked out their feeble lie from the night before, or if he had become lonely in the absence of his bodyguard and gone slightly Mad himself.

"But that's not important, nor why I'm here. Come with me. It's time." Andrews walked to the door, opened it, and waited for Mary-Anne and Caitlin to follow. Caitlin instructed Jaxon to stay, told Jamie to keep an eye on him, and closed the door behind her.

As they walked through town, their number grew. At first, it was simply Caitlin, Mary-Anne—dressed head-to-toe in Mabel's outfit as the sun was high in the sky—and the pastor. But then Caitlin noticed others joining them.

"Firestarters?" Caitlin whispered.

Mary-Anne nodded.

One-by-one, their number swelled until, by the time they'd reached their destination, there were at least fifteen men and women. All were dressed in black, each with their own tattoos.

"Reckon we can send a complaint to their stylist?" Caitlin said. "All black? Very unoriginal."

"What would you recommend?" Mary-Anne replied.

"I don't know. Rainbows? Colors? Anything so that they don't look so bland. They look like a shadow has shit all over them."

Mary-Anne stifled a laugh.

They walked on in silence, the pastor leading the way out of town, past smoking remains of buildings, across a stretch of fields, and to a house the likes of which Caitlin hadn't seen before.

It looked to have once been a farmhouse that could have housed a family of thirty. The roof had caved in, and the glass in the windows was nothing more than a memory.

"Talk about your fixer-uppers," Caitlin said, eliciting a small giggle from Mary-Anne as they walked on in. The vampire took her hood down as they entered the shade.

"What a shithole," Mary-Anne confirmed.

"Did you *see* your place?" Caitlin asked, poking out her tongue.

They continued inside, the pastor leading them all to a large room filled with candles. The furniture at the edge of the rooms was thick with dust, but the table and chairs in the center looked to have been used recently.

Perhaps this is a regular occurrence for the Firestarters? Headfirst into their HQ, we go.

Her heart fluttered. *Is this where the governor is hiding?*

The Firestarters each took a seat around the table. Caitlin caught Christy's eyes and looked away quickly. There was a gap on the pastor's right where, presumably, Clob would have sat. A few of the Firestarters looked curious, an unspoken question in their minds though no one had the guts to ask.

Just where is the big guy?

"Praise be unto the flame," Andrews said, bowing his head and clasping his hands in prayer.

"Praise be unto the flame," the Firestarters chorused.

"Praise be unto the fire."

"Praise be unto the fire."

"From the ashes shall rise a new dawn."

And so it went. With every proclamation and every sentence, the Firestarters chorused the words. Caitlin and Mary-Anne followed suit, afraid that any minor indiscretion would arouse suspicion.

Not that it really mattered. Every Firestarter had their eyes firmly closed. Their devotion seemed whole and unwavering. The hairs on the back of Caitlin's neck pricked up as she realized the truth. *These people are all completely in Pastor Andrews' control.*

At last, they finished with a round of "Amen."

"Thank you, brothers," Andrews said, lacing his fingers on the table in front of him. "And welcome to us all on this glorious occasion.

"As you may have noticed, we have some new blood with us today. Please welcome Miss Moxie Curtis and Miss Detta Slystock. Visitors from afar. Defenders, warriors and, soon to be...*Firestarters.*"

Caitlin and Mary-Anne jumped slightly as every Firestarter beat the table and cried "Into the flame!" The pastor flicked his wrist towards a candle in the center of the table. A sprinkle of something dark found its way into the flame, and it ballooned in a flash of light before shrinking back to regular size.

"Let us take a moment to celebrate our new blood and revel in joining others to our cause, fighters of freedom and protectors of Ashdale. Those who would lay down their lives for a better tomorrow, as is the mission of the *Firestarters.*"

Another flash of light initiated another beat on the table.

"Brothers and sisters!" Andrews said, rising with his arms wide. "It is time to bring these strangers into our midst, to mark them with the mark, and to set them loose upon their journey into salvation. Do you all accept these women to our brotherhood? Do you all accept their blood-line into our sanction of purity? Do you all..." He paused, and his face grew dark. "Take responsibility for their life, their death, and all that is known, so that the Firestarters rule eternal?"

"Into the fire!" they roared as one. Animalistic cries mirrored faces creased with primal emotion.

Caitlin smiled weakly and turned to Mary-Anne, who mirrored her exactly.

"What have we gotten ourselves into?" Caitlin side-mouthed.

"At least Pooch isn't here. Imagine how he'd cope with this," Mary-Anne replied.

"But first!" Pastor Andrews said, cutting off the rallying cry so silence dropped into the room. "Let us pay tribute to our fallen comrades. Those who have fallen into the darkness where no flame can light."

"No..." one of the Firestarters whispered, their bottom lip trembling as they looked at Clob's empty seat.

"That's right," the pastor said, his eyes flicking momentarily to Caitlin and Mary-Anne.

He didn't detail their deaths, only acknowledged their passing. Several of the Firestarters held back tears, while others remained straight-faced, as if no such news could, in any way, affect their emotions.

Then they were led outside. Each Firestarter held a candle—except for Mary-Anne and Caitlin—it seemed this was an honor only given to those who had been officiated into the group—and Christy, who dragged a chair. Mary-Anne pulled her hood back over her face. They moved in single file, heading through the back door and into a wide garden with high fences and overgrown shrubbery on all sides. The sun was thinly masked by cloud. In the center of the garden stood two man-sized and man-shaped holes.

And beside each...

"Oh shit," Caitlin said, catching Mary-Anne's arm.

"No."

Beside each pit was a charred corpse, one considerably larger than the other.

"If they've searched the house for the bodies, then they'll have seen that there aren't as many bodies as we said there'd be," Caitlin whispered hurriedly into Mary-Anne's ear.

The vampire counted on her fingers. "There should be five."

"And there's only two."

The Firestarters lined up around the edge of the pits.

"We're fucked," Mary-Anne said.

"I guess that depends," Caitlin responded, hurrying now as each Firestarter took their place. "Surely, if we were fucked, they'd have killed us by now. Also, the counting completely depends on who the search party was. If it was Christy, we're in luck. If it was anyone with scrambled brains, we're fine."

"So the odds are in our favor?" Mary-Anne grinned.

They both looked quickly around the group, trying to gauge how smart the Firestarters were from their looks. Even if they were a bunch of brainwashed fuckheads with an affinity for setting everything they could aflame, that didn't mean they were all dimwitted and dull.

The girls took their place in a gap in the middle of the line.

The pastor gave a rousing eulogy for each victim of the fire—Clob's considerably more heartfelt than Yusuf's. After he finished, two Firestarters with thick jaws and green eyes —twins by the looks of them—moved to stand beside each body.

As Andrews uttered the final farewells, each brother turned to the bodies and kicked them into the holes. They landed carelessly with a thud before the brothers each took a shovel and began piling dirt over them.

"May the afterlife be ever kind, and may they find their way..."

"Into the fire," those gathered chorused, their voices more gentle this time.

"Now, with death comes life. And with life comes beauty," Pastor Andrews said, his attention shifting to Caitlin and Mary-Anne. "And, boy, do we have some beauties joining us today. Moxie. Detta. It's time. Are you ready to join our band of brothers in the sacred flames of eternal life?"

He clapped his hands, and the fire roared into life. A neat circle, running the perimeter of the garden, appeared. Despite her best efforts, Caitlin jumped. She looked to either side of the garden where the brothers stood with torches pressed to the ground.

They stood up in perfect unison.

Pretty fucking creepy, really.

"Yes," Caitlin said. "I am ready."

Mary-Anne hesitated a moment. Shrugged. "Sure. Me too."

"Then let us begin." Pastor Andrews seemed delighted with their response.

He invited them both to the center of the circle. Christy stepped forward and placed the chair down. Caitlin took a seat.

"Now, this may sting a little," Andrews said as a young woman with muscles which many men would envy stepped forward. In her hand was a pot of dark ink, and in the other, a needle.

"Are you sure that's sterile?" Caitlin asked as the woman knelt down and took Caitlin's arm in her hands. "If I come out in a rash I'll be sending you the doctor's bill."

"Of course. We wouldn't have it any other way," Pastor Andrews replied.

"What do you sterilize it with?" Mary-Anne asked.

The woman nodded at the flames.

"Ah. Of course."

It hurt a little, at first. Caitlin gritted her teeth to hold back the sounds of pain. But as the woman set to work, dipping the needle expertly between the pot of ink and her flesh, she soon grew numb to it. Small beads of blood joined the ink, and occasionally, the woman would dab at her skin with a cloth.

When it was finished, Caitlin twisted her arm to look at it properly. It was actually a fine piece of art. She had never even considered the idea of a tattoo before. Tattoos in Silver Creek were less than sanitary, often leading to infection and gangrene as back-alley artists failed to keep their conditions free from dirt and dust.

Nor had she ever really wanted one. But, as much as the conditions in which this tattoo was acquired were less than ideal, she took it as a sign that she was one step closer to her goal. One step closer to the inner sanctum where Trisk was hiding, and she could end his reign.

Besides, she looked pretty badass.

"Okay, you're up," the woman said, wandering back over to the ring of fire to heat and clean the needle.

Caitlin admired her tattoo, then turned to Mary-Anne.

In an instant, her face dropped.

Mary-Anne was outside. In the *daytime*.

A vampire out in the fucking sun. Now what?

What the fuck would happen when the Firestarters pulled her sleeves up and started tattooing?

"Detta, are you ready?" Pastor Andrews asked.

Beneath her hood, Mary-Anne shook her head.

"No need to be scared. It's not as bad as it looks." He guided Mary-Anne by her shoulders and sat her in the chair. Caitlin's gaze was fixed on her friend, her mind working in overdrive to see what she could do to try to get out of this.

The woman returned, dipped the needle in the ink, and went to grab Mary-Anne's sleeve.

Mary-Anne pulled away.

Pastor Andrews pressed on her shoulders. The woman grabbed again, more forceful this time, and managed to expose a small square of dark skin to the sunlight. As she leaned forward to begin tattooing, Mary-Anne screamed.

"What?" Pastor Andrews uttered. "What the fuck is going on?"

Mary-Anne's skin began to burn, and a small feather of smoke filtered into the air as the skin began to blister and bubble.

"Ma. *No!*" Caitlin urged.

But it was too late. Beneath the black of Mary-Anne's hood, she could see the red of her eyes shining through. Murmurs rippled through the gathered Firestarters. Mary-Anne ripped her arm out of the tattooist's grasp, dragging the needle across her skin which ripped more of the material.

"The devil! The devil has come!" the pastor cried, stepping backward in shock. "Burn her. Burn her *now!*"

The Firestarters were ready, diving in as one unit. They charged, jumped, and bounded towards Mary-Anne, their fears pushed to the backs of their mind as years of pack mentality kicked in.

All except Christy, who held back, letting the others lead the charge. She seemed too afraid to attack the people who had saved her parents and too afraid not to.

But she needn't have worried. Mary-Anne had already moved.

Using all her speed and strength, she hurtled forwards, shoving the tattooist so far backward that she fell into the ring of fire. The woman's hair caught fire and she screamed, patting and fanning to quell the flames on her head.

Mary-Anne sped towards her, grabbed her wrist and dragged her beyond the fire and into the house.

"Don't let her get away," Andrews shouted, then saw Caitlin at his side. "And her. Get them both. Moxie has delivered the devil to Ashdale!"

His face was white, clearly panicked. He stumbled backward, almost tripping over his own garb as he stepped away from Caitlin.

Several Firestarters peeled off and gave chase to Mary-Anne, while at least half a dozen went for Caitlin. She pulled back her cloak and drew her sword—the gleaming beacon of hope which filled her heart with confidence. Compared to their shitty weapons, her blade was queen.

A woman jumped at her from her left. Caitlin took a

step back and watched her hit the floor. A swift kick to the head put her out for the count.

"One down," Caitlin said, maybe a little too cocky because she felt a searing pain across her wrist. She followed the thin black line of the whip to where one of the brothers stood with a sickening grin on his face.

Another lightning strike of pain seared through her as a second whip wrapped around her other wrist.

"Son of a bitch," she cried, dropping her sword to the ground.

The brothers leered. Somewhere behind her, she heard the pastor cry, "Now, no need for blaspheming, harlot."

Caitlin used all her strength and pulled. Her muscles ached, and sweat peppered her brow. Christy and two other Firestarters stood around her now, each holding their weapon menacingly. The woman on the floor moaned and rolled onto her back.

Caitlin struggled again, but it was no use. She fell to her knees.

"See?" Andrews crooned, approaching only once he saw that Caitlin was secure. He circled in front of her, bent down, and picked up Caitlin's blade.

"Fuck face!" Caitlin cried.

Pastor Andrews turned the blade over in his hand, examining every inch. "A delicious specimen. Where did you pick up this treasure?"

"I plucked it from your mom's vagina," Caitlin retorted.

He winced. "I imagine it's quite effective cutting through heads?"

"Why don't you set me free and we can find out."

Andrews began to laugh. Quietly at first, but it grew

louder until he was in a fit of hysterics. He turned to the other Firestarters who joined in, guffawing along with their leader.

A scream of pain from inside the house made them fall quiet.

"It's a shame, really, Moxie. It would have been nice to have someone with your talent and...looks on the team." The pastor stroked the tip of the sword down Caitlin's chest, revealing a large part of her cleavage. "Still. I'm sure you won't be missed. No tears spared for wanderers and vagabonds."

Holding the sword with both hands, he stretched back. He brought the sword down hard, stopping inches from Caitlin's neck as a loud crack shot through the circle.

"Huh?" he cried, looking in bewilderment at the whip around his wrist. The leather tugged sharply, and his hand flew backward, dropping the sword once more to the ground.

Christy picked it up in a heartbeat, pulling the pastor so hard he fell. In one smooth motion, she hacked at the brothers' whips, slicing through them to release Caitlin before tossing the sword back to her.

Surprisingly calm, Christy flicked her hair out of her face. "Let's get you out of here," she said, dragging Caitlin by the hand through the fire before the reality of what had just happened could sink in.

As they leaped across the flame and into the house, they heard the pastor shouting. "After them, morons. Cut off their tits and leave them in a jar." The mob surged forward, oblivious to the brothers who brought their torches to the corners of the house and watched the flames grow.

CHAPTER EIGHTEEN

Ashdale Pond, Old Ontario

They found Mary-Anne in a large room at the back of the house.

Her eyes were bright in the shadows. Her hood was down, and her face beaded with blood as she held the woman firmly in her grasp. She hadn't killed her, but she'd definitely used her as a sippy straw.

All the other Firestarters were either dead or standing paralyzed in the corner.

"Ma," Caitlin said, catching her breath. "Is now really the time for a snack?"

"Why not?" Mary-Anne replied.

Caitlin nodded at the other Firestarters.

"Oh. Them? They're cool, aren't you guys?" The Firestarters nodded enthusiastically. "I showed them what I'm capable of and they stopped in their tracks. Pleading like little girls, weren't you?"

"What was the scream we heard?"

Mary-Anne looked down at the tattooist. "That was this one. Tastes delicious, but she doesn't half make a noise."

Rushing footsteps sounded behind them. Caitlin and Christy leaped across the room to Mary-Anne's side. She held the woman's hair in her fist threateningly.

The Firestarters who had chased Caitlin and Christy stopped in their tracks the minute they saw Mary-Anne. She was certainly fearsome to behold, all fangs, blood, and red eyes. Caitlin grinned, feeling the tide turning.

The pastor was the last to join them, appearing behind his minions with a smug grin until the vamp flashed a bloody smile his way. Then, he turned to flee.

"Where are you going in such a hurry?" Mary-Anne asked as she dropped the woman and sped to the other side of the room, blocking his escape. "Feeling spooked?"

His eyes widened. *"Get her,"* he shouted at the Firestarters. "Get *them!*" He pointed wildly at Caitlin and Christy.

No one moved.

"Not a set of balls between the lot of you," Caitlin said, stepping into the middle of the room. "You preach about power and loyalty and camaraderie, then your courage falls flat at the sight of an itty-bitty vampire."

"Heathen!" Andrews cried. "Jezebel! The devil has indeed come to take Ashdale. Come to drag us back from our salvation. To take us all and hold us in sin. They called them the Holy Trio, but we saw it all along. The destroyers of the governor's mission."

Rallied by the man's words, one brave Firestarter pulled a small cleaver from his side and sprinted at Caitlin. In one fluid motion, she swung her blade and slit the man's chest.

His eyes opened wide as he fell to the floor and lay there without moving.

"Anyone else?" she asked. When no one responded, she lowered her blade and continued, growing ever aware of the smoke smell seeping in from outside. "Speaking of the governor, we're in need of a little parley with the big man. What do you suppose are the odds of you taking us to him? We can promise to repay you kindly."

The pastor spat on the floor. "You've got nothing that we could want."

"Erm...how about your lives? Unless you fancy ending up like your friend down here on the floor?"

Caitlin waited patiently for an answer. She could hear the fire outside growing louder now, and if she wasn't much mistaken, could she see the flames in the other room. Smoke began to filter through, clothing the ceiling as she nudged a response from the man before her. "Well?"

Another stepped forward with a thick, grizzly beard and a skinny waist compared to his broad shoulders.

"Don't you say a fucking word," Andrews instructed.

The man hesitated, apparently struggling with his thoughts for a moment before saying, "It's impossible. No one but the pastor has seen the governor in days. Not even Pastor Andrews knows *where* he is."

"What did I just fucking say?"

"Yet you blindly follow his rule?" Mary-Anne asked, looking more at Christy than the others. Christy looked at the floor.

"It's not our place to question the words of higher powers," another Firestarter—a woman this time—

answered. "Our place is to deliver and obey. Without the worker bees, the queen will die."

"Queen B's," Mary-Anne remarked, a joke only she seemed to understand.

"But it is your place," Caitlin said. "It totally is. You can't spend your days taking commands without question, being told what is right and what is wrong, and trusting whichever crazed psychopath comes your way to tell you what to do."

"Watch how you speak about the gov—"

"Oh, yeah, yeah. We get it. The governor is the prophet, come to deliver the town, blah, blah, blah. Why don't you sip a bit of reality, fuck-face, and think about it? All of you. *Think*." Caitlin began to count the points on her fingers as she spoke. "Who benefits the most from Trisk telling you all he's some kind of supreme being? Who went from being a shit-scooper to leading congregations and acting like a goddamn monarch? Who has his every wish come true—"

"Erm… Kitty Cat?" Mary-Anne interjected.

"Hold on. Who has his every wish come true, brought to life by a group of obedient, black-clothing-wearers willing to burn towns and ink their skin because he says so?"

The tattooist raised a hand weakly, "Actually, that was my idea."

Caitlin looked at her own tattoo, still sore and bleeding lightly. "Bitchin'."

"*Moxie*," Mary-Anne urged.

"What?"

The vampire nodded behind her where the flames now

crept in. "We should probably wrap this up and get moving."

"*Fine*," Caitlin moaned. She turned to each Firestarter in turn, talking to them as though she was a mother telling her kids to come back to a safe place if they got lost. "Now, we're going to take your pastor and use him as a divining rod to locate the governor. He's got to be around here somewhere. If any of you care to join us, feel free. If you feel it's too much to break the habit and come to the side of the good guys, then more fool you. Your HQ is burning, and you're leaderless. Get some sense, people."

And with that, Caitlin left. Mary-Anne placed her hood back over her head, ripped a bit of cloth from another Firestarter to wrap around her arm, which had already healed, and dragged Andrews behind her.

The only Firestarter to join them was Christy. Shortly after that, the house was swallowed in flame.

"Holy shit. Are you kidding me?"

Jamie's jaw dropped when he opened his front door. Mary-Anne had raced ahead with the pastor, taking as many shortcuts as she could to avoid drawing too much attention to herself.

Of course, she still left several confused residents in her wake.

"Move," Mary-Anne said simply, dropping Andrews on the sofa.

"Are you kidding me?" Jamie repeated, looking around and clearly flummoxed. "You've *captured* Pastor Andrews?"

"No, I'm here of my own free will," the pastor said sarcastically.

"Give it a rest, fuck-nugget," Mary-Anne snapped, ripping a length of cloth from the man's garbs and gagging him. "We may need you to talk, but until Kitty-Cat gets here, I want you to stay schtum, okay?"

He raised an eyebrow.

"Oh, that's right. Moxie ain't her real name. It's Kitty-Cat, or Caitlin for short. Seems the world is full of liars, right?"

Caitlin knocked shortly after. Jamie ran a hand through his hair, mumbling under his breath. He opened the door, his eyes widening when he saw Christy standing behind Caitlin.

"Wha—" His voice broke. He coughed. "What are you doing here?"

Caitlin looked between them both, understanding finally dawning in her head. "Oh, of course. This is a romance scene, right?" She patted Jamie on the back. "I'll leave you guys to it."

Jamie blushed and stepped aside to allow her entry. Christy followed, a coy grin on her face. Jaxon sprinted up to Caitlin and jumped into her arms.

"Ah, I missed you, too, boy!" she said, scratching behind his ears. She looked around the room. "Where's Mabel?" she asked, half-expecting the old woman to hobble in at any second.

"Out the back, watering the plants," Jamie answered.

"I didn't see any plants out there."

"Nope," Jamie said simply, taking a seat. "So, are you going to explain what exactly is going on?"

"Want the short or the long answer?" Caitlin said, searching her mind for an easy explanation.

"Long," Jamie replied.

"Well," Caitlin drew a deep breath. "We traveled through a forest, found a crazy guy in the woods who lived in a house of compacted metal and that his wife had turned Mad, though he still kept her around. We continued to Ashdale in the hopes of finding the governor—y'know, on account of him being a shitbag who used and manipulated my brother and me, threatening to kill us both. It turned out he had given directions to a sociopath to breed hope and delusion into the townspeople who lived like a herd of sheep.

"Found a way to join his cult, set Christy's parents' house on fire—with them still inside. Saved her parents but killed two of his best men so had to send Kain with Patricia and Felix back into the woods to stay with trashcan man until the dust all blew over."

She took another breath. "Got inches away from joining the cult and finding a way to the governor without any need to create any mess until old sweet-fang—that's what Kain likes to call her—suddenly remembers she can't sit out in the sun and get tattooed because she's a friggin' vampire, so she goes on a rampage. Next, she flees, eats part of a person, we manage to trap the pastor and all his cronies, and now, we're using him as a signpost to get us closer to Trisk so we can finally clear his evil from the land forevermore. Amen."

They all sat in stunned silence.

"Couldn't have said it better myself," Mary-Anne slow-clapped, breaking the spell.

"Any questions?" Caitlin asked.

Mabel wandered in then, her hands covered in dirt. She wiped them down her dress, sat down in her favorite chair, then looked at everyone in her living room in surprise. "The turnips needed turning," she explained as if it were the most obvious thing in the world.

"Which brings us to…" Caitlin dragged a chair over to where the pastor sat and pulled the gag down from his mouth. "We don't have time, and my patience is running thin, so tell us everything you know."

Andrews looked the most terrified Caitlin had ever seen him. His gaze kept flicking to Mary-Anne and the blood crusted and painted on her face. "I don't know where the governor is."

"Bullshit," the vampire responded sharply.

"Not at all." Andrews suddenly looked ashamed. "He's in *hiding*. Even I don't know where he is right now."

"You must have a way of communicating with him. I find it hard to believe that you're out here running rogue off one conversation with Trisk while he sits back in his hole and watches." Caitlin grabbed his hair and pulled to tilt his head back, her other hand hovering in open threat on the handle of her blade.

The man stared unblinkingly at Caitlin. He looked to be about to say something when, instead, he hocked a loogie straight into her face.

Everyone in the room tensed. Caitlin heard Jamie gasp.

Caitlin let out a hollow laugh and wiped the loogie with the back of her sleeve. "Men… They never learn." She moved backward and motioned for Mary-Anne to take her place. "If you won't listen to a woman, I'll have you listen to a vampire."

The pastor's eyes widened as Mary-Anne walked over slowly and straddled his lap. She grinned, taking his head in both hands. She felt him stiffen beneath her, leaned in close to his ear, and spoke quietly. "Talk. Before I take this head, rip it off, and use it as a fucking bowling ball."

"What's a bowling ball?" Pastor Andrews asked.

Mary-Anne grinned and began pulling.

His face settled into a strange mix of pleasure, confusion, and pain. The tendons in his neck grew taut as Mary-Anne pulled. His face grew red. Only at the moment when Caitlin thought the skin would begin to fray and break did he suddenly exclaim, *"Fine*. Fine, I'll tell you what I know."

Mary-Anne stepped back triumphantly, leaving the pastor to sit awkwardly with a small bulge in his crotch.

"Still got it," the vamp remarked, brushing her shoulder.

"So, the governor?" Caitlin probed, impatient now to end it.

"I really don't know where he is."

Caitlin half-drew her sword.

"But I know how you can reach him," Andrews added quickly. "Stump is your key. I send my messages through him."

"The tiny guy at the Cloak & Dagger?" Jamie asked, instantly falling silent again as all eyes turned to him. "He gives me the creeps."

Christy giggled and placed a hand on his knee, turning his face an even brighter shade of crimson.

"That's the one." The pastor nodded vigorously. "Send a

message through him, and you should be able to reach Governor Trisk."

"Or we could tie him up and threaten to pop his head off, too?" Mary-Anne suggested.

Strangely, he laughed at that. "Good luck. If there's one man you'll never break, it's Stump. There's something…not quite right about him. He'd rather eat the big one than break his own moral code."

"Sounds like a challenge." Mary-Anne looked intrigued.

"No," Caitlin said, putting an abrupt end to whatever flight of fancy her friend might entertain. "When was the last time you sent a message to him?"

Andrews seemed to wrestle his own thoughts before surrendering. "Early this morning."

"And what did it say?"

He would say no more other than that he had requested a meeting with the governor at the Cloak & Dagger, room fifteen, later that day and before congregation.

"*That's* why the room smelt so familiar," Caitlin said. "What was I thinking? I should recognize the governor's stench anywhere." She closed her eyes, drew back memories of the smell, and saw herself in Trisk's chambers back in Silver Creek all those weeks before. She could still feel the burning rage as she had hit him and he had shoved her. *Hard.* The humiliation as he commanded Caitlin and Dylan to bring Mary-Anne back to join the ranks of his guards at Silver Creek under pain of death.

"Looks like we know where to go, Kitty-Cat," Mary-Anne said. "Lover girl, you in?"

Christy blushed, removing her hand from Jamie's knee. "Sure."

"Don't worry, she's saving that whip for you." Mary-Anne winked at Jamie who colored yet again.

"What time did you give the governor?" Caitlin asked, looking out the window. The sun was beginning to set, the sky turning a mottled mix of reds and oranges. It was beautiful, a striking contrast to the ugliness of the world.

"A little after sunset."

"Let's get moving, then," Caitlin said to Christy and Mary-Anne. Jaxon barked, then licked her face excitedly. "Yes, you can come, too."

"Why room fifteen?" the vampire asked suddenly.

Andrews shrugged. "It's a nice number."

"Well, that clears that up." Caitlin wrapped her cloak about her, watched as Mary-Anne put her hood back up, twisting at the tears in her fabric to close the holes that might expose her skin to further sunlight, then pointed at Jamie and Mabel. "You keep an eye on him, okay?"

Jamie's face dropped. "You're leaving *him*, with *us*?"

"That's right, fuck face." Pastor Andrews grinned. "Don't worry, though. It's not like my Firestarters will be looking for me. Let's see how long you can keep me quiet when these guys are all gone—"

His taunts were cut short by a deep metallic clang as Mabel smacked him over the head with a pan. "Go on, dears. We'll keep old soppy-dick safe and quiet."

CHAPTER NINETEEN

Silver Creek Forest, Old Ontario

The forest was thick and unfamiliar, trees boughs blocking nearly every inch of sunlight. A strong smell of damp and moss permeated the air as the group stood at the base of the ancient pine and waited.

"Anything?" Dylan called up.

They paused, waiting. He rummaged around, reaching and clawing for the top. If he went *too* far up the tree, he risked his weight snapping the branches as the strength of the pine tapered to its point in the sky. If he didn't go far *enough*, then there wasn't a great deal of sense in him climbing up at all. All he'd see would be green, green, and more green.

"Tom?" Dylan asked again.

No answer.

"Tom?"

Silence.

Dylan rolled his eyes and looked at Laurie. "Sergeant?"

A gruff voice called down to the Revolutionaries. "We're on track."

Laurie giggled. Ash joined her, catching Laurie's eye. He stopped immediately when Alice glared at him.

A wave of relief fell over the group—or, at least, those who had begun to wonder if they were even going in the right direction. The forest seemed to take on a freakish sameness with every step.

"Great. Come on down."

Sergeant Tom Hitchcock shimmied his way down expertly, landing with a soft thud on the forest floor. Leaves and twigs crunched underfoot, dried and dead from lack of sun or water.

"The smoke is getting thicker," he said, adjusting his eyepatch and straightening his back. "There must have been a big ass fire somewhere. That smoke was thicker and blacker than any I've seen yet."

Dylan's thoughts turned to Caitlin. His group had made great speed thus far, only having to stop occasionally to rest or take down a cluster of Mad-infected fuckers. They had lost one of their crew along the way, but that only made them all the more determined. But Dylan wished they could be there already. He was growing uneasy, wondering with every step if Caitlin was even alive anymore.

What would he do if he made it to Ashdale and discovered she had been killed there?

Or what if she had never made it at all?

"Rest time is over. Let's keep moving," he instructed. A few of the Revolutionaries sighed, but most obeyed without hesitation.

Laurie walked off ahead, side by side with Tom. Alice and Ash walked behind, he trying to look everywhere but at Laurie's ass. If Dylan wasn't mistaken, her gait was exaggerated, and he wondered if it was for Ash's eyes only.

Suddenly, Alice pulled her man to the side. She shoved him against the back of a tree and placed her lips on his. He tensed at the unexpected action but soon softened into the kiss. Dylan grinned and kept moving.

"What was that for?" Ash asked when she finally removed her mouth.

Alice considered her words. "I know I've been acting coy and like this doesn't mean anything to me. But it does. I...like you. I need you to know that."

He smiled and tucked a lock of hair behind Alice's ear. "I do."

Alice blushed and lowered her head. "I'm not as pretty as her."

Ash's touch was gentle as he tilted her chin up and stared deeply into her eyes. They shimmered like clear pools. "You're everything and more."

"Then why do you keep staring at her? Why can't you peel your eyes away?"

It was a fair question. Ash took a moment to think.

"You know how, if somebody tells you not to look at something, you immediately want to look?"

"What a shit excuse," Alice retorted, her expression hardening.

"Okay, look behind you," Ash said.

"Fuck off."

"Fine. *Don't* look behind you."

Alice turned to see two red eyes a short way behind her,

moving toward them both. She pulled out her twin blades and cut the Mad down before he had a chance to cause any damage. He fell impotently to the floor at their feet.

Ash's smile returned. Smug. "Told you."

Alice couldn't help but return her own grin. "I fucking hate you."

"Save some of that passion. It'll come in handy." He winked and kissed her deeply.

They stopped when they heard someone up ahead call them both. With a final kiss, they ran back to the others.

The Revolutionaries continued through the forest, their steps light and measured. As they moved through the brush, they barely noticed the steadily increasing presence of tin cans and scraps of metal caught in the foliage.

No one noticed the small man with the ten-gallon hat as he aimed his shotgun through the shadows.

Ashdale Pond, Old Ontario

The streets were eerily quiet as they sped through the town. Doors were closed, and curtains were drawn. A steady haze of black smog obscured their vision, the acrid cast-off of the charred cinders of the Firestarters' HQ.

Caitlin pawed at her stinging eyes, silently thankful that the smoke muted the last rays of the day's sun. Mary-Anne was beside her, coughing into her black material. Jaxon kept his head low, seemingly unaffected by the discomfort. Christy merely squinted and walked in silence.

Before long, the creaking sign of the Cloak & Dagger came into view, appearing out of the smoke as rocks and islands might once have for and sailors and pirates at sea.

Caitlin had read about the ocean and seen pictures of its vast mass of water. As a child, she'd wondered if she'd ever see it herself one day.

One thing at a time, she thought before saying, "Come on. Let's get this over with."

Her heart pounded with anticipation as she walked into the tavern. She could sense him now, could feel Trisk's presence inside. As she approached the bar, she looked at the floorboards above, wondering if he had received the pastor's message. He might even be up there right now, his great blubbering mass of stomach spilling over the sides of his chair.

Once more, her memory flashed back to that fateful day in Silver Creek and the oil and grease that stained his skin. The women he 'entertained' in the bedroom flashed through her mind with the vivid picture of the spilled wine which trailed down his stomach.

Trisk's strength when he had shoved her back into her brother, anger and rage on his face, reminded her he was no pushover.

When they reached the bar, Caitlin leaned across and looked down low for Stump. He wasn't there.

"What's the problem?" Mary-Anne asked, lowering her hood.

Caitlin stared at her face in shock. "You could have at least washed the blood off your face. You look like you've just gone down on a girl during her moon phase."

Mary-Anne tutted. "I hardly had time to wash, did I? Between that bonfire on the outskirts and speeding your prize back to Mabel's, when did you expect me to shower? Should I have shaved while I was at it?"

She nodded to her crotch.

Christy stifled a giggle behind her hand.

"Where's the little guy?" the vampire asked.

"I don't know," Caitlin said in a hushed whisper. She looked around the room, noting that the place was almost empty. "He can hardly be collecting glasses, can he?"

"Why don't we just go upstairs?" Christy asked.

Mary-Anne answered, her voice bored. "Because we don't have the key."

"No, but we do have a vampire with super strength," Caitlin teased. "You think you can tackle an itty-bitty door?"

"I fucking hate you sometimes."

They moved to the stairs. Jaxon sniffed the ground as he went, taking a great deal of interest in a small crack in the floorboards. He lingered, his nostrils wide, growling until Caitlin encouraged him to carry on. "Not now, boy. We're going upstairs."

"No entry without a key," a voice grumbled from behind them as Christy's foot hit the first step.

They turned, looking around for half a second before noting that Stump stood in front of them.

"There you are," Caitlin exclaimed. "We were looking for you."

"No key. No entry," Stump repeated, his face an expressionless mask.

"In that case, can we have the key for room fifteen, please?" Mary-Anne asked, sounding more sickeningly sweet than Caitlin had ever heard her.

Stump's eyebrows raised. He disappeared behind the bar without a word. They heard the jangling of many keys before he returned, squeezed between them, and headed upstairs.

With questioning looks at each other, they followed. The stairs creaked beneath their feet, loud in the silence, and soon, they stood outside the room.

Stump turned the key in the lock, opened the door, and again, they were met with the musty scent of sweat and body odor. Caitlin felt the rage boil inside her but managed to keep it controlled. She peered through the darkness, looking for any sign of movement before Stump lit a candle and stood at the side of the room.

Caitlin led the group, half-drawing her sword and craning her head around the room. Aside from Jaxon's sniffing, silence shrouded the small group. She opened the door to a side room—also empty—and felt frustration replace her anger.

Where the fuck is he?

"Anything?" Christy asked.

Mary-Anne sniffed the air. "Nope. No one."

"I don't understand," Caitlin said. "Why wouldn't he come? Andrews is his only conduit to the townspeople. What reason would he have to stand him up?"

"Because the governor is dying," Stump said simply. His presence took Caitlin by surprise. He had stood immobile the entire time she had searched the room to the point where she had forgotten he was there.

"I'm sorry?" Mary-Anne's face had turned curious.

"What do you mean, dying?" Caitlin asked.

Stump remained silent.

"Tell us what you know." She exploded, drew her sword, and touched the blade against Stump's neck. She could feel her emotions taking over now. She wouldn't let the small man stand in her way.

But he didn't move. He didn't blink. Instead, he simply drew his own knife—a pretty little thing with engraving along the blade—and tapped Caitlin's sword aside.

"You can't draw words from a dead man."

"You can't tease women from the grave," Caitlin replied.

A flicker of a smile touched the corner of Stump's mouth. He put his knife back into its pouch and began walking out of the room. "Follow me."

They did.

"You have *got* to be kidding me," Caitlin exclaimed, her words muffled by the edge of her cloak drawn over her mouth.

The place was a hovel. After following Stump down some steps and through a tiny door which led to a secret room beneath the tavern, none of them could quite believe what they were seeing.

The stink was nauseating. The floors were strewn with straw which looked sticky and a strange shade of pink. In the corner were a pile of blankets morphed and shaped into a cocoon in which someone had previously slept. A tiny table stood in the corner and a bucket at the far wall, but little else.

"Why did you bring us here?" Mary-Anne asked. Caitlin couldn't imagine how Mary-Anne and Jaxon were experiencing this room. Both vamp and dog's smell were infinitely greater than that of Christy and Caitlin's.

Stump walked over to the bucket and kicked it. A dark trail of what smelled like piss but looked like bloody tar seeped along the floor. "This is your governor's quarters. This is where he has been resided in secret, biding his time, fighting the disease."

"My governor? He's *your* governor now," Caitlin said.

Stump didn't acknowledge that comment.

"He slept *here*?" Mary-Anne looked horrified, as well she might.

Stump nodded. "Late at night, he came, his hair wet and sodden from the rain. Afraid he was, though he wouldn't admit that to be true. Wrapped in a dark shawl, he crept to the Cloak accompanied by the pastor, begging Stump for a place to stay. A place hidden and quiet in which he could work, hide, and recover. The pastor left him in my charge. There was a fear already in his eyes, though he didn't know why at the time."

"You?" Caitlin said. "You've been guarding Trisk?"

"Caring is more of the truth," Stump responded with a shrug.

"Caring for what?" Mary-Anne asked. "From what I can see, the man is more than capable of taking care of himself. He created an entire following through Pastor Andrews in no time at all, utilizing fear and using the whisper of his name as a means to create a gospel. What does that sagging ball-sack have to fear?"

Stump's face grew dark. "What else is there to fear these days, other than the Madness?"

Caitlin's face fell. She looked around at the pink patches in the straw and the sticky stains on the floor and around the walls, noting the hint of decomposition now in the air which always drew her back to a time, years gone, when her parents had passed. For a brief moment, she was a young girl standing outside the bedroom door, listening to the sounds of the Madness taking hold, the smells of the dead seeping through the gap beneath the door.

"You mean...the governor..."

Stump nodded. He told them about the small cut on the governor's shoulder—a wound received as he had run through the forest, narrowly avoiding a swarming cluster of Mad in the darkness and escaping with only a single mark. The Madness had begun to spread, causing the sores and marks within hours—marks easily hidden by clothing as Trisk began to lay the roots of his lies in the town. The diminutive man related how he had created an elixir, a potion of his own devising, which seemed to have slowed the effects but would not last forever.

"That's impossible," Caitlin said. "Nothing can delay the Madness."

"What's in that potion, Stump?" Christy asked.

Stump detailed the ingredients—a mixture of seeds, oils, and fats—all reputedly used to slow the blood and decrease the heart rate. He explained how the sores still came, and the wounds still bled, but his feat of experimentation had afforded the governor an extra few weeks more than the traditional incubation period of merely a few days.

"So, it slows the nanocytes..." Mary-Anne mumbled to herself. "Causes them to move slower in the blood and reduce the rate at which the affliction occurs."

Caitlin looked at Mary-Anne, intrigued despite the other emotions warring within her. It wasn't the first time she'd heard that word over the years, but with knowledge limited to a token selection of books among her people at Silver Creek, she had never truly understood what they were. "What are nanocytes?"

"A bigger question than I think I have time to answer right now." Mary-Anne shook her head but continued. "In short, nanocytes are the reason why vampires and Weres exist today. A microscopic alien technology lives in the bloodstream, affecting the biology to create the strength and powers that we have. It is, I believe, also the reason for the ushering in of the Age of Madness, though I've yet to find an explanation as to why."

"Then why would you think that?" Christy asked.

"Because I feel it in my gut," Mary-Anne replied, tapping her stomach. "Those affected with the Madness have eyes which glow like my own. It only makes sense that it's the same curse which runs through our own veins."

Caitlin's head spun. She wasn't sure which was more difficult to understand. That there was a microscopic alien technology floating around in Mary-Anne and Kain's bloodstream, or that Stump had found a way to slow the Madness down in the governor's body.

"Why would you save him?" Caitlin asked at last. "If he was dying, why would you risk your life to save him?"

Stump shrugged. "He paid me coin."

"Then why are you telling us all of this? Why betray him now?" Christy scowled her open displeasure.

"Because there is no more coin."

"What do you mean, there's no more?" Mary-Anne asked. "Stump, where is Trisk?"

He shambled over to the corner of the room. There, the

floor looked cleaner, and shapes left in the faint layer of dust indicated that something had been stacked there until fairly recently. Judging by the look of the marks, Caitlin thought they might have been boxes of some kind.

Stump stood in the clean space. "The answer can be found in coin."

"*We don't have any—*" Caitlin began.

Christy fished into her pocket and pulled out a couple of coins which she tossed to Stump. He caught them with little effort and dropped them in his pocket.

"Well?" Caitlin urged.

As Stump spoke of the governor's plan, Caitlin, Mary-Anne, and Christy's faces fell. Caitlin thought back to her dream of fire and flame, remembering the sound of the Trisk's laughter and the bangs which had awoken her from sleep.

CHAPTER TWENTY

Ashdale Pond, Old Ontario

Shit, shit, shit, Caitlin thought as they sprinted through the town. *We picked the wrong fucking moment to send away our werewolf.*

"Slow down," Christy moaned from somewhere behind. "I only have short legs."

But Caitlin wasn't listening. Jaxon streamed along beside her, keeping up easily, his tongue flapping out the side of his mouth. Mary-Anne set the pace just ahead of them all, no longer burdened by her hood as they raced into the night.

Smoke still hovered around them. There was little light to see by, but Caitlin followed the vampire, completely at ease being led by her companion.

What the fuck were they thinking? At a time when they needed *more* people to help get Trisk, they had sent some away.

You needed to. How else would Christy's parents survive? The plan was to operate in secrecy. To take the governor down without anyone else noticing. A covert mission—

Yeah, look how great that worked out.

It disturbed Caitlin how empty the town seemed. She guessed that everyone would be at the church now, waiting for their glorious pastor to give his sermon and fill their hearts with hope. Hands in their laps, no doubt, as they prepared their buckets for a delicious spoonful of gullible.

"It's a good thing you know where *you're* going," Caitlin called ahead to Mary-Anne, blinking and rubbing the smoke from her eyes.

The vamp grinned and took a hard left. They could hear Christy somewhere behind them, but Caitlin didn't have time to slow. She would catch up, sure enough. Christy had the advantage of knowing the town like the back her hand—she had been there for years, after all.

When they reached Jamie's house, Mary-Anne burst through the door, near enough smashing the damned thing from its hinges.

Jamie jumped up, startled. He had been asleep on the sofa. On the floor, tied from neck to toe in rope, was Pastor Andrews, and Mabel's snores could be heard from way upstairs.

"Come. Now," Caitlin said, kicking Andrews in the side as she passed.

Jaxon began growling at the pastor as he blinked stupidly.

"What's going on?" Jamie asked.

"We have to go—*now*," Caitlin instructed. "Go, get Mabel. Hurry her fucking ass up unless you don't want her to see the morning."

As Caitlin waited in silence with the pastor, Mary-Anne swept around the house at speed, looking for fire pokers, cutlery, or anything that could be used as a potential weapon for the pair upstairs. Christy arrived a minute later, her breathing labored and chesty. It seemed the smoke had begun to take its toll on her.

"Nice of you to join us," Caitlin teased.

"Fuck you." Christy scowled her obvious displeasure.

When Jamie and his Nana came down the stairs, Mabel seemed more bewildered than ever before. Her hair stood up in odd directions, her nightgown was caught up in the back of her pants revealing a very pale, weathered ass cheek, and she muttered incomprehensible words to herself.

Jamie looked darkly at Caitlin. "Nana needs her rest. It's the only thing that keeps her sane. Mind telling us what's going on?"

Caitlin looked from Jamie to Mabel. She sighed. "You need to get Mabel out of the village. It's the governor—"

Pastor Andrews' ears pricked up.

"What about him?" Jamie asked.

Christy answered. "It's fucked up, Jay-Jay. He's gone Mad."

"He's always been a bit kooky to me," Mabel said, a light coming back into her eyes briefly. "Strange man. Handsome at the start. The years have not been kind."

"No. He's gone *Mad*," Christy emphasized. "He's contracted the Madness. It's eating him alive. He's at death's door, his mind's gone. He wants to lead one last sermon before he...before he..."

"Before he what?" Jamie urged.

"Goes out in a blaze of glory," Mary-Anne finished simply.

Mabel gasped and clapped a hand to her face. The light in her eyes extinguished. "Does the reverend know?"

"I prefer 'pastor,'" Andrews said.

Jamie rolled his eyes.

They packed a quick bag of necessities—food, clothing, and the like—and were soon back out the door again. Caitlin cut Pastor Andrews' legs free but made it clear he was to follow Jamie and Mabel and not run away.

Jamie and Mabel prepared to separate from Mary-Anne, Caitlin, and Jaxon as they neared the edge of the village. Ordinarily, they'd have been able to see the church from where they were stood, but the smoke was too much, and in the dark of the night, they could see nothing.

"Take care," Jamie said, supporting the pastor awkwardly. "And if we don't see you again—"

"You will," Caitlin said. "You will."

They lingered a moment. Mabel's eyes had glassed over again, and she looked tired. Caitlin felt a sudden pang of guilt for waking the old woman in the middle of the night until she remembered that Mabel would have been woken by one of the pastor's goons anyway. At least soon, she could stop all that bother—she hoped.

Christy hesitated a moment before flinging herself into Jamie's arms. Her eyes were filmed with tears, and Caitlin wondered whether that was from sadness or from the smoke.

"I'm sorry," Christy said, then pulled away and kissed Jamie on the lips. The pair softened, falling into the romance of it all before Mary-Anne coughed and broke the spell. "I never meant to join them, Jay-Jay. The pastor had my parents from the start. It was all to keep them safe."

"I know," Jamie said as they fell back into another smooch.

"Seriously?" Mary-Anne hissed a breath of displeasure. "That's enough tonsil-tennis. It's not like we're on a time limit or anything."

Despite it all, Jamie and Christy smiled. "I'll come back for you," she said.

"About bloody time," Mabel said with a wink.

Then they were gone, into the smoke and out of sight with instructions to find one of their sheds on the outskirts of town and hide up until the chaos had passed. Caitlin hoped it wouldn't come to that but already knew in her heart that there would be a lot more madness before the night was over.

Caitlin peered through the church window. As expected, the whole damn town was inside.

"What do you see?" Mary-Anne asked, hovering behind where she acted as lookout.

Faces. Hundreds of expectant faces. Restless faces which fidgeted and turned to those beside and behind them as they grew impatient in their wait for their authority figure. Usually, by now, the pastor would be in full swing, the church echoing with his sermon.

His absence and the break in their normal routine left them vulnerable and uncertain.

"Can you see him?" Mary-Anne said, tuning her ears in to try to hear more.

"No. There's no one there."

"Unsurprising, really. The pastor's halfway out of town by now."

Caitlin looked incredulously behind her and was about to make some quip to match Mary-Anne's when she heard a throat clearing inside the church, followed by a gasp as everyone fell silent.

A man emerged from the back of the church and hobbled toward the lectern. He was cloaked virtually head to foot, his face shadowed. Slender and malnourished—she could see that much from the way the cloak all but fell off him—the only parts of his face on display were the crook of his nose which jutted out from the folds of the linen and the shape of his lips which looked calloused and riddled with ulcers.

Caitlin watched as those gathered inside the church shuffled nervously in their seats.

The man scanned the room, then cleared his throat once more. A great lump of phlegm caught on the ring of his fist which he wiped casually on his cloak. When he spoke, his words were measured and calm.

"Welcome, one and all" he began. "And what a beautiful evening it is to join together and hold congregation."

"Where's Pastor Andrews?" someone called from the crowd.

A flash of anger passed over the man's face as he searched for the culprit but couldn't identify him among those gathered.

"To tell you the truth, I hardly know myself," the man

replied. "But fear not, for you are in the hands of a power far greater than the pastor himself. A man with the power to change your fate forever and help usher in a new world far beyond what you've ever known."

A wicked grin grew on the man's face.

A ripple of unease spread through the crowd.

"Who are you?" another voice shouted.

The man beamed, then, as if he had waited for that question since his arrival.

"I'm glad you asked," he said, gripping the sides of his hood. "For in the absence of the pastor comes your governor."

He lowered his hood in one swift motion, eliciting an explosion of murmurs, gasps, and cries of disgust. Even Caitlin left all sense of pretense behind, cupping her hands against the windows and peering in, nose to the glass. She waved for Mary-Anne to join her.

"Dear Queen Bitch and all that is good and pure," Mary-Anne muttered.

Trisk was hideous, his face a canvas of sores and blotchy skin. Great craters of pus and blood dotted his features. His eyes were bloodshot with bags hanging so low beneath them she was sure he could lick them. His hair had fallen away in patches and looked like it was hardly holding on to his scalp.

But that wasn't the worst part for Caitlin. That was saved for the gaunt expression on his face. The man who had once been cherry-cheeked and fat now looked as if he had been left out in the sun to melt. There was barely anything left of him, merely skin clinging desperately to bone.

"What the…" Caitlin said, her words trailing away.

"Monster," someone declared.

"It's the devil," another shouted.

"*Flee*. It's the Madness."

Several others stood up, pointing and shouting names at Trisk. He waited patiently until the noise began to grow. Then he roared in a voice which echoed around the room, "*Silence!*"

Those who were brave enough to stand stopped talking, and some fell back into their seats.

"I am no monster," he said. "Though my flesh has been tarnished, my mind is still pure. There is no monster here."

"What happened?" a woman asked. Caitlin watched her shrink back into her chair as the man's eyes met her own.

"I have been tested, and I have passed," the governor said. "I have indeed been inflicted with the Madness—"

Another ripple of murmurs cut him short.

"*But,*" the governor interjected loudly, regaining control. "I have passed the test. The Madness which affected my system but a few weeks ago has yet to take me into its clutches. The Lord himself has placed his hand on my soul and protected me from its grasp. What you see before you is an image of the Lord's work."

"More like the Lord's scrotum," Mary-Anne remarked. "He looks like a tree had sex with a shriveled piece of fruit."

Caitlin wanted to laugh at that but couldn't. She was transfixed, not merely by the governor himself but by the softening expressions on the faces of the congregation. She couldn't believe it. They were *buying* it. Though Stump had performed some kind of strange and wondrous miracle on the governor, he had said himself that he would still die soon. The elixir *slowed* the affliction. It didn't cure it.

"It's a miracle," a woman in her fifties gasped, standing and holding her hands to the sky.

"Hallelujah." Another joined in, holding her child in her arms as she stood.

"You don't have to be pretty to be a living miracle," a younger woman said, slapping at her partner who tried to drag her back into her seat. "Magic and wonder have indeed come to the governor. God bless ye, man."

"I've got a bad feeling," Mary-Anne said. When she turned, Caitlin was already running to the front of the building. "Son of a bitch."

Caitlin took the corner and was greeted by the backs of the two door guards. They were so transfixed by Trisk that they didn't even notice her dart between them, bursting into the church and only pausing when she was halfway up the aisle.

"Absolute-swamp-ass-chicken-turd-dumbfuck-dick-slapping-bull-shit," she said, her arms out wide in disbelief. Another silence fell, and all eyes turned to her. She barely even noticed their attention. Her gaze caught and held the governor's.

His face dropped for a moment and brought her a surge of satisfaction. He hadn't expected her to arrive. Hadn't even considered the possibility that Caitlin would find him in Ashdale, she was sure of that.

"Caitlin Harrison..." he whispered.

Caitlin turned to face the crowd. "Don't listen to a word this man says. Your governor is *evil*. The very definition of the word. His whole regime thrives on lies, deceit, and terror, and you're handing everything to him on a plate."

"Says who?" a man shouted from somewhere near the back. "A newcomer to our town? What do you know of the governor, Moxie?"

"Because he was once my governor. A lazy shit who ruled the town from afar, let us suffer, threatened our lives, and sent my brother and me out into the forest to capture prisoners under pain of death."

Nice one, Kitty-Cat. Best not mention the vampire just yet.

"You lied to us?" the man asked, turning to Trisk.

"Not a lick."

"Liar!" Caitlin yelled.

"What reason would I have to lie to you all?" Trisk asked, prowling back and forth behind his lectern. "Have you not enjoyed prosperity in the weeks following my arrival? Have you not all gathered as a community and lived the best days you've seen? Am I not a living embodiment of a miracle?"

He sneered as confusion fell on the faces of the congregation. It was clear to Caitlin that they were mired in uncertainty. Who were they to believe? A nobody woman who had brought danger to their doorstep and now threatened to topple their whole belief system, or the sore-pocked governor who had seemingly performed nothing short of a miracle and provided a reason to keep on living. To them, it must seem that he'd provided hope at a time when there was none.

"Stick with me, my flock, and by all that I swear is good and holy, I will rid these lands of the Madness. I will mass-market my elixir to help those who are suffering. Already,

I've tested the drink on those who are long fallen, and some semblance of life has been restored. Stick with me, and I swear to you all that we will leave these dark days together."

Trisk finished by punching his hand into the air. There was a moment of silence before a few members of the crowd punched their own fists in emulation. Then a dozen. Then more until all but a few had stood, their eyes shining with inspiration as they looked upon the decrepit man.

"Bring back my husband," a woman shouted.

"Heal my son, please," a man boomed.

"All of these and more," Trisk proclaimed, both hands now in the air. "For freedom."

"*For freedom*," the congregation chorused.

"For hope."

"*For hope*."

Caitlin looked around, bewildered. She shouted, but her words couldn't be heard above the din of the congregants. For the first time since she'd entered the church, she noticed that Jaxon and Mary-Anne hadn't joined her. She was alone, surrounded by a sea of people. And it wasn't until the crowd began to simmer down and two figures emerged from the back of the church that her heart truly stopped.

The brothers from the ring of fire. They're here?

They walked in ceremonious step, a large box carried between them. Piled high in the box were what looked like brown balls, almost spilling over the edge. They placed their burden near the governor's feet, then took a step back, lacing their hands behind them. Somewhere in the shadows at the far back of the room, Caitlin saw more movement.

Trisk reached his hands in front and lowered them, the crowd falling obediently quiet at the gesture. They craned and arched their necks to get a better look at the contents of the box.

"Brothers and sisters," Trisk said. "It is time to begin our work. Time to begin the revolution anew. To cleanse the world, we tear down the liars and the cheats—those who have falsely accused us and done us wrong."

He pointed at Caitlin.

"The harlot standing before you is the false one. A woman of poison tongue and deception."

"Moxie? Is this true?" a woman asked nearby. Caitlin turned to see Clarissa, the girl she had rescued from the wreckage of the car, seated on her mother's lap. The woman looked up at Caitlin with wide eyes.

"What? Of course not."

"*Liar!*" The governor exploded, glee on his face. "Even her name is false. Why would you pretend to be anyone else if you're not a deceiver...*Caitlin Harrison?*"

Clarissa's mother clapped a hand to her chest.

Caitlin felt herself flush with anger. She wanted more than anything to sprint up the aisle, launch herself at the man, and cut his throat where he stood. But, what then? Escape an angry mob of townsfolk who all believed she'd killed the prophet?

No. She had to be more tactful. She had to buy time. *Where the fuck is Mary-Anne?*

Caitlin took a small step back, turned on her heel, and began to run from the church.

"*Seize her*," Trisk cried, spittle flying from his mouth.

She charged for the door, only then realizing that the shadows that moved around the edges of the room were actually men and women in jet-black cloaks. They lined the aisle in single file, blocking the door.

Caitlin pulled to a halt, put a hand on her sword, then thought better of it. She looked out at the freedom of the town over the shoulders of the Firestarters and saw two red eyes staring back at her. She could just make out Mary-Anne's face as the vampire winked and placed a finger over her lips.

She thought she could see something else, too. Two faint throbs—amber eyes immediately behind her.

CHAPTER TWENTY-ONE

Ashdale Pond, Old Ontario

The whole farce seemed a bit unnecessary.

The Firestarters bound Caitlin's hands and ankles. Those whom Mary-Anne had scared half to death in the house seemed to take great delight in manhandling Caitlin and dragging her out into the space outside in front of the church.

In all their excitement, they never touched her sword.

"Really? I tell you to get some sense, and you come back to join the side of the governor?" she said, rolling her eyes and thrashing her body to make tying her all the more difficult. "When you grow a pair of balls, you should call me. We could grab lunch. I could smack you with a rock and make you see real fucking sense."

"Shut your pie-hole," one of the Firestarters said as he took a length of rag and forced it into Caitlin's mouth. "In case you didn't notice, the governor is back. With him, we can do great things."

Caitlin spat the rag out. "You mean like twiddle with each other's assholes?"

She gasped as her head was pulled back and she was gagged.

From the edges of the shadows, the Firestarter brothers emerged with what appeared to be the trunk of a moderate-sized tree. They grunted as they stood it on its end in the center of the clearing. One brother took to digging a small hole while the other balanced the trunk. Those within the church poured out and into the torchlight, gathering in a large circle around the Firestarters.

Caitlin cast her eyes around the circle, looking everywhere again for a sign of Mary-Anne's glowing eyes. Though she trusted the vampire with her life, she wondered what she was playing at. How far did this farce need to go before they went ape-shit and took control of the situation?

And was that Kain that she had seen? Perhaps her tired eyes were playing tricks on her. Kain would know better than to disobey orders and leave Christy's parents in the unpredictable clutches of Psycho Joe.

No. Just Joe. Jesus. Kain was really starting to rub off on her.

The crowd parted to allow Trisk through. "Fetch kindling," he said to those Firestarters standing around the edges of the circle. "I want to watch this bitch burn." He tossed one of the clay orbs from one hand to the other. Caitlin saw a small hole from which a thin trail of black powder leaked. With every toss, the governor's hands grew a tad dirtier.

His followers obeyed, slowly building up a small stack

of bracken and twigs at the base of the trunk. When the brothers were done fixing the trunk into place, they each grabbed one of Caitlin's elbows and tied her to the post.

She looked once more for Mary-Anne. Her heart began to quicken.

Come on, bitch. This isn't funny anymore.

Mary-Anne watched from the safety of the shadows, a smile on her face and a plan in her head.

"What are we waiting for?" Kain grunted into her ear.

"The perfect moment."

They watched as the Firestarters trotted off to the edge of the woods and came back with more kindling. The two brothers who had escaped Mary-Anne's wrath busied themselves with tying Caitlin to the post.

"Which is when?" Kain asked.

"We don't want to go in too quickly and startle them all into a blind attack. You heard them in the church. They all think *we're* the bad guys. You think you'll be able to tell them otherwise when they stampede against us and choose to fight first, ask questions later?"

"We can take them," Kain said.

"Maybe. But I'd rather do as little killing as possible. These people don't deserve to die. Just those sick Firestarter fucks and the walking, bleeding scrotum with legs." She looked Kain up and down and whispered. "Besides, don't you think Were Kain would be a lot more effective than the skinny fuck you're pretending to be?"

"You know I can't—"

"I know, I know," Mary-Anne teased. "I just love to see you squirm."

Kain took a step forward, watching uneasily as the last of the Firestarters came back.

"Two hundred to two," Mary-Anne said. "I don't like those odds."

Kain grinned. "Oh, I think our odds are better than that."

Caitlin looked down at the pile of wood beneath her. It had reached several feet high. She wondered what it would feel like when the flames licked her toes and the heat rose.

Trisk stepped into the center of the circle. Caitlin couldn't quite believe it was possible, but he looked even more hideous in the torchlight. Weeping sores shimmered in the flames, and she was pretty sure, as he laced his hands together, several areas of skin simply peeled off and slopped to the floor.

"And so we come to it. The sacrifice of the traitor to lead the world into the new, the great, the revolution," the governor said, addressing the crowd as he placed the orb delicately in his pocket.

Caitlin leered at his jab, knowing how much it would anger her for him to use her own words against her. She'd sent those same words with a Silver Creek guard to deliver to the governor himself when he ruled supreme over their little wooden town.

He advanced, a figure of horror and power. "Remove her gag."

The brothers, who now stood on either side of Caitlin, pulled the gag from her mouth.

"You've been a pain in my ass for far too long, you little twat. Now, any last words?"

"I would've thought your ass knew only pleasure," she jibed. "Get these boys to show you how it's done. They like a good bit of meat buried in their holes." She spat then, a thick glob of saliva landing directly in the governor's eye.

He pawed angrily at his face, irritating the sores which oozed and exploded with his touch. His face was a bubbling pot of lava, but it did not seem to hurt him. All sensory recognition of pain must have gone when the Madness came.

Caitlin exploded into laughter. The brothers reached up to place the gag back over her mouth.

"No, don't," the governor instructed. A shadow crossed his face as he sneered at her. "I want to hear her suffer. Every last scream."

If looks could kill, the look she gave him then would have had him down on the ground in seconds.

Trisk addressed the crowd again, his arms wide. As he moved about the space and drew nearer to the crowd, Caitlin couldn't help but notice that they withdrew in total awe of the man—but also in total fear of going anywhere near him. He boomed verses, talked of the brighter future, and had them all riled up and ready for the great burning of the traitor.

"Without further ado, let us sacrifice the harlot," he finished. He withdrew the orb from his pocket and tossed it once more between his hands. "And let us introduce the new world with a new technology, in a style which would make our Lord clap his hands."

He clicked his fingers, and the Firestarter nearest to him offered a torch. The governor reached out with his free hand and took it.

Which was when the explosion came.

A scream echoed through the crowd as he reared back in pain. A blinding flash of light startled him as the orb fell from his hand to the ground. He looked in disbelief at the hand with which he had reached for the torch. It was no longer there, and in its place was the blackened stump of his wrist with flames licking up his sleeve.

Trisk held up his other hand, noting the trails of powder coating his palm.

"*Idiot!*" he scolded himself aloud, then muttered, "So much for safe and watertight. That Stump is going to get it—"

"Governor, are you all right?" several voices asked from the crowd. One of the Firestarters leaned down to gather up the orb, the torch in his other hand dangerously close to the powder.

"*Stop*. Fool," the governor said, kicking the Firestarter to drive him back. The torch fell to the floor, extinguishing itself on the night dew of the grass.

The Firestarter leered back at him.

"Aw, don't you hate it when that happens," Caitlin teased. "Always sad when the explosion *comes* too early."

"Enough of this shit," Trisk said, wiped his hand on the grass, and took a new orb from the box the brothers had carried out and placed beside him. "Let's light this bitch up."

He nodded to his henchmen who each touched their torches to the base of the pyre. Immediately, Caitlin began to cough, her skin already sweating from the flare of heat.

If you're thinking of jumping in and saving me, now would be a good time, Ma...

Trisk started to laugh, a hollow chuckle which disintegrated into a splutter. He reared his hand back for the throw, muttered, "Payback is a bitch," then launched the orb into the flames.

In the split second before the orb landed, a streak of red light appeared through the crowd.

Not that anyone saw it though, Caitlin realized as if removed from her conscious self. They were too busy clapping their hands over their faces. In the space of a heartbeat, the people were pushed back into each other from the force of the explosion. The gunpowder drank the fire greedily. Several screams resounded and, above it all, the maniacal laugh of a governor gone mad dancing in triumph.

CHAPTER TWENTY-TWO

Ashdale Pond, Old Ontario

The screeches of surprise went on for some time after the explosion died down. Townsfolk held their hands to their ears, and some cried. Many fell onto their asses and watched in wonder as the fire burned.

Yes... Burn motherfucker... Burn... Soon, they will all burn...

The twisted smile remained on the governor's face as he waited for Caitlin's screams. He waited for the desecration and destruction of the bitch who had torn it all apart, the one who had invaded his safe space and toppled his tower. She'd made the fire rain down on the world he had known and forced him through the woods on that fateful night.

He remembered it so clearly, that moment when Hank, his captain of the guards, had informed him of Caitlin's arrival with her mini-battalion as they stormed the gates. Fear had ripped through his chest, the same feeling he resented her so much for. *How dare that bitch make me feel this? How dare she force me into a corner?*

The survival instinct had kicked in. He knew when to run and when to fight. Halrod wasn't a stupid man, after all, and he had fled through the secret passages of his quarters and out into the wild without a whisper.

The darkness had greeted him. Leaves and twigs had clawed at his face as he ran, guided by the position of the stars and the moon, towards a place where he could regroup and feel safe. Another bundle of fuckwads with malleable minds waited, those who would cower before him and do his bidding. It would be a refuge, a place to build toward a larger destiny in which he would band his towns together and lead a revolt against the revolters. Against Caitlin, and the fuckers she had brought to her cause.

He would watch the whole damn world burn before he'd allow her to take it from him.

And it was there, in the thick of the forest, when the eyes had appeared. They had no doubt been drawn by the trample of his feet, heavy with panic, and the gasping of his breath as his lungs screamed for oxygen. It was there that they came.

A couple at first, then infinitely more. They were fast but clumsy, and he was faster, but his stamina ran thin.

He had torn through the brush, batting away the hands that reached for his shoulders, doing his best to block out the screams and the grunts and the cries of the Mad who wanted nothing more than the skin off his back. The delicious satisfaction they would derive from digesting and drinking the blood which surged within him drove him on in desperation.

"Back, scum!" he had cried as he turned to see most of them fall behind.

All but one.

That fateful one.

One scratch, that was all it took. One small break in his skin and there it was. The discharge from the Mad's sores mixed with his own blood and began to take hold.

The governor had bowed his head, doubled his concentration as fear and adrenaline shot through his body, and somehow, managed to lose them. Anger and terror rose from within as he blocked the scratch from his mind and careened toward Ashdale. That was the place where he would begin again as he rebuilt his empire and fought back against the bitch.

All of this and more flashed through Trisk's mind as he watched the fire burn, burn, burn Caitlin Harrison in its pyre. With patience born of Madness, he waited for those screams to erupt.

Waited.

And waited.

But nothing came.

"Talk about cutting it close to the wire," Caitlin said the second Mary-Anne put her down. "Any longer, and I'd be burning more than Kain's pecker when he pees."

"Unnecessary," a voice said through the smoke.

Caitlin's face lit up when she saw Kain emerge. She ran and hugged him, taking him by surprise.

"Woah, easy now. Didn't think you'd miss me *that*

much," he said, relaxing into the hug. Jaxon sprinted towards them and jumped up at Caitlin.

"Jax!" Caitlin said, bending down to tussle his head.

"Shhh," Mary-Anne urged.

"What are you doing here, Cornswaggle? What have you done with Christy's parents?"

"We're here," Felix said as he and Patricia came nearer. "And we're here to fight."

Caitlin looked up, and her mouth dropped. They were all there. Several dozen figures came into sight with smiles on their faces and weapons in their hands. She beamed as she spotted Dylan, Ash, Alice, Vex, Belle, and the rest of the Revolutionaries, as well as two others she hadn't seen before—a grizzly man with an eyepatch and a woman she would easily reconsider her heterosexual tendencies for. She was one of the most beautiful women Caitlin had ever seen.

"Hey, sis," Dylan said, holding out his arms.

Caitlin ran to him and kissed him on the cheek. "What are you doing here?"

"We couldn't let you go out into the wild and take all the ass-kicking for yourself, could we?" He grinned.

"What about Silver Creek?" Caitlin asked.

"It's in safe hands," he said, winking at Ash beside him. "Sully's got it covered."

She couldn't believe it. Just a few minutes ago, she had been alone, surrounded by an angry mob while tied to a pole, and now...

"Joe?" Caitlin said suddenly, not quite believing her eyes.

"*Keep it down*," Mary-Anne insisted, but Caitlin wasn't listening.

Joe stepped out from behind Belle, his shotgun held loosely in one hand. "Yous wants helps, so heres we comes."

"What about Violet?" Caitlin asked.

"She's nots be going anywheres for some time. I cans help yous, yes, I can, and makes the worlds a touch safer, then that's what Joe's going to dos."

A tear came to Caitlin's eyes. All along, the plan had been to operate in secrecy, but even now, they had all somehow known that she would need them. It would be the group of them who helped bring some sort of order and justice into the world, not her alone.

"I don't mean to be a limp dick, but we need to get a move on. We won't have long until the governor notices that there's no—"

Mary-Anne stopped as a cry of anguish roared into the air. The haunting sound resembled the shriek of a gutted pig mixed with a ghoul. "*Noooo! Where is she? Where is she?*"

There was a rumble of distant chatter as the townsfolk joined the governor's confusion. Then, seconds later, Trisk roared, "To hell with that bitch. To hell with them all." The sounds of several more explosions filled the air, mixed with the mingled cries, gasps, and tears of the crowd.

"I think that's our cue," Mary-Anne said.

"Hey, that's my line." Caitlin frowned.

The vampire motioned for Caitlin to go ahead. "I think that's our cue," she said. "Revolutionaries. Let's roll."

Caitlin sped through the smoke with renewed confidence, knowing that she had her team on her side. This was it. It might not have totally gone to plan, but this was what she had been waiting for.

Before she could reach the front of the church, she saw figures appear in the smoke. Dark, ill-defined silhouettes of Ashdale citizens fought with each other, fear taking them in its grasp as they panicked and their survival instinct kicked in.

It was a far cry from the herd mentality they had displayed when Caitlin had led the horde of Mad to them.

"Watch out," Kain cried as a large man charged at Caitlin, panic written all over his face. He raised a fist and threatened to clobber her in the face, but she ducked the blow easily.

The man was thrown off-balance, and Kain sent him to the floor with a tap on his head.

"Bop!" Kain exclaimed, then was instantly distracted by another group of townsfolk swinging their arms in aimless defense.

Caitlin sped through, listening the whole time for Trisk. She dodged and evaded several more townsfolk, drew her sword, and parried the blows of a Firestarter as he stumbled through the smoke, blood dripping from the corner of his mouth. With little effort, she took him down and managed to find her way to the front of the church.

Or what was left of it.

The building was engulfed in flames. The wooden structures which had held it together were nothing more than crackling fire. Smoke streamed thick and black into the air as she pulled her collar over her mouth like a mask and squinted for any sign of her target.

"Couldn't keep away, could you?" a voice came from behind her.

Caitlin turned, her eyes stinging, and could make out the shape of the Firestarter brothers. Their skin was dark and ashen and their clothes tattered where flames had caught and wood had flown and cut from the bombs the governor had tossed in all directions.

"You know me, lover boys." She winked at them. "I've somehow always been attracted to the biggest pricks."

"She's funny." One of the twins chuckled before falling into a fit of coughing.

"She'll be funnier when she's dead," the other exclaimed. "Hand her body to the governor, and we'll be laughing right into paradise."

"Even after this, you're *still* on his side?" Caitlin asked, stunned.

"'Til death do us part," the second brother said.

They ran at her, their sneers turning to determined grimaces. The first brother held a mace in his hands and swung it hard at Caitlin, who blocked the attack but was forced off-balance. The second followed up with his bare fists, one of them connecting with her cheek.

White light bloomed in her vision, and she could hear a whine in one ear.

"Sons of bitches," she said.

"Harlot," they replied.

Caitlin held her sword in both hands, swung it wide, and went for the fucker who'd punched her. He jumped back but the blade connected, opening up the skin on his arm and unleashing a faucet of blood which sprayed in all directions.

She was sure she could hear some of it hiss as it sprayed into the flames.

The brother with the mace looked in horror at his twin's arm and charged, grabbing her around the hips and forcing her backward into the fire. They landed with a heavy thud, the heat of the flames instantly scorching. Caitlin summoned all her strength and twisted around, turning the brother onto his back. She straddled him.

"I always did like it hot and heavy in the bedroom," she said.

He screamed as the flames bit into his clothes, licking his skin. Caitlin scrambled off, feeling the skin on her knees begin to burn, and turned in time to see the other coming for her, a large, jagged piece of wood in his hands.

His eyes were devoid of anything else but anger as he drew his arm back to throw the wood like a javelin.

That was when Kain appeared.

"Kitty-Cat, we thought we'd lost..." He trailed off, noticing her attacker. "Hey!"

Kain, followed by Jaxon, sprinted at him, his eyes a dull amber as his mind seemed to focus on nothing else but taking him down. He struck the man in the side, the javelin falling to the floor beside them. Kain reared a fist back and smacked him in the face. "Save that shit for the vampires," he said, nodding at the wooden plank.

Jaxon chomped into the fucker's leg.

"Hey," Mary-Anne shouted from somewhere nearby. "I heard that."

The brother behind Caitlin rose suddenly, half his skin

stuck to the floor. He took one look at Caitlin, Kain, and his brother and sprinted off into the smoke. His mouth seemed frozen open around the screams.

The noise around them was deafening. Caitlin heard several more explosions from somewhere in the smoke, followed by more screams. The smoke caught in their lungs, and the fire raged on in the church. Caitlin could hear her Revolutionaries as they battled the Firestarters and subdued the townsfolk—or those that they could, at least.

Kain threw a final punch at the remaining brother, who fell unconscious, then stepped up to Caitlin's side.

"Shall we check the church?" he asked.

Another explosion rang in the distance.

"No point," Caitlin said. "He's this way, come on."

Kain tugged Caitlin back. "Are you crazy? We need to regroup. We can't run through that ourselves *and* find the governor before he chucks a bomb at us."

Caitlin thought about this a moment. He was right. If they charged straight at Trisk, who knew what would happen? He was clearly on edge, tearing down everything around him because there was little left of him before the Madness took hold. He wouldn't think twice about sending a bomb their way, taking himself with it. Then what would they do?

"Okay, I've got an idea. But you're not going to like it."

"Shoot," Kain said.

"I need you to transform."

"What? No."

Caitlin sighed. "We need to get to the governor fast before he realizes that we're there and takes the chance to blast us into tiny little pieces. I've read about the speed of the Weres. We need you to transform."

"Can't the vamp do it?" Kain moaned, looking at the thick tufts of hair on the backs of his hands, lasting evidence of his slowly fading ability to switch between forms.

"I'm a little busy!" Mary-Anne called again. There was the sound of metal on metal, then a scream.

"I need you both. We'll flank him from both sides. Whoever gets there first, wins."

Mary-Anne appeared from the smoke and sped towards them. She stopped as she reached their side. "Ooh, sounds like some fun. Come on, Pooch. Let's see the puppy bark."

Kain looked at them both as if he couldn't believe what they had suggested. His shoulders sagged as he gave in to the idea.

"Fine. But if I can't change back into a human after this, I'm dropping a deuce in your shoes every morning for the rest of your life."

"Sounds like a fair trade," Caitlin said.

They both stood back and watched as Kain concentrated, his eyes bursting with amber as his body began to warp and twist.

CHAPTER TWENTY-THREE

<u>Ashdale Pond, Old Ontario</u>

Caitlin wasn't sure what she had expected, but the end result was damned impressive.

In the place where Kain stood moments before was one of the largest wolves she had ever seen. His back reached the middle of Caitlin's stomach, and with a body covered in fur of golds and browns, Kain was flawless.

Well, almost. There were small bald patches around his paws, and his tail was crooked. Caitlin put that down to the difficulties he had explained in transforming and how, since the Madness had come, Weres struggled to keep the transition smooth.

"Ready to go?" she breathed.

Kain nodded and nudged at her legs.

"You want me to ride?"

"Maybe when this is all over, you two should get a room," Mary-Anne jibed.

Kain growled a response. Jaxon sniffed around him before bursting into his own barks.

"Come on, then," Caitlin said and climbed cautiously onto Kain. "What about Jaxon?"

"He'll slow us down," Mary-Anne said as she sped off into the smoke.

"Jax, go find Dylan, okay?"

Jaxon cocked his head, one ear raised as if he listening, but he did not move.

Kain growled and barked at Jaxon. The next thing Caitlin knew, Jax was off, running towards the shouts and the voices.

She gripped tightly into Kain's fur. He turned his head around as if asking for permission to go. "All yours, Mr. Cornswaggle." Caitlin winked. A small gasp escaped her as Kain took off, running so swiftly that her breath caught.

Figures hidden in smoke whirled past them. Caitlin closed her eyes to avoid the sting. They heard another explosion—nearer now—and headed in that direction.

Soon enough, the houses came into view—or what parts of the houses were left. Everywhere Caitlin looked, there was nothing more than rubble and flame. The houses which had stood proudly in the sun on the day she had snuck into Ashdale and met Jamie were now nothing more than memories. She saw beds and memorabilia sizzling in the fires. Occasional mini-explosions boomed from liquor and old flammables caught in the chaos as the hungry fire consumed all.

And still, they ran on, not quite catching up with Mary-Anne but following the governor's trail. As terrible as the destruction was, there was a strange satisfaction in knowing that Trisk made the trail easy to follow.

After a short time, Kain slowed.

"Why are we stopping? I can't hear..." Her words faded away as she, like Kain, cocked an ear.

Someone was singing—a jovial song, something Caitlin hadn't heard before.

It seemed a strange contrast, the jolly melody of the governor's song lilting against the backdrop of carnage and destruction. She saw him up ahead, merely a faint outline at first as they crept forward, doing their best to remain on the edge of visibility in the smoke. Trisk skipped and sang, laughing between words. As he reached another house, he plucked an orb from the box he dragged behind him—now apparently half empty—and held a torch to a length of string dangling from between the orb and the lid, then threw it.

And explosion boomed and was met with raucous laughter from Trisk, who seemed oblivious to all else now but his fun.

"Easy now," Caitlin said quietly as Kain growled. "Wait for Ma, first."

But where was Mary-Anne? She looked around her, but it was near impossible to see her friend with the flying debris from the bombs and the smoke whirling around them.

The governor clapped excitedly, a delirious expression on his face. His tongue darted out of his mouth and licked at the liquid oozing from the sores on his lips. Another bomb. Another explosion. Another whoop.

Where is she?

"Yoo-hoo!" Mary-Anne's voice called out from somewhere ahead.

Trisk froze midway to grabbing an orb. He sprang up

suddenly, looking in all directions as Caitlin shrank back into the veil of smoke.

"Hey! Blubberguts, come get me," Mary-Anne teased.

Whirling in panic, Trisk lit the fuse and launched the bomb in the direction he believed the voice to come from. Mary-Anne appeared from the opposite direction, streamed past him, and booted him in the stomach.

He stumbled backward.

"Bitch!" he cried, lighting another bomb and tossing it after her.

Caitlin and Kain moved quickly out of the way, feeling the air push with heat against them as they dodged the trajectory. Mary-Anne sped past them and muttered, "Whenever you're ready, guys."

She tore back towards the governor, knocking him aside once more. Despite her speed, Caitlin could see she was careful to only touch him with her shoes, obviously not wanting to make contact with the sores and blood on his skin unless she could help it. One misaligned hit and who could say a drop of pus or blood wouldn't fly through the air and into one of many orifices?

Caitlin and Kain geared up, ready to run. They paused as Trisk picked up the box, emptied the orbs all around his feet, and crouched down low.

"Next time you come near me, I'm blowing you to king-dom-fucking-come," the governor declared, holding the torch precariously close to the pile of bombs surrounding him. "Come and get me, bitch."

Dylan hadn't felt this alive in years.

Having had to sit on the fence during the last battle, he felt the adrenaline race through his body now. This was what it was like to feel alive. Fighting for justice. Helping those in need. Destroying evil. Not sitting in prisons or hiding behind the walls of Silver Creek while his sister led the charge. It was this. The feeling of—

Argh! Bitch, Dylan moaned as he looked for the culprit who had thrown the knife. It had whizzed by him, catching his skin so that a small patch of red now bloomed on his shoulder.

The woman grinned, tossing another knife between her hands. She was pretty, standing in her black cloak with her dark hair about her. But Dylan figured she'd be prettier lying unconscious on the floor.

She chuckled and tossed the blade.

Dylan had been prepared for that one. He reached for his sword—a gift from Mary-Anne after the battle—and blocked it mid-air, sending it clattering to the floor.

He smiled as her face dropped. She held up her hands. "Please. I didn't mean it."

"What do you mean, you didn't mean it?" Dylan said. "You tossed *two* knives at me." Despite himself, he couldn't help his eyes wandering to her chest where a teasing eyeful of cleavage was exposed. The woman noticed this and leaned forward to exaggerate the effect.

"I panicked," she said in a slow, crooning tone. "I couldn't tell the good guys from the bad guys."

Dylan advanced, his sword held in front. She recoiled and fell onto her ass as she tried to scurry away.

"No, please..."

"I'm not going to hurt you," he said, extending a hand to help her up.

The woman looked into his eyes a moment. She accepted his help and rose to her feet. "Thanks."

"Don't mention it. Now, just help us calm these fuck-nuts down. We need to gather water. Quell the flames. Not running around in a panic with our heads in the smoke—"

Dylan cut off as the woman's eyes widened. He was confused until the woman fell once more to the floor, wrestling with the creature which had attacked her. She struggled and then stilled, the knife which she had hidden and intended to stab Dylan with in a sneak attack resting loosely in her hand.

Dylan marveled at the bite marks around her neck as Jaxon barked and shook his body. She struggled and gurgled in the dog's grip until she eventually stilled.

"Well... Good boy?" Dylan said.

Jaxon barked.

"Come on, let's round up the others. Can you sniff them out for me?"

As if understanding every word, Jaxon turned and ran into the smoke, pausing long enough along the way for Dylan to follow as they left the Firestarter dead on the floor.

He couldn't believe what a mess the damn place was. As he ran through the smoke, he managed to calm a few townsfolk down. He worked as quickly as possible to get the message to spread, talking to any who would listen to tell them that Trisk had gone. Also, he urged them to gather on the outskirts of town where they'd be safe—at least in the short term.

Dylan assigned several Revolutionaries the task of leading those who needed help and to protect them on the outskirts. Along the way, he took down several folk in black cloaks with expressions on their faces so determined he knew that if *they* didn't die, *he* would. He heard the report of a shotgun as the strange, deranged fellow they'd met in the woods sent bullets flying.

Through the smoke, he spotted Vex and Belle whirling around each other, working as a team to take down those who fought and to talk to those who wanted nothing more than safety. He even saw Ash and Alice fighting back to back with the pretty newcomer not too far away, her hair whipping in the wind. They fought with a couple of people who, after a second glance, Dylan realized displayed glowing red eyes as they reached and clawed for their faces.

Great. It's not enough to have a psychopathic governor and a band of twisted Firestarters, but we've drawn the attention of the Mad, too?

Though, as he made his way around the chaos, he only saw a few Mad, and they were taken down easily by the Revolutionaries—apart from one who chomped on the body of an old man who had fallen to the floor.

One lop with the sword and she was taken care of.

After finding himself back at the church for the third time in a row, Dylan began to grow concerned. He was sure he'd searched everywhere when the fight was taking place, but he had seen no sign of Caitlin, Kain, or Mary-Anne.

Where are you, sis?

Ash ran out of the smoke, gasping for air. The sounds of the fight were fading, but the crackle of fire continued all around. "I'm pretty sure that's most of them," he said. "I've sent Vex, Belle, and Alice to search the field once more, and Tom and Laurie have gone back with the others to keep the townsfolk in order. They're terrified, like sheep watching their field burn."

"Have you seen Caitlin?" Dylan asked.

Ash shook his head. "Nope. I haven't seen Kain or Mary-Anne, either."

"Shit," Dylan said.

"They'll be fine," Ash encouraged him, though the confidence in his words didn't reach his face. "They've made it this far."

Dylan jumped as several more explosions sounded somewhere in town.

Dear God, I hope so.

"Not so big now, are you?" Trisk grimaced. "Amazing what fear can do to paralyze the enemy, eh? I've used that tactic most of my life, and it's served me pretty well so far."

Caitlin hardly realized she was holding her breath. The governor was crouched so low it looked like he was some kind of bird squatting and protecting his eggs. The fire burned in his hand, so close to the bombs that Caitlin couldn't believe they hadn't lit and exploded.

Kain whined beneath her.

"Steady, now…" she whispered.

Caitlin felt Mary-Anne's presence before she saw her. The vampire materialized at her side.

"Great kick. No goal," Caitlin said.

"You try kicking a hundred-pound football. See how far that gets you." Mary-Anne held her sword tightly in her hand. "Give the word, Caitlin, and I'll slice that fucker's face off."

"We can't," she replied, thinking hard. "If you do that, the flame will drop and the town will explode anyway."

"Then what do you suggest, Kitty-Cat?"

When the idea hit Caitlin, her face lit up. She looked down at Kain and said, "I've got it. Ready to tag-team, boy?"

If Caitlin didn't know better, she'd say the werewolf smiled at that.

"Come and get it." The governor laughed—his loudest and craziest yet. He scratched his head, and a large chunk of flesh slid into his hands. He looked at it with a dead expression and tossed it on the floor.

After a rapid briefing from Caitlin, Mary-Anne set her feet firmly in the sand, turned to the others, and nodded to show that she was ready.

"On the count of three," Caitlin said. "One. Two. *Three.*"

Mary-Anne and Kain sped into action. The surprise on Trisk's face was hilarious in itself. Had it not been for the imminent threat of the fire touching the orbs and creating an explosion so large that it might have swallowed the entire town, she might have laughed.

"You sons of bit—"

But that was as far as he got. Like a baseball player from the old world, Mary-Anne tore at him, managing to smack the torch out of his hand so fast and hard that it flew through the air, extinguishing its own flame from the revolutions as it spun.

It all seemed to happen in slow motion. Trisk grasped his hand in pain, his eyes widening as he saw Kain running straight at him. Caitlin knew he made a terrifying sight. Saliva coated his jaws, his snarl terrifying as he bent low to the ground before pouncing and soaring over the dumbstruck man. The governor craned his neck and watched her sword flash silver. Beyond the gleaming sword, looking down on him, was a face that Caitlin could see filled with rage and hate.

"Caitlin fucking Harrison." An excruciating mix of emotions bubbled across his face before the blade cut through his skin, cracking bone and slicing his brain in two.

There was no pain and no screaming, only instant blackness and death.

Kain landed so softly it was hard to believe that a moment ago, they had been several feet in the air. Caitlin turned to look at Trisk but could hardly recognize him as he crumpled in a bloody pile amongst the orbs.

"You did it, Kitty-Cat," Mary-Anne said, appearing at her side.

"No," Caitlin said, feeling a wave of relief washing over her. *"We* did it." She looked down to examine her sword, now slick with the governor's blood, and wiped it clean on governor's shirt and smiled.

"You know, Moxie, every good sword which has achieved great deeds needs a name," Mary-Anne said.

"Moxie," Caitlin repeated with a smile as Kain began to transform back into his human form. "I think that'll do just fine."

CHAPTER TWENTY-FOUR

Ashdale Pond, Old Ontario

The town worked together to quell the flames. Carrying buckets of water from a large pond just outside the town, they passed them along in single file, working hard through the night until the smoke cleared and the final embers died.

Caitlin worked with Mary-Anne, Kain, Dylan, and Christy to lead the town on the cleanup effort. Those who were injured had their wounds taken care of as best they could. Those who had died were buried around the wreckage of the church. The few remaining Firestarters who had the sense to join the good guys before it was all over lent a hand where they could.

"It's going to take a shitload to rebuild all of this, Kitty-Cat," Kain said, standing by Caitlin's side. There was more hair on the backs of his hands now, a reminder that his transformation days were limited.

"So?" Caitlin replied.

"So? You've seen how many houses the governor blew up, right? It'll take forever to put this all back together and give the people their homes back."

"So?" Caitlin repeated. "These people don't deserve to have their lives back and live in peace? They don't deserve help from their fellow man to have a decent standard of living? Are we *wasting* our time helping them?"

"That's not what I meant."

Mary-Anne chuckled.

"What?" he said defensively.

"Look at you bow down to the human girl. Anyone would think you hadn't just turned into a gigantic wolf and helped tear the governor's face off."

Kain frowned and growled at Mary-Anne.

"Whatever it takes, we'll help them," Caitlin said.

"But, how?" Dylan chipped in. "We'd need more wood, which means more woodchoppers. We'd need more weavers for clothes, more carpenters...the list goes on. And we've got to get back to Silver Creek at some point. I love Sullivan, but I had only planned on leaving him for a week or two at most. This could take months."

Caitlin grinned, staring out toward the edge of the town and the line of trees where Silver Creek forest began.

"What's the smile for?" Dylan asked.

"Kitty-Cat's got a plan," Mary-Anne said, pulling her hood over her face as the morning sun struck the horizon in an explosion of oranges and golds.

"We connect the towns," Caitlin said. "Cut through the forest. Fell the trees. Open up a road between Silver Creek and Ashdale. We can use the wood to rebuild the houses.

We can make the route faster and send our men and women to help. We have merchants and traders who could help. Let's join the two. Let's open the world up again."

She looked out over all the people bustling around Ashdale Pond. She could see her Revolutionaries helping townsfolk, men and women working together to collect treasures and debris from the rubble of houses. She saw Joe standing nervously in a crowd of strangers, clutching his gun close to his chest. It all made her smile—so many people now joined by a cause and soon, their cause would be all the greater.

But first, there was one thing left to do.

"Call together the CoR," Caitlin said to Dylan and Kain. "Meet us at Mabel's in ten."

As they walked away, Caitlin heard Dylan say, "Who's Mabel?"

To which Kain replied, "Oh, you're in for a treat."

***

Mabel and Jamie's house stood a few houses away from the devastation. She hadn't realized it at the time, what with the amount of smoke and fire, but the house had been barely several bombs away from total destruction.

As they approached the front door, they heard the sounds of furniture falling and items smashing to the floor. Caitlin's heart stopped as her mind went to the worst-case scenario.

Oh shit, the pastor has escaped. He's attacking them both. What if they're already dead?

Caitlin had sent the Mary-Anne to find Jamie, Mabel, and Andrews after the fighting but struggled to believe that they'd be back at the house already.

What the...

But she needn't have worried. For as she opened the door to the house, Jamie cried out in alarm. "Hey! Woah, hey!"

She paused in the doorway, stunned. Mary-Anne and Kain stepped up and sniggered behind her.

"Sorry," Caitlin said, a smile creeping onto her own face as Jamie and Christy untwisted from each other's naked bodies and flapped around the room to retrieve their clothes. "Didn't mean to disturb...this. If you like, we can come back in a minute. Let you guys finish off?"

"Good on you, mate!" Kain roared triumphantly.

"Eurgh, and with the pastor right there on the floor," Mary-Anne added, pointing at the still form of the man tied and snoring on the living room floor.

Jamie turned a violent shade of crimson, but the smile never left his face. Not once.

When the CoR finally did arrive, they were joined by several new recruits—Tom, Laurie, and Joe. Caitlin smiled as she looked around them all—her team—and laid out her plans of uniting the towns.

Jamie and Christy sat on the panel, appointed by Caitlin to be the new representatives of Ashdale Pond. Caitlin, Kain, and Mary-Anne—whom folks had already started calling the "Holy Trio" again—would announce the new leadership to the town later that day and spread news of the union of the two communities.

"You know, it's not going to be easy. Even with more people involved, there's no telling how many Mad are in that forest. It's going to be dangerous work," Tom said, his voice like gravel as he pulled back his eyepatch and scratched the small bowl where his eye had once been.

"The things that are most worthwhile usually are," Caitlin replied. "But as our number grows, and as more towns unite, the safer we can feel."

"Unless every town we come across is filled with God-fearing pyromaniacs led by sociopathic nobodies with superiority complexes," Kain added.

They all turned to look at Pastor Andrews, now seated in the corner of the room. He shrugged. "What?"

The Council of Revolutionaries fell about laughing. It was a beautiful sound, Caitlin thought. Despite all that they'd been through, she couldn't help but feel optimistic. The governor was gone. Justice had been brought to Ashdale Pond. And, soon, the doors to Silver Creek would be open to the public.

Fuck yeah. Caitlin smiled, relaxing into her chair.

"Nice tattoo, by the way, Moxie," Kain whispered to Caitlin. "Really rock 'n roll."

Caitlin laughed. "What's rock 'n roll?"

"Elvis? The Rolling Stones? Mick Jagger?" He rolled his eyes. "I sometimes forget how young you are. Old music from a time long ago. My parents made me listen when I was just a kid. Before I went all wolf and teeth."

Even Mary-Anne smiled then. "Those were the good old days."

"No," Caitlin said, rolling her arm over and inspecting the burning church etched into her skin. "The good old days are yet to come."

EPILOGUE

Silver Creek Forest, Old Ontario, Four Months Later

The wolf sniffed at the forest floor, his nose deep into the tangles of bushes and vines. Even in the shadows under the canopy of trees, his eyes burned a vivid orange.

As he lifted his head, he caught a scent—*the* scent he had been looking for.

His tail wagged in excitement. He sped through the brush in near-silence, padding expertly over thorns and brush. The scent grew ever stronger, making his heart beat so fast he could feel it in his own ears.

Voices sounded, now. Lots of them, which seemed a strange thing in the middle of the forest. For miles and miles, it seemed, all the wolf had encountered were odd clusters of Mad which he had avoided with ease. But to find a whole group of people in the forest who didn't smell Mad was a most unusual thing.

He slowed, keeping as low to the ground as possible until he saw them through the trees ahead. Some men had axes. Some women carried swords. Most were busy patting the ground into a firm path several meters wide.

Were they making a road?

And there, sitting with his back to a tree, a hood low over his face as he snoozed and let the others do the work, was the man he had hunted for months, now.

The wolf turned on his paws and sped back through the forest, weaving between trees, scaring a nearby deer who pranced off into the undergrowth. He only stopped when he reached the others.

The three creatures waited patiently, picking berries off a tree—a bear, a panther, and another wolf. Their amber eyes turned to greet him as he concentrated with all his might and transformed before them into the form of a naked man. He was the youngest of them all. Tufts of fur clung to his body, but he figured he still had a fair number of transformations left in him.

He blinked, and the bear was gone, replaced by a tank of a man with ripped abs and bulging biceps covered in scars and a thick carpet of hair.

"Anything?" the man who had been a bear asked.

He grinned and nodded. "We've found him. We've found the traitor."

The dark smile distinctly resembled the bear he'd so recently been, his teeth jagged and worn. *At long last, Kain Sudeikis. At long last.*

FINIS

THEY FIGHT. THEY LIVE. THEY ROT.

Eight years ago, an infection hit London, before spreading outwards. 90% of the population was either contained by the military, trampled during the riots, or infected by the disease.

A disease that came to be known as **The Rot.**

Colin Bolton survived the incident but not without losing everything he held dear to him – his life, his love, and his humanity.

Now, he's living at a farmhouse, acting as a bodyguard for a new surrogate family. Life is stable. He's making do. He's *surviving*. That is… until a vagrant scavenger comes knocking at the door, desperate for food and water.

An encounter that will spin Colin's life into chaos once more, bringing him face to face with a murderous family, the dead and the dying, and the failures of his past.

THEY ROT is the first book in a brutal new series of post-apocalyptia set in Great Britain. It's brought to you by Willcocks and Kondor, two of the groundbreaking authors behind the iTunes chart-busting podcast, The Other Stories, and the story studio, Hawk & Cleaver - A digital story studio bringing you the best new stories to watch, read, sniff, and absorb.

Available at Amazon

AUTHOR'S NOTES - DAN WILLCOCKS

AUGUST 20, 2018

What do you get if you cross a window cleaner and a giraffe...?

...

Thanks so much for making it all the way to the end of this book. It's been an absolute whirlwind of a journey, not only with Caitlin and her crew (who, by the way, might just be my favourite kickass band of characters I've ever created), but with Michael and the guys behind the scenes as well.

When I started writing, I could never have foreseen this journey. I remember sitting down at a keyboard in early 2015 and just toying with sentences, playing with a few paragraphs, and wondering what life would be like as a full-time writer.

I imagined the classic scene: me, sat at the vintage oak writing desk that was far too heavy to ever lift out of the room (God knows how it got in there!). I imagined myself smoking a cigar, a whisky in one hand, and a typewriter clacking away as the pages dinged and made their way through the roller...

Who was I kidding!

There is something romantic that comes when you think about the writer's life. But—and here I may shatter some illusions completely—that's not what it's like at all.

As I write these author notes I can safely tell you that I'm sat, cross-legged, on my sofa. There's a coffee in front of me, and a bowl of porridge. It's 6:45am and I'm getting ready to start the day-job. I've already made my way through book 3 of this series (*oh my God, oh my God, you're in for a treat!*), and I'm already thinking of the writing I'll be doing on my hour lunch break at work.

Somewhere upstairs I can hear my 3-year-old snoring. In about 15 minutes I'll be up, dressed, and cycling into the heart of my city.

No cigar—I don't even smoke!

No whiskey—such a shame, but I discovered morning drinking doesn't exactly help my morning bike-rides go any faster.

No typewriter—okay... so this one I'd *love* to have. Did you know they do USB plug-in typewriter keyboards?

I digress...

I suppose all this is to say that, if I can do it, *anyone* can write. Anyone can do this. It took a long while for me to build the routine of writing, and it's with the encouragement of other writers that I realised how easy it can be to just... do it. My end goal was never to write an international bestseller—thank you *so* much guys!—but it was simply to tell stories. And that's all I continue to do.

As per my last author notes, I wanted to add a few extra

nods of thanks—though there may be some unfamiliar names in here.

Last week myself and the writers from Hawk & Cleaver (my story studio responsible for the chart-busting podcast, The Other Stories) celebrated 2 million downloads on our podcast. Not only that, but the damn thing has also been optioned for possible TV adaptation, too.

That's not to say it's definitely going to happen... but we're certainly moving in the 'write' direction (see what I did there?).

So a massive thanks to Ben Errington, Matt Butcher, and Karl Hughes who continue to contribute to an amazing podcast and deliver amazing content. And, particularly, to Luke Kondor, my original writing collaborator, for all the work you put in to producing the podcast, and for being an absolute rockstar to work with. If it wasn't for you, I know I wouldn't be here now.

And, most of all, thank you to you, dear reader. Without your eyes on the page I would just be another crazy guy in his bathrobe, drinking himself silly with whiskey, and wondering why there's pee-pee on the Twister mat.

Oh! And in case you were wondering...

A window cleaner who doesn't need any ladders!

(I know, it's terrible. But I'm a dad now and terrible jokes are all I have...)

Until next time.
Dan

First, THANK YOU for not only reading this story, but also reading through the back to our *Author Notes*, too!

Right now, I'm in the AC Hotel (San Jose) about six blocks from the Convention Center where WorldCon 76 is being held.

This is the first time I've ever attended this con.

It started Thursday and will finish on Monday, and I have seen a few interesting things I NEVER expected to see. One of them is the Han Solo carbonite block that was used for the Star Wars film *Return of the Jedi*.

Another was someone cosplaying Leeloo from the movie *The Fifth Element* (a favorite of mine.) Now, I'm fifty, pushing fifty-one years in a few weeks, so there was no way I was going to tell the young woman playing Leeloo that I thought it was cool that she was playing the character.

(No way I'll be accused of being a creepy guy, thankyouverymuch.)

However, I found that my not saying anything was

kinda sucky on two levels. The first was my reaction of embarrassment (I thought it was cool she was playing a character I really like in a movie, and my embarrassment grabbed the excuse that it might be seen as creepy as a reason to not say something). Why?

Fear of rejection, of course.

When you look up "Fear of Rejection" on Wikipedia, they should have my picture there as an example. I'm not nearly as bad about the fear as others who suffer (and don't leave their homes.) Rather, I fear walking into rooms with people I don't know. My first reaction is to find a corner and hide.

The second level of sucky is that the person put in effort to look like Leeloo, and I missed an opportunity to show that someone appreciated it. I'm sure I could have said something nice in passing, waved, and walked on (I assume that is normal reaction and etiquette. It's my first time at a larger con.)

So, for those of my readers who love cosplay, I salute you. You bring much fun to the cons! And while I work on my rejection issues, know that many of us appreciate the work you put into your costumes and some of us wish we had the ability to pause the embarrassment button in our lives and live it up like you do.

Keep cosplaying,

Michael Anderle

They Rot (Book 1 of 'The Rot' series)
They Remain (Book 2 of 'The Rot' series)
Lazarus: Enter the Deadspace
Twisted: A collection of dark shorts
Sins of Smoke

The Caitlin Chronicles
Dawn of Chaos (1)
Into The Fire (2)

Dan's Facebook Group
https://www.facebook.com/groups/832626480256677/